MY FAVORITE LOST CAUSE

ELIZABETH O'ROARK

1

———

MAREN

Persephone wasn't a victim.

Sure, she was abducted by Hades. Sure, she had to give up a couple seasons on Earth. But that descent into shadow was necessary; it's how she found her true self, how she came into her power.

That's what has happened to Charlie, my stepbrother. He's descended into shadow—a drunken, noncommunicative shadow that's kept him from the last four family dinners—but he'll eventually emerge better than he was.

His dad, Roger, says it's just a bender, but that I should check anyway.

It's still unclear to me why *I* was the one asked to perform this welfare check. It should have been Roger—they actually share DNA. Even my younger sister, Kit, would be better—if he refused to let her in, she'd probably kick down his door. Effective, if nothing else. I agreed because Charlie has a better heart than anyone gives him credit for, and I want to be sure it's handled with care. Or perhaps it's just that I struggle to say *no* to anything asked of me.

When the driver arrives at Charlie's building, glinting like a knife in the summer sun, I grab the tray of juice in my lap and tell him not to wait.

This might take a while. Or no time at all if Charlie doesn't let me upstairs, which is a strong possibility. I'll risk it.

I greet the doorman and make some inane comment about the weather. Kit hates my little social niceties. *You don't need to be everyone's best friend*, she's said a million times. But I like being liked. And mostly, it works—Charlie is the only person who can't be swayed. It's not that he hates me—it's just that he doesn't allow himself to be won over.

So I probably won't win him over today.

I give the woman at the front desk my name and identify myself as Charlie's sister, though it's not technically true.

"Can you tell him it's urgent?" I add when she calls upstairs. Because he's very, very likely to send me packing otherwise.

This strategy works. A few moments later, I'm inside the elevator and heading for the tenth floor...without a clue what I'll say when I arrive.

I already know he's going to be a dick to me the entire time I'm trying to fix things, but underneath all that...there will be a wound, because Charlie's real issue is that he cares and doesn't want to. That he would fight to the death for all of us and can't stand to let on.

I knock and he opens the door for me, running a hand through his unruly brown hair. His eyes are only half open, he needed a shave a month ago, and he's in nothing but a pair of boxers.

None of these things should look quite as good as Charlie makes them look.

"To what do I owe this unprompted, incredibly early visit I never agreed to?" he asks, without suggesting I enter.

"It's noon, Charlie," I reply. "And you could have at least put on some clothes."

He raises a brow. "I *did* put on clothes."

I blink. I never took Charlie for a *sleeps in the nude* kind of guy.

Yuck. Moving on. "Are you going to let me in?"

He pinches the bridge of his nose. "This really isn't a good time, Maren. Can I call you later?"

It's unlike me to push. But Charlie—as debauched as he is —doesn't typically sleep 'til noon and dodge his father's calls. Something has gone wrong, and I can't leave until I know what it is. "I brought you some juice. It'll help with the hangover."

He runs a hand through his thick hair until it's practically standing up straight and plucks the green juice from my hand. "This juice doesn't even go with vodka."

"Charles," I say sternly, "don't you dare add vodka. Let me in."

He finally steps aside, and I get my first hint as to why he really didn't want me here. This place looks like a frat house at two in the morning. Pizza boxes, wine bottles, his suits, news-papers...a broken lamp rests atop a partially collapsed book-shelf. It's like the morning-after scene in *The Hangover*, minus the lion in the bathroom, although, to be honest...I haven't gone into the bathroom, so the jury's out.

"And here I was worried you might have company," I say faintly.

"I did," he says with a shrug. "I think she's gone. If you spy a dead female, give me a small heads-up before you call the police."

"I'm not sure how I'd spy anything with all the shit on your floor."

He flops into a leather chair, letting his head fall backward as he closes his eyes, which have dark circles beneath them. "This visit is already so much fun," he groans. "Why are you here?"

What the hell has gone wrong? Is it a job? Has he finally

gotten his heart broken? He's not ready to tell me, whatever it is.

Charlie acts like a guy whose life is lived entirely on the surface, but I've always suspected that almost none of it is. A simple fifteen-minute visit was never going to earn me real answers.

Which means I need an excuse to prevent him from ushering me out.

I clear a chair of the suit strewn across it and take a seat. "I've come to you with a proposition," I lie.

He opens one eye. "I'm hoping it's sexual, but that seems optimistic."

"We're stepsiblings, so that's extremely optimistic." *Think, Maren. Why would you need to stay here when you've got a condo twice the size of this apartment, and multiple family members with spacious homes?* "I need to stay here for the next few days. My apartment's being fumigated."

I'm pretty proud of this one. Maybe I'm not as terrible at lying as I thought.

"That's even less exciting than I thought it would be, and I knew it would be incredibly unexciting."

"I'll be the best roommate," I wheedle. "Like a wife minus the sex."

He blows out a breath. "Sex on demand is the only part of having a wife that appeals to me, however."

"Sex *on demand* isn't actually a part of marriage, just so you know. I wouldn't want you to find out once you'd gotten down the aisle."

"It would take much more than sex on demand to get *me* down an aisle," he replies. "And why the fuck do you need to stay here? Go to your mom's. Go to Kit's."

I anticipated this objection, and he's absolutely right. My mother lives in a massive, three-floor condo in the best section of town. She has far more space than Charlie does.

"My mother is currently fighting with your dad...you know how that is," I tell him. It's a lie, but it's the case so often that he won't even question it. My mother loves drama, and poor Roger is continually jumping through hoops to make her stay. "And... Kit moved into Miller's place, and they're still in Nepal—not that I'd be willing to sleep on their couch if they weren't."

This one is entirely true. It's been awkward, having my sister date my ex. Mostly because everyone keeps giving me pitying, uncomfortable looks like Charlie is now.

If Miller had just been a guy I dated a decade ago, that would be one thing. Unfortunately, I had to be all *Maren* about him. I had to pine. I had to go hardcore Taylor Swift-level wistful and claim he was the one who got away. I tend to do this —to latch onto the idea of someone. For a long while it was Miller and more recently it was my husband's friend, Andrew. It's not that I want these men in particular—Andrew's married, and I hadn't seen Miller in a decade—and it's not that I'd cheat on my husband. It's just that sometimes I need a reminder that there are men in the world who are kind, who'd be good to their wives.

And if I forget, I'll allow Harvey to be worse to me than he already is.

"Fine, fuck. Whatever. You can sleep in the spare room. But your puppies need to stay somewhere else. Those are the least domesticated animals I've ever seen, and I've gone on safari twice. And don't cockblock me." His tone is accusatory, as if this is something I do all the time. "I don't need you having a long conversation with some girl I've brought home."

He lazily runs a hand over his flat stomach—I can see a hint of his happy trail and shift in my seat, struggling to refocus. "So don't suggest to your one-night stand that giving it up for a guy who's going to kick her out first thing in the morning isn't her best move."

He exhales wearily. "Yes, Maren, that is a prime example of

the sort of conversation I don't need you having with someone I am about to fuck. And don't befriend anyone afterward either. I make a lot of effort to ensure that the women I'm seeing don't get the wrong idea. Are we clear?" He rises from the chair, his boxers sliding low as his abs flex. I really wish he'd put on some clothes.

"I'm not even sure what we'd talk about anyway, aside from your disastrous decision-making ability."

"You married Harvey," he replies, heading back to his room. "So don't get me started on decision-making ability."

I guess he might have a point.

When his door shuts, I truly allow myself to take in the disaster that is his apartment. It's a tribute to how insanely handsome Charlie is that any woman he's brought up here for the past few weeks hasn't run off screaming in terror. The kitchen is a sea of dishes that never arrived at the sink. There's an open pizza box, its contents mummified, and so many partially drunk glasses of wine that I'm surprised he can still find anything to drink out of.

I rise, hunting beneath the kitchen sink for a trash bag, then start throwing stuff away.

What happened to you, Charlie? And how do I fix it when you won't admit anything happened at all?

2

———

CHARLIE

When I wake in the afternoon, Maren is gone, and the fucking apartment is clean. I am not surprised by this—I knew Maren wouldn't be able to help herself. It's part of her whole Disney princess thing—she wants to dance around my apartment like Cinderella, beloved by magical singing mice while bluebirds float around her head, making the world a better place for everyone but herself.

I text some friends who are as useless and lazy as I am before I hop in the shower. When I reach the bar, the afore-mentioned friends—most of them functional alcoholics like myself or straightforward alcoholics without the functional part—have sequestered an outdoor table, and I've soon got a girl in my lap who I will definitely be taking home later.

Is it weird that she looks a bit like Maren? Perhaps. Maybe it'll make Maren uncomfortable enough to leave early. No good can come of this roommate situation, and it's easy to see how a whole lot of bad could come out of it instead.

"A toast!" shouts Winslow, setting a tray full of shots on the table before us. He's already hammered at four in the afternoon. Quite a feat given that he was at work until an hour ago. "To Charlie, because I've never seen a guy as drunk as he was last night convince a sober woman to come home with him."

I grab one of the shots, though I'm not sure that was much of a compliment. First of all, it's a bad sign when I'm getting more drunk than *Winslow*. Second...the girl I brought home? I couldn't pick her out of a lineup. I don't know her name. The thought *I've got to slow down* is overshadowed by the thought *I can slow down once my life doesn't feel like shit.*

I'm sure Maren would have something to say about that. Maren would tell me things can't feel better until I stop making them worse. She's full of sage advice for everyone but her-fuck-ing-self.

"Huh?" asks the girl in my lap. "Who's Maren?"

I didn't realize I'd said it aloud. I squeeze her hip. "Absolutely no one."

She giggles for no discernible reason. I can already tell she'll be a screamer, and if I were the biggest asshole ever, I'd make sure she screamed loud enough to wake Maren. Certainly, if my surliness isn't bad enough to drive her away, the sound of me railing her lookalike would do the trick.

I'm not that much of an asshole, right?

Right?

"I need another shot," I say.

FEMALE LAUGHTER WAKES ME. Never a good sign.

I peel my eyes open, but my bedroom offers few clues. It's a disaster, sure, but it's been a disaster for a while. I vaguely remember the girl in my lap at the bar, and a bottle of wine opening after we met a friend of hers in the lobby, but then? Nothing. It troubles me, this gap. Mostly because threesomes don't just fall in your lap. They're the sort of memories that will keep you warm in your old age, but you've got to actually remember them. I really need to clean my shit up a little.

There's more laughter. Dammit. A hundred bucks says that Maren's making them a nutritious breakfast while she administers STD tests. And now, these two nameless girls are happily settled into my apartment rather than tucked into a cab the way they should be.

I throw on sweats and trudge down to the kitchen, where Maren and two Maren-lookalikes are all busy drinking from large mugs and eating...muffins. Where the fuck did they get muffins? *And* those oversized mugs?

"Good morning," I say with a forced smile.

"I didn't know you wore glasses, Charlie!" one of them cries gleefully.

Unsurprising, since we met ten hours ago, and I still don't know your name.

"I can't believe Maren Fischer is your stepsister!" squeals the other.

They're loud. And cheerful. Was I the only one who was drunk last night? Should I worry that I was taken advantage of?

"Yes, lucky me," I say, shooting daggers at Maren, who beams back at me with her clear blue eyes and pink-flushed cheeks. A living blonde Barbie doll as always, with a kind word for everyone she meets.

Except...I've got Maren's smiles memorized, and this is a new one. It's not the brave, false one she wears when her husband ridicules her or the patient one she wears whenever Ulrika, her insane mother and my tiresome stepmother, says something ridiculous. Nor is it the unfettered, happy one I spy sometimes when I've made her laugh.

This one has an edge. And might be vengeful. Did I intentionally make a lot of noise last night? It seems...possible. I'm not the best version of myself when blackout drunk.

One of them starts asking Maren why she's no longer

modeling, and I can see that this hangout is never going to end. "I'm sorry to cut this short, ladies, but I've got a"—I scan my brain for a lie Maren won't be able to refute—"meeting."

"A meeting?" Maren asks. "Who would you need to meet with on a Sunday?"

Apparently, she *can* refute it.

But so can I. "Tokyo."

Her raised brow and that glimmer of a smirk on her mouth scare me, because behind Maren's Mother Teresa act lies an evil streak. I'd enjoy watching it unleashed. Just not at me. And not right now.

She glances at her watch. "It's eleven at night there."

Of course she remembers all the time zones from her modeling days.

Dammit. "Yes, they are finishing up dinner then calling me on Zoom."

The girls, whose names I still don't know, make pouting faces but gather their things and say goodbye. Maren hugs them in that way of hers—easily affectionate and genuine—and they seem sadder about leaving her than me, but she's been far nicer to them than I've been, which is fairly typical.

Maren wants everyone to love her but never seems to grasp that some people's love isn't worth earning. Like that of these girls she'll never see again.

I wait until the door shuts behind them and turn. "What the fuck, Maren," I groan.

"You deserved it after what I had to listen to last night." She throws her head back. "Oh, God, Charlie, yes, yes, yes!"

"You're good at faking an orgasm," I reply, turning toward the coffee maker before she realizes exactly how good she was at it. "Not surprising. I bet Harvey gives you a lot of practice."

"Would it kill you to have had breakfast with them?" she asks. "Would it kill you to get to know them beyond the moment you blew your load?"

Fuck. My favorite appendage was beginning to settle until she used the expression "blew your load." It was unusual phrasing from Manhattan's sweetheart. Is there porn involving Barbie or a Disney princess getting railed from behind?

Probably. I'll check later.

"Maren, my life is hard enough without your bullshit. And you've broken every single rule I set, so it's time for you to go impose on someone else."

"Charlie, we need to talk—"

"Not really a good time, since you're leaving and I'm about to host a fictitious Zoom meeting at eleven p.m. in Tokyo."

"I'll go if you tell me what's so hard about your life, and that wasn't an opening for you to talk about your dick. Tell me what's wrong." There's something genuine in her voice but firm at the same time.

Knowing I'll regret it, knowing she's still not going to fucking leave, I cross the room and grab the letter.

3

MAREN

harlie thrusts a typed letter in front of my face. I half expect it to be a lawsuit or test results because I can't think of anything else that would trigger his current distress. *Dear Charlie*, it begins, *If you're reading this, it means that I'm gone.*

Immediately my gaze drops to the signature line: *All my love, Mom.*

My eyes jolt up to meet his. His mother *died*? She wasn't even old. And how could no one have told me? I mean, for fuck's sake, Roger could have mentioned it when he sent me over here to do the welfare check. "I'm so—"

He shakes his head, his jaw tight. "Read it."

I don't want to read the letter. I don't want to see this painful thing in all its glory. Because even if Charlie didn't see much of his mom after she left for South Carolina, I know he loved her. Roger has never been allowed to voice even the mildest complaint about her without Charlie leaping to her defense.

Dear Charlie,

If you're reading this, it means that I am gone. I'm sorry to be letting you know this way, but I didn't want our final memories together to be sad ones. I've gone to the little retreat in Panama, where we buried Zoe. I've asked them to cremate me and spread my ashes over her grave, so there's nothing to be done. My executor has been instructed to send this on to you as soon as he has word. There's not much to leave you with, aside from Riverbend.

Do you remember that summer you spent here after high school? I loved that summer so much. You'd get up early and run on the path around the inlet, and you were so full of promise and hope. I don't see that in you anymore. I didn't push you because I was scared, but now that I've got so little time left, I know I was wrong.

That's why I'm saddling you with this dying wish of mine, one I know you'll resent. I want you to go down to South Carolina and make the house into everything I dreamed it could be. And don't just hire a crew: go down there and be a part of it. Get your hands dirty.

You could ignore all of this—I'm not there to stop you— but if you ever loved me, you won't. You'll let me be the parent to you I wish I'd been all along. One willing to make you suffer a little in order to come out happy in the end.

All my love,

Mom

I'm crying by the time I reach the letter's conclusion. No wonder Charlie's been taking this so hard. In one fell swoop, his mother burdened him with this job he doesn't want, and also let him know that she died disappointed in him.

She had a hard life—Roger said that she never recovered from the death of Charlie's little sister years ago—so as much as it upsets me that she's left all this on Charlie, I'm also heartbroken for her. She died thinking her son had failed, but also that she had failed too.

"Charlie, I'm so sorry," I begin again. "I...I'm...I hadn't even heard."

Charlie pulls his cup from the Keurig and dumps some cream in it. "No one's heard. I haven't told anyone, not even my dad."

I blink. Obviously, Charlie's parents are no longer together, but surely when your child loses his mother, someone gives you a heads-up?

"Why haven't you told anyone?"

He scowls in the direction of the half-eaten muffins and coffee cups still sitting on the table. "Maybe because I didn't want someone over here plying the women I bring home with muffins and suggesting that I'm lying when I try to usher them out."

I wonder if he's cried about this even once. I wonder if every single time he gets choked up, he decides he'd better take a drink or have a threesome.

As if on cue, he sets his coffee down, crosses the room, and grabs a bottle of Jack.

"Don't give me that look," he says, screwing off the top. "Hair of the dog. And we had an agreement. I told you, now you leave."

I bury my head in my hands. I told him I'd go...but I can't leave him like this. "Do you...need to go to Panama?"

"Already went," he replies, taking a quick swig before he recaps it. "Two weeks ago. She apparently had cancer. She knew it for a year and never said anything, not to me, anyway, and now there's nothing there to even say goodbye to." He sinks into his big leather chair, and I follow, taking a seat on the ottoman directly in front of him.

"What are you going to do?"

"About the house? Nothing. I can't move to South Carolina and refurbish the whole place by hand. And stop looking at me like I'm a tired toddler who needs to go to bed."

He's *acting* like a tired toddler who needs to go to bed. Maybe that's why I have this desperate urge to take care of him when he's being a total prick.

I reach out and let my hand rest on his knee. It jumps, as if he's reflexively repulsed by my touch, but I don't pull it back and he doesn't insist.

"Charlie, you've apparently been drinking yourself into a stupor for weeks and living as if you're on borrowed time. Don't you think it might have something to do with the fact that you're conflicted?"

"Conflicted?" he groans, uncapping the whiskey again. "Unless you've built some sort of portal to the past where I can go say goodbye to my mother, there is nothing to be conflicted about."

"It was your mother's dying wish that you go fix that house, and I think what's happening here is you feel guilty not doing it."

He sets the bottle on the table beside him and pushes it away. "Why the fuck would I feel guilty? It was an insane request on her part. A developer has already offered me millions, every building on the land is a wreck, and clearly, we aren't discussing a woman who had her head in the right place if she'd choose to die without even saying goodbye."

He's furious, and beneath that, he's hurt. That's why Charlie has always been able to tug at my heartstrings like a master violinist. Because under every snide, shitty thing he says to me, I've always sensed something sweet but broken. Which makes sense: he lost his little sister, but in some ways, he lost his mom, too, when she left.

I slide my hand into his. His remains limp, not returning my grasp. "I'm not saying that you *should* feel guilty. I'm saying that you already do, and maybe it's better to face that than it is to bury your head in the sand, or in your case, bury your head in a bottle of whiskey and multiple vaginas."

"I think that I could continue burying my head in bottles of whiskey and multiple vaginas pretty successfully. I doubt that you have done either, but both are a delightful way to spend an evening."

A strange, unexpected heat flashes through me, one I don't want to consider too hard. I know for a fact that I am not interested in burying my face in a vagina, but the fact that Charlie *is*...well, yeah, I'm not going to think about it.

"There will be plenty of future opportunities to indulge in both those hobbies," I tell him. "But this sort of feels like the moment in a movie when a character can go really wrong or can turn shit around, and I'm pretty sure whiskey and drunk threesomes are not in the turning-things-around plotline."

"Maybe you and I watch different movies," he says. "Let me get my laptop. I'll show you some favorites."

I laugh, even though I shouldn't. Two seconds from now he'll hurt my feelings, and before I've recovered, he'll make my heart break for him. Some guys are a comedy, some are tear-jerkers, and some snidely condemn everything about you. If Charlie were a movie, he'd be all three.

"Look," he admits, "I know I've got to slow down. I mean, Jesus...I don't even remember last night or the night before. The worst could have happened."

"Having one of them murder you in your sleep?"

He frowns. "No, that's like number three on the list."

"What could possibly be worse?"

He holds up a hand. "Number two, getting someone pregnant. Number one, getting someone pregnant with twins. Can you imagine me as a father?"

I actually *can* see Charlie as a father. He'd accidentally make jokes about masturbation and porn in front of his toddlers, and his kids would get kicked out of preschool for profanity, but he'd also be fiercely protective and sweet beneath all that grouchiness.

"Anyhow," he concludes, "I'm going to drink less, and you can now leave as promised."

Oh, Charlie. He has every conceivable asset—he's gorgeous, he's charming, he's smart—and he's just throwing it away. Why?

"Don't give me that look, Maren," he growls.

"I'm not giving you a look."

"Yes, you are. You are definitely giving me a fucking look."

I swallow and he rolls his eyes.

"And don't swallow either." He rubs a hand over his face with a disgruntled laugh. "I never thought I'd hear myself say that to a woman. But don't swallow like that."

I can't win with him. He's mad if I speak, he's mad if I'm nice to his overnight guests, he's mad if I'm sympathetic. I'm about to concede defeat when he releases a weary exhale.

"Fine, I'll go take a look. I'm not promising anything. My guess is the place needs to be razed, and I'm not doing a total rebuild if that's the case. I have a job."

I ignore that. Charlie does some kind of venture capital thing that I don't totally understand—he's currently bankrolling some new team in San Antonio—but his time is his own. He can go anywhere he wants.

"It's in South Carolina, right?"

He slouches back in his chair like a beaten man, as if even the prospect of revisiting the state has exhausted him. "Yeah, near Beaufort."

I close my eyes and picture it—sea pines, a sandy beach, the soft pulse of waves against the shore. I have no idea what it's actually like, but I want to be there regardless. I need a break from my life here—Harvey's demands and his constant complaints, the way my life has narrowed to nothing but him and this baby I don't yet have. "Can I come?"

His head jerks. "With *me*?"

I knew he'd object, but I didn't realize the prospect would

be absolutely incomprehensible in its horror. "It might be good to have someone with you, Charlie, and—"

His jaw locks. "Don't you have your husband and the dogs to deal with?"

"Harvey's out of town. The puppies can stay with Lori. And I've done a lot of design stuff, Charlie. I have no idea if I'm good at it, but—"

"Of course you're fucking good at it," he growls.

I fight a smile. The minute anyone insults me, he's my angry knight in shining armor. Even if I'm the one hurling the insults.

"Aren't you about to do IVF?"

"Next month," I reply, no longer able to meet his eye. I'm excited about IVF and dreading it at the same time. Apparently my ovaries won't produce eggs without some help, a fact I wish I'd known before we spent two years trying to get pregnant. I want a baby. What I don't want are the months of waiting, or the list of my failings from Harvey if it doesn't work, along with the not-so-subtle reminder that he'd already have a kid by now if he'd married someone else.

Charlie studies me for a long moment, and then his shoulders sag. "You can come, but the second I hear the word *shiplap*, you'll be driving your ass back home."

An idle threat if I've ever heard one—Charlie knows I barely drive.

My smile is wider than it should be.

I'm doing this to help him escape his misery. But it might be a brief escape from mine too.

$$4$$

MAREN

The trip comes together in a matter of days. I thought Charlie would fuck around for weeks or months stonewalling me, but I'd underestimated his desire to *"get this bullshit over with,"* as he so charmingly phrased it.

I think most of the bullshit is me. My presence. For a man who is generally patient and charming with everyone else, he is neither with me as we plan the trip, but as long as he shows up at the airport, I'm okay with that.

I manage to squeeze in brunch with Kit and convince her to get her hair and nails done before she returns to Everest, where Miller is planning to propose, unbeknownst to her. At least I assume that's what happening, since he had me help pick the ring and was hell-bent on getting it before he left for Nepal.

I tell Roger that Charlie is fine, which isn't true, but news about his ex-wife's death can't come from me and Charlie isn't ready to share it. It also works better for me—if my mom knew I was going on this trip, she'd find a way to make it into something it absolutely is not, and poor Roger would pay the price for it. We love Roger—he's a stabilizing influence and the best thing to happen to our family in a very long time. Kit and I run ourselves ragged trying to keep our mother from ruining the relationship, because she makes very bad decisions when Roger's not around. Of course, if he'd been around when she met my dickhead father—a now-famous artist who took off before I was born—I wouldn't exist. So I guess occasionally, it has its benefits.

I drop my gorgeous babies, black yorkipoos, off in Brooklyn with Lori, dog sitter to the stars, on my way to the airport. While I'm heartbroken at the idea of leaving them for a week, the puppies themselves are ecstatic, tripping over their own feet as they bolt toward the open back door of her place.

"Should it hurt my feelings that they don't care about being left here?" I ask with a sad laugh.

Lori elbows me. "They're going to be excited while they're here, and they'll be excited to see you again in a week. I know you love them like babies—we both do—but they aren't human you know."

I fight my wince. I've been accused before of treating the puppies as if they were my children, and the implication— though I know Lori isn't saying that now—is that it's because I've been unable to get pregnant.

Maybe it's just that I worry they're as close as I'm going to get to having children.

Harvey calls when I'm on my way to the airport, wanting to know if I canceled the housekeeper and picked up his shirts before I left. He always treats me like a worthless assistant he hasn't had time to fire when he's pissed off.

When this elicits no reaction from me, he revisits the argument he made when the trip first came up.

"I can't believe you're doing this, and I really hope it doesn't fuck up IVF. God knows what kind of shit is in the air down there—it's in the south; the place is old. It's probably full of mold. You shouldn't be traveling at all, and you sure as hell shouldn't be traveling with *Charlie*."

I was willing to be civil until now. "You think *Charlie* is going to harm the quality of my eggs?"

"No," he says, "but I think Charlie is eager as fuck to get you alone in an isolated location."

I slap a palm to my face, stunned. "He's my stepbrother. He's been in my family for a decade."

"As if that would stop him," Harvey mutters.

Except I've been on a hundred modeling jobs with creepy men in isolated places, and he didn't say a word—so this has less to do with Charlie's moral flexibility than it does Harvey's fear that I'd be *tempted* by it.

"I guess you're lucky my commitment to our marital vows is a little stronger than yours," I reply.

He hangs up, which is as close as Harvey ever comes to admitting I'm right.

The driver gives me a curious glance in the rearview mirror. I can't be the first client he's overheard fighting with her husband, though I might be the first he's heard accused of wanting to fuck her stepbrother.

Fifteen minutes later, my bags are checked and I've gotten through security. It's a relief to see Charlie already seated at the gate—long legs stretched in front of him, so handsome that every woman in the vicinity is doing a double take and the teenager over at the nearest newsstand is surreptitiously taking his photo.

Adjusting the overstuffed Goyard on my arm, I move his way until he glances up, studying my face. "How did it go?" he asks.

In my head I hear Harvey saying *as if that would stop him.* "How did *what* go?"

"Dropping off the dogs," he replies. "What else?"

"You might have been referencing me saying goodbye to my spouse."

His laughter is so smug that I want to swing my purse at

him. "No, I was referring to things you actually love. So it went okay?"

"You don't care about my dogs."

"No, I don't," he says, "but you do."

Because he cares about the things that are important to me.

My heart feels as if it's being squeezed by a tiny fist. Harvey didn't ask.

Harvey has never asked once.

CHARLIE

We land in Charleston, and I try not to visibly wince at how much it's changed. It's a major airport now. I should know this. If I'd fucking bothered to visit my mother once over the past few years, I'd know a lot of things.

Maybe I'd even have known she was sick, though she hid that pretty fucking well the last time she was in New York. Jesus, maybe she didn't hide it well even then. Maybe I just had my head so far up my ass that I didn't notice the signs.

What else can you assume when your mother doesn't bother to tell you she's dying and has someone else spread her ashes?

We pick up the rental car and head out, skirting Charleston for points south. I remember this drive being tree-lined and rural. Now it's a fast four-lane road dotted with big box stores and fast food and I barely recognize it.

More guilt. More arguing with myself about the guilt.

Her house was a pain in the ass to get to. I'd always resented that she'd left—I'd thought the onus to visit should be on her, given that she'd abandoned me for her new home—and she said she liked coming to New York.

It doesn't matter. You still should have come back. You were all she had left.

Maren is privy to none of this, and she's just fucking determined to love this trip—she's been gasping over the trees and the Spanish moss and the names (Cuckold's Landing is a favorite) the whole way here, and the closer we get to Riverbend—the landscape finally as rural as I remember—the more deeply she seems to fall.

"You lived here for a summer, right?" she asks, her eyes glued to the window.

"When I was eighteen," I grunt. "My only way into town was a bike, so it basically meant no drinking and no girls for three months."

She raises a brow. "I think you could use another three months without drinking and girls, to be honest."

"I'd be more inclined to listen to those suggestions if they were coming from someone whose life was any better than my own."

It's a low blow, but I've never seen a marriage quite as miserable as Maren's. Every time Harvey opens his mouth, it's to deliver some new way to make her smaller. When I return from a family event, my jaw aches from clenching it.

We reach Oak Bluff, the town nearest Riverbend, and her infatuation grows. Where I see decay and annoyances, she sees something else entirely. The tiny diner is pronounced *adorable*. The old-timey swirling barber pole is also adorable. The town's administrative building and the Stop-n-Shop are *super cute*. I sort of wish Oak Bluff had a brothel just so she'd be forced to admire it somehow, but none of this bodes well for convincing her I should sell the place off as soon as we arrive.

"Tell me about Riverbend," Maren says, glancing my way. "It's old, right?"

"Yes."

She pokes me in the side. "Stop being so informative. How old?"

"Turn of the century, I think. Like, 1899 or thereabouts."

She gives one of those dreamy sighs of hers. "Is it a mansion? It must be, if they gave it a name."

"It's a dump," I reply. "Actually, no, it was a dump years ago, and now I'm sure it's worse."

The statement falls on deaf ears, like I knew it would. Maren is a dreamer. She never sees anything for what it is, only its potential, which is how she's managed to renovate two condominiums no one even wanted and flip them for millions of dollars. Her current place is so amazing it's been in magazines.

But that's also how she wound up with Harvey, and no amount of faith could renovate that guy.

A gravel lane canopied by Spanish-moss-heavy live oaks marks the start of Riverbend, plunging us in shadow.

"Charlie, I have chills," Maren says, lifting her forearm to show me goose bumps. "It's like something out of another century."

I had chills when I first saw it too, though for different reasons. No females for three months was a death sentence to an eighteen-year-old. It would be a death sentence to a thirty-two-year-old as well, which is why we're not staying long.

That summer didn't end up being terrible. Eventually I got used to the long days, to the quietness of it. My mom had me and a kid from town building these two pre-fab cottages along the water, side by side—she always said it was so that we'd have a place to live while the house was being renovated, though I suspected it was just to keep me busy—but it was sort of cool, seeing them come together, watching an actual home constructed and knowing I'd been a part of it.

I was frequently bored, but peaceful in a way I hadn't been

in years—not since before my sister's diagnosis. And yet, for some reason, I returned to New York and remained there. Sure, I'd learned my lesson. I never got another DUI, but everything else? I guess my mother's letter basically said I hadn't learned the lessons I was supposed to.

Doesn't mean I'll learn them this time either, however.

"Wow," Maren whispers, rolling down a window and reaching her arm out, as if she wants to grab one of the gloomy trees. "This is crazy. *Charlie.* Wow. I have a good feeling about this place."

"You sound like the naïve girl in a horror movie," I warn her. "The one who dies first."

After another thirty seconds, the house comes into view at last and that queasy guilt in my stomach worsens. What was once a stately old Southern mansion, complete with a broad front porch, is now...a relic. The kind of place you chance upon and wonder why the hell it's still standing—the stairs are caving in, windowpanes are broken, the roof sags dangerously, and a massive tree branch juts out of its center like a flagpole.

This isn't a house my mother abandoned a few months ago. It's a house that seems to have been abandoned since I last saw it.

How could this much destruction take place over the course of twelve years?

My mother couldn't have been living here.

God, I *hope* she wasn't living here.

A better son would have known what was happening. A better son would have come back to see her.

The last time she came to visit me, she prattled on about endless bullshit that didn't matter—her friend Marianne's granddaughter and the clerk at the Stop-n-Shop. Now I've got to wonder if it was just so I never got a chance to ask her about anything real.

I pull to a stop in front of the rotting stairs, ready to suggest we just go find a hotel. Beaufort and Hilton Head aren't far. The structural engineer will get here within an hour and condemn the place, and we'll find a five-star hotel and be done with it. Hot girl with a Southern accent for me, while Maren spends the night on a call with her puppies or watching informational videos about microplastics in the water supply. We'll get out of Charleston in the morning.

"Ohhhh," Maren says, however—as if she has stumbled upon the Taj Mahal by accident. "Oh, Charlie, look at this place."

"By which you must mean, 'Charlie, yes, it's just as terrible as you said it would be,' yet I'm not hearing that in your tone."

"*Terrible?* It's an abandoned mansion surrounded by oaks! I feel like Odysseus, chancing upon the home of a god."

"I've got no idea what you're talking about, but I can promise you there aren't any gods in there. I'd bet my ass there's a family of squirrels, however."

Maren is clearly experiencing something entirely different, as she's out of the car and *fuck*—

"Maren, wait!" I shout, darting out of the driver's seat and lunging in her direction. My warning comes too late. She is already on the stairs, one of which promptly starts to crack underfoot. She flails and hurtles backward, like a tree pulled out at the root.

I barely manage to catch her before she hits the ground.

She swallows, staring up at me with wide eyes. "I didn't expect that."

"That the stairs were going to cave in?" I'm winded, and I don't think it's from lunging three feet. She could have broken her fucking spine. "Clearly."

"No," she says with a breathless laugh. "I didn't expect you'd bother trying to catch me."

Of course she didn't. We probably ought to keep it that way.

6

______

MAREN

Charlie is full of surprises. If he was anyone else—meaning not my stepbrother, and also not Charlie Dalton— I'd say it was almost romantic, the way he lunged to save me.

He brusquely sets me on my feet like a misbehaving child. "Let's get something straight," he barks. "You don't take a step on the property until we know it's safe, clear?"

I ignore his tone, walking to the other side of the stairs. There is something about the house. It calls to me, pulling me inside it. From the instant it came into view, it's felt momentous...a sort of promise that my life is about to change.

I can't say this aloud—not to Charlie, who is inclined to ridicule me even when I am saying perfectly rational things. But...*this place.* The trees hang heavy with Spanish moss, and the warm air is soft as velvet on my skin. There's so much noise, but none of it is manmade— a whisper against my ears rather than a bruise. I'd almost forgotten what it could be like, out of the city. I'd almost forgotten how much I've missed it.

I take a careful first step and find myself lifted by the waist and removed from the stairs entirely.

"Maren, it's as if you didn't hear me two seconds ago. I'm going first." He releases an aggravated sigh as he starts to climb the stairs ahead of me. "I can already tell we'd be better off just burning the place down."

Does he really not feel how timeless this is? These trees, this house, this magnolia-scented heat...all of it existed a hundred years ago. I could be Zelda Fitzgerald right now, a debutante enjoying one last dance before all the boys leave for the First World War. I could be Daisy Buchanan, pining for Jay Gatsby.

I take a deep breath and the house says, *Come, take another breath and another after that. Let me put you back together.* Which is yet another thing I can't tell Charlie. He seems like the type who'd object to a talking house.

The porch floorboards sag under my weight but don't give way. Charlie watches, nostrils flaring, until I'm safely beside him before he pulls out a key.

The smell of mildew wafts out of the house the second he opens the door. I dismiss Harvey's voice in my head, the one warning about the damage this will do to our future offspring, and follow Charlie into the tiled foyer.

The stale air seems to rustle, a hostess straightening her skirts as callers enter. The tiled floor is filthy, and the ancient floral wallpaper peels in curls off the plaster behind it, but I bet the sconces are original. Same with the brass chandelier overhead.

A thousand lives have been lived in this home, and at least some of them were happy. I picture a young mother here a hundred years ago while her small children run past, their laughter echoing in the halls, deepening as they grew.

I swear to God it feels as if I belong here, as if I've always belonged here, as if I was that mother or perhaps one of those children but I—

"Earth to Professor Trelawney," Charlie says, and I blink, so lost in my thoughts I almost forgot who I was with.

I bite my lip. "Wow. I thought *I* was the dork, but you've just surpassed me with the obscure Harry Potter reference."

"I'm pretty sure the fact that you know exactly who I meant puts us on equal dork footing."

"It was inaccurate anyway. I see myself more as a Luna Lovegood type. The blonde hair, etcetera."

"Well played. You're back to being the dorkiest. Now, stop daydreaming and admit what we're both thinking: this place is a lost cause."

I blink again, shocked. "A lost cause? No. I..." How does he not see it? Even without this overwhelming sense that I belong here, the value of this place is obvious. We're standing in the foyer, and ahead of us, a grand staircase spills upward toward the second floor, twisting in two separate directions at the landing, a stained-glass window at its center. To both our left and right are massive rooms with views out to the grassy lawn and water on the other side. It has great bones, yes, but it also holds something else. It's like this...jewelry box of past lives and rich memories. Can't he see that?

Of course he doesn't. This is Charlie. He notices hot girls and nice cars and the gleam of Jack Daniels over ice. Here, he only sees cracked plaster and the loose wires hanging off the walls and the water-damaged ceiling. He might also be noticing the...

"Holy shit. Charlie, tell me it wasn't your mother who put in that carpet."

Because they didn't even do wall-to-wall carpet at the turn of the century, which means there's probably hardwood beneath the nasty gray shag rug in the room to our left.

"That was always there as far as I know."

"My God. Why didn't your mother ever pull it up?"

He shrugs as if it couldn't possibly matter. "Maren, believe me, the carpet is the least of my concerns. Have you not noticed the fucking water damage...What the hell are you doing?"

I've fallen to my knees on the carpet and am digging through my purse. I brandish a tiny pair of nail scissors, which I'm fairly certain I wasn't supposed to have flown with, and jam it into the base of the carpet, clipping at whatever holds it together. Under normal circumstances, I doubt manicure scissors would have worked, but the carpet is so dilapidated that it gives way with little resistance, spewing dust into the air as I slice.

"Maren, I repeat, what the fuck are you doing?"

I can't pull it back, but I'm able to stick my finger through the hole I've created. "Charlie, it's hardwood. Probably wide-plank hardwood. You could totally refinish these. I'd do a nice honey stain. It would brighten this place up a—"

His groan stops the flow of my words. "Maren, has the mold in here already gotten to your brain? I'm not worried about *refinishing the floors*. The roof is caving in and half the windows are broken. It's probably not even sound, and if the structural engineer weren't already scheduled, I wouldn't even bother hiring one. It's just going to get torn down."

"*No.*" I climb to my feet. "Charlie, you can't tear it down. Please."

His teeth sink into his lower lip as he searches for a polite way to tell me no. "Mare...we'll see what the engineer says, but I think you're not grasping how much work saving this place would take, if it's even possible."

I think *he's* not grasping how much work a home like this *deserves* and I don't know how to persuade him if he doesn't see it already.

Nothing changes as we take in the rest of the house. When I gush over the real, wood-burning fireplaces, he groans over the signs that a family of birds has been entering through the chimney. When I point out the elaborate molding along the ceiling, he points out the wasp's nest in one corner.

Charlie refuses to let me go upstairs with him, which he claims is for my safety but is more likely because he doesn't want me falling more in love with this place than I already have. I have to fight myself to do as I'm told because that sense I had—that the house wants me here—is even stronger now.

And it wants me *upstairs*, in particular.

I wait impatiently, listening to the thud of his steps above me, and the oddest sensation washes over me. A chill, goose bumps and then...delight. A giddy thrill, the sort I haven't felt in a decade at least. It's the way I used to feel in high school as my friends and I got ready to meet the boys from Collegiate at the one club that would let us in.

As if something magical is about to happen—something I'll never forget.

It eases away as he starts down the stairs, like a bashful friend darting from the room, but...something remains behind.

It feels a bit like hope.

Charlie shakes his head, his pessimism unchanged. "All six rooms are in terrible shape."

"I don't care," I say on a breath. "Don't you see what it could be? I'll help you. We'll bring it back."

He tugs at his hair. Frustrated with me, no doubt, but making far more of an effort to hide it than Harvey would. "Look, I don't know what's going on with you here, but renovating this place will cost millions. All my money is tied up in the stock market and that team I'm funding in San Antonio. And we're only here for a week. How much do you even think we'd accomplish? A job like this will take *years*."

"I'll help," I blurt before I've thought it through. "And I have my trust fund. I can use that. And Henry loves you. I'm sure he'd—"

Charlie stops me with a gentle squeeze of the bicep.

"Maren, I'm not using your trust fund, and I like Henry, but I'm sure as fuck not asking my stepmother's *ex-husband* for a loan. You see how incredibly awkward that would be, don't you?"

I guess he has a point. But I have a point, too, albeit an entirely intuitive and possibly illogical one.

This place isn't meant to be torn down. Somehow, in the next six days, I've got to convince him to save it.

7

CHARLIE

Maren has clearly watched one too many movies in which a couple of people with hammers build an entire home in a day's time. And despite her earnest promises about helping me, she's probably never even changed a lightbulb.

She emerges from the kitchen with that same optimism.

"The stove works," she concludes. "And the refrigerator could use a good cleaning, but it's running." My mother had so much faith in my return that she didn't bother shutting off the power. Not her wisest move.

"Excellent. So I'll still spend millions rehabbing this house, but we can hang onto the appliances from 1970. That's great news."

"It won't be millions," she argues, heading to the laundry room to my left. "And some things matter more than money."

This is the kind of thing the Fischer girls with their trust funds say quite often. "You know who says that? People with a lot of money."

She blows out a weary breath. "You're so cranky today. Is this because you've had to go twenty-four hours without alcohol or because you've had to go twenty-four hours without sex?"

I glance at my watch. "It's actually only been sixteen hours for one, and eight hours for the other. So no. And I'm not cranky. I'm just trying to provide a counterpoint to the lack of logic coming from your side. Mare, this is not happening."

"We'll see what the engineer says," Maren tells me cheerfully, opening the washing machine door as a truck rumbles over the gravel in front.

I stride toward the heavy wood door. "This isn't a negotiation."

"We'll see," she replies as if it *is* a negotiation, one in which she holds all the cards.

A lifetime of being hot has created this problem. She's so accustomed to getting her way that she can't hear the word *no*. And there's a weak part of me that has always struggled with saying it to her myself—she's gotten her way with every-fuck-ing-thing she's ever asked of me, but crashing in my apartment for a weekend and saving a centuries-old house are incredibly different requests, and one of them requires a year of my life and at least a million dollars.

So I'm gonna have to get better at saying no. Fast.

When I reach the porch, the engineer is getting a bag out of the cab of his truck. I'm half inclined to tell him he doesn't need to look around at all, and then he turns toward me and—

The guy who's my height and has the build of a college quarterback is the same skinny kid I worked with here for an entire summer. "*Elijah?*"

His eyes crinkle. "Long time no see, Charlie. You got old, man."

I laugh, shaking the hand he's extended. "So did you. How are things? I had no idea Oak Bluff Construction and Engineering was you."

"Yep, it's me," he replies. "Sorry about your mom. I just heard."

Yeah, you and me both. "Thanks."

Elijah's eyes widen when Maren steps up beside me, which is a pretty standard reaction when Maren steps up anywhere. There are lots of women who look better in magazines and TV than they do in real life. Maren is the opposite—the sort of beautiful you can stare straight at yet not quite believe is real. Her eyes are bluer than Photoshop could make them, her skin creamier, her hair shinier. You want to take a second look, a third, just to figure out the trick.

"Elijah," he says, extending his hand. "I worked here with Charlie one summer. You must be Charlie's..." He glances at the massive rock on her finger.

"Sister. Hi, I'm Maren. And are you trying to tell me that Charles Dalton actually did good, honest work at one point in his life?"

"I'm not sure how *good* it was," Elijah says with a laugh, putting his boot down hard on a joist, watching the boards sag in response. "And I'm pretty sure he was here under duress—you'd gotten a DUI or something, right?"

I throw a hand over Maren's mouth, anticipating the motherly scolding she's about to offer. "Before you start, I got a DUI on a *golf cart*, which I didn't even know was a thing. You can apparently also get a DUI while on a bike or horseback."

Maren pushes my hand away. "These are things only Charlie would know," she says to Elijah. "You must have learned *so much* from him that summer."

"I aged about a decade over three months," he says, "but that was mostly due to Charlie's haphazard building skills."

He's grinning; Maren's laughing. She's already doing it—making everyone fall in love with her. This place is actively falling in on itself and she'll soon have him claiming it just needs a fresh coat of paint.

It's irritating. And cute. It irritates me that I find it cute.

"Okay, let's take a look," he says. "I'm sure you're aware this place already needs a new porch and a new roof. Hopefully that's the worst of it."

"Clearly you haven't seen the interior, then," I reply, and Maren elbows me.

"This place is amazing," she gushes. "Obviously, you've been inside, so I don't even have to tell you how stunning it is, but—"

"Maren," I growl. "Stop. Let him decide for himself." Because the next words out of her mouth are definitely *money's no object* or *I'll just die if we can't fix it*. And if he's half as weak as me, he'll find himself offering to take the job on for free just to make her smile.

On second thought, maybe I *should* let her talk.

Elijah walks through the house, knocking on walls, stomping on the floor, examining the windows, and flipping on light switches—Maren wants to believe this is all about tearing out some shitty carpet and replacing the wallpaper, but the cosmetic damage is the least of my concerns. Half the floors in the house sag when you put any weight on them, and I don't know much about construction, but I doubt that's a good sign.

"There are problems," Elijah says, "but the real issue will likely be the basement."

I frown. "It has a basement?" This seems like something I'd have known.

"A house this old probably has a root cellar rather than a real basement. You'd access it from the outside."

We go out back to a trap door that abuts the house, one I somehow never noticed during my few visits here.

Elijah climbs down a ladder in the darkness and turns on a flashlight for us.

"You don't need to come down," I tell Maren as I begin my descent. "It's probably pretty creepy."

Her eyes light up. *Creepy* is apparently an enticing word for her, which perhaps explains how she wound up with Harvey.

I reach the basement—dirt floor, dirt walls with plant roots bursting through—and turn to follow Maren's descent. Her shorts are riding up just enough to spy the curve of her ass. I cut a warning glance toward Elijah, and he politely looks away.

"Wow," Maren whispers, taking it in.

"Until about 1920 or 1930, most homes didn't have refrigerators. This was where they stored stuff to keep it cool. If you could afford it, you'd get a big block of ice delivered and keep it in sawdust to lower the temperature."

"I can't imagine, even with ice, that it got that cool," says Maren.

Elijah shrugs. "Dairy and meat were mostly fresh or could survive a day down here. But other stuff would last a lot longer. Canned goods, vegetables ..."

"Bodies," I add.

Maren's head jerks from me to Elijah. "That was a joke, right?"

He shrugs. "Until a couple decades ago, it was sort of the norm around here to store a body in the house until burial."

Maren's eyes go wide. "And...*did* people die in this house?"

He glances from me back to her—a look that asks if he should tell the whole truth, to which I shrug. "I'd imagine so."

This hasn't diminished Maren's enthusiasm for the house at all. Her eyes glow in the dim light. Everything that should send her screaming seems to have the opposite effect instead. Again, though...Harvey.

Elijah stays behind to finish examining the basement while Maren and I climb back up the ladder. When he rejoins us, he suggests, with a polite glance in Maren's direction, that we stay put while he checks out the attic since he's not sure how structurally sound it is.

"I don't know if contractor porn is a thing," she says with an appreciative purr once he's out of earshot, "but if so, he could be making a lot more money doing something else."

My teeth grind. "Maybe this would be a good time to remind you that you're married."

She laughs as she heads toward the covered back deck. "I'm married, not dead. I still have eyes."

We sit side by side on the stairs, and she stretches her long legs in front of her. She has the smoothest skin I've ever seen, skin that begs you to glide a hand over it.

"I bet they had amazing parties here," she says dreamily, looking over the grassy slope splayed out before us, which leads down to the water.

"*Who* had amazing parties?"

"The family who lived here at the turn of the century," she says. She didn't know shit about this house until an hour ago. Now she's the Oak Bluff historian, if historians are people who craft tales entirely from their own imaginations. "I bet they had amazing parties and played croquet on this lawn, and the kids ran around catching fireflies." She smiles as if she's watching it happen.

"Maren, you don't even know that a family owned it. Maybe it was some crotchety old confederate widow who remained pissed off until death that the North won the war. Maybe it was the KKK meeting house. Maybe it was a brothel."

She exhales heavily. "It wasn't a brothel."

"And you know this *how*?"

She hitches a shoulder. "Pure economics. You said there are only six rooms upstairs. They'd need more rooms than that to cover the mortgage."

I laugh unwillingly. "It's funny the way you go from saying things like 'some things matter more than money' to providing an accurate ratio of overhead-to-income when it suits you."

She ignores me, leaning back on her palms, staring at the

water with shining eyes. I think I finally know what Maren looks like when she's in love. "I adore this house," she whispers.

"I picked up on that."

She sits upright and places her hand over mine. "Charlie... do you really feel nothing inside there? Nothing at all?"

I feel as if every asset I possess is about to be bled dry. It's on the tip of my tongue to say it, but I hold back. Because this is Maren, who is a burst of springtime in the dead of winter and... she genuinely loves this house. She loves it in that same gentle, all-encompassing way she loves her mother and her sister and her dogs and perhaps even me, and though I can't imagine caring deeply about any of those things, I like that she does.

But none of that changes the fact that I don't need this place and don't want to be here a moment longer than necessary.

"I don't know, Maren. It's hard to see past some stuff."

"What stuff?"

My jaw shifts. I didn't want to get into this, but Maren will find a way to force the issue, so I might as well. "That my mom was living like this," I finally say. "Or more to the point, wasn't living here at all, and I didn't even fucking know. I should have come back to see her."

She leans her head on my shoulder. A whole day of travel and her hair still smells like roses. "Why didn't you?"

"I don't know." The words are so quiet they're barely audible. "Life got busy. It wasn't easy to get here, and she always offered to come up." Those are shitty answers, but not nearly as shitty as the truth: that I didn't come because I just didn't care enough. My mother suffered about as much as anyone can suffer—she lost an eight-year-old she adored to cancer—and I couldn't take a week out of my worthless life to visit.

Maren sighs. "I hesitate to say this, because it feels manipulative, but I'm going to say it anyway. I'd say it even if I hated the house: you feel guilty, I think, and you're going to keep on feeling guilty if you don't fix it up."

"You're right. That does seem manipulative."

She laughs and nestles closer. "You know I'm right. If you forget about the time it'll take and what it might cost, picture yourself back in New York after each outcome and tell me how you'll feel."

"I'm pretty sure I'm going to keep feeling like shit either way," I argue. "Only significantly poorer in one of those scenarios. And what am I supposed to do with this grand Southern manor after it's all fixed up? I'm never getting married. I'm never having kids. I'm sure as hell not going to vacation here *alone*. It's just gonna sit vacant and decay all over again."

"I'm not saying you can't sell it eventually," she replies. "But your mom wanted to see it shine again. You can do that much and decide the rest later."

"We still have no idea what it'll cost."

There's a polite cough from behind us. Elijah stands there, looking somewhat uncertain. Perhaps because I'm sitting here *cuddling* with the girl who introduced herself as my sister.

Maren lifts her head and smiles at him, sunny and untroubled, because she's affectionate with everyone and has never noticed that *I'm* only affectionate with her. "How was it?"

"So, from a structural standpoint, it's salvageable," Elijah says, "but there's pretty significant water damage in the basement—you'll need to underpin the back left corner, and there's some necessary remediation to keep it dry going forward. There's also a fair amount of water damage in the attic because that roof has been in bad shape for a while. We're talking replacing joists and redoing the upstairs ceiling. Plus the roof, obviously."

"That's not that bad," Maren says cheerfully.

Fuck my life.

"Maren," I growl, "that's a lot. And none of that makes this a house anyone wants to *live* in."

Elijah runs a hand through his hair. "Yeah, it's far from

livable. You've got radiant heat, which is pretty standard for the time it was built, but you'll need to replace the copper pipes to get it up and running—not that heat tends to be a big issue here. HVAC is shot, however, and a house of this size really needs two systems, not one. The bathrooms are in bad shape; a lot of the wiring isn't up to code. I'll write it all up tonight."

"Ballpark?" I ask.

"Basement—forty-five grand. Rest of the structural stuff, maybe another four hundred. Soup to nuts with high-end finishes, somewhere around a million. I can get you a quote if you're interested."

"But it sounds like it's safe for us to sleep here," Maren urges.

Elijah and I both gawk at her.

"You're planning to *sleep* here?" Elijah asks, his voice stained by incredulity, and why wouldn't it be? Maren's got thirty thousand dollars in jewelry on a single wrist alone. Even if Elijah doesn't know that the bracelet is Cartier, that the watch is Chopard, that the purse she casually tossed on the porch floor probably costs more than his truck...privilege comes off her in waves.

She's not someone who sleeps in a house like this.

"No," I say.

At the same moment, she says, "Absolutely."

I turn to face her. "Maren, he just said the *roof* could cave in."

She hitches a shoulder. "Then we'll sleep on the first floor."

I groan. I already know there's no arguing with her, so I'm not sure why I'm continuing to try. "There's only one decent mattress upstairs."

"Then we'll drag it down here."

"You seem to be ignoring the part about there only being one mattress. Though if you'd like to sleep here alone and let me go to a hotel, I can be persuaded."

She shivers. As much as she loves the idea of this house being possessed by the spirit of a very happy family who threw lavish parties, she doesn't love its dead inhabitants *that* much.

"We can share a mattress for tonight and go get some kind of blow-up thing tomorrow," she argues. "It's just one night. We'll see if we can get blankets and pillows in town."

Elijah glances away, as if he feels he shouldn't be listening in. Probably because the incredibly hot girl who claimed to be my sister is now talking about sharing a bed with me.

"Come on," she says, "it'll be like a campout."

"Spoken by someone I guarantee has never camped."

She grins as if she already knows she's won, and that makes sense.

Of course she's fucking won.

And if I don't get her ass out of here, I'll be playing croquet on this lawn alone next summer, trying to figure out how I just blew a million dollars on a house I never wanted in the first place.

8

___

MAREN

Even in my earliest memories, I have a sense of being on the outside. Perhaps because it was so obvious that Henry, my stepfather, preferred Kit to me. He tried hard not to show it, but there was something in his gaze when he held her, something I'd now claim was reverence. *I can't believe I'm a father*, he'd said when Kit came home, unaware that I was in the room.

My mother, my father, this tiny new baby—they were the family unit, inside the windows of a warm and cozy home— and I was the beggar sitting just outside the door.

I've worked hard to become adaptable and pleasing, trying to make sure I have a place wherever I find myself. Oddly, Charlie is the one person I've never felt compelled to do this with. Even though he's sort of a dick during dinner, and he continues to be a dick at the Stop-n-Shop, I have no urge to back down at all.

"We could be at a five-star hotel, Maren," he says, walking behind me as I throw some poor-quality sheets into our cart. "We won't even have A/C."

If anyone else said this, under these circumstances, I'd cave.

I'd apologize and scramble to see if we could still find rooms. With Charlie, though…I just don't. "Fortunately there are lots of broken windows so that will take care of the airflow."

He throws his head back like a sulking teen. "Come on. We'll go to Hilton Head. You can get some incredibly over-priced massage and spend tomorrow sitting out at the beach drinking a nice glass of hydrogen water or whatever the latest fad is, which I will mock you for until I'm too drunk to be witty. That's fun for us both."

"You're not that witty sober," I reply, slightly stung by the hydrogen water comment, though I shouldn't be. This is who I am now. Or who everyone *thinks* I am. Some health-obsessed stoic so busy pureeing vegetables and researching fluoride side effects that she's forgotten how to have fun. "I know it seems incredibly lame, but I don't have a lot of adventure in my life, and this feels like an adventure. Harvey didn't even want me to come on this trip. He was talking about how the air quality might affect my eggs."

Charlie rolls his eyes. "That's because he's a gaslighting prick."

I ignore this. I gave up trying to convince Charlie to tolerate my husband years ago.

"My life has gotten narrower and narrower with every month we don't get pregnant," I continue. "And I just want to do something big, something wildly different, even if it's only for a few days. Does that make sense?"

He pulls the spatula I just grabbed out of the cart and sets it back on the shelf. "Then do something wildly different, Mare. Eat a bunch of candy, drink your weight in margaritas—go to some nudist resort and lie out naked for a week. If you're going to expand your horizons for a few days, there are more fun ways to do it."

"This *is* fun. It's an adventure. I'm camping out in this amaz-ing, definitely haunted old Southern mansion with my cranky stepbrother, and possibly helping him pull a house together. I'll make us shitty meals on that old stove, and we can tell each other ghost stories at night. It's...something I'll never be able to do again. Can you please try to enjoy it?"

He laughs begrudgingly. "Okay, but if I was right about it being a brothel and all the ghosts are dead prostitutes, you might regret the way I attempt to enjoy it."

I briefly picture Charlie with a ghost prostitute, which is surprisingly titillating. "Please don't dry hump the mattress until we're no longer sharing."

I buy several things Charlie insists we won't need—two clean pans, the spatula I put back into our cart, a set of cheap plates—and then we go to the grocery store, where I buy more stuff Charlie insists we won't need. I think he's mostly disturbed by the vegetables.

It's dark by the time we get back to the house, and...it looks a lot less charming and a lot more haunted by moonlight. Our jokes about the ghosts we'd encounter tonight were funnier when they didn't seem probable.

The chandelier only has one working bulb, so we put sheets on the mattress in the dimmest light imaginable, and then I brave the downstairs powder room to pee and brush my teeth.

Both the toilet and sink are cracked. I've run a cleaning wipe over the surfaces, but everything remains filthy. I'm not sure why I didn't take him up on the hotel. I really, really want to shower.

He waits until I've slid between the sheets to hit the lights, and then lands on the other side of the mattress.

"So are we telling ghost stories now?" he asks. I can just make out the flash of his teeth in the moonlight.

"It seemed a little more appealing when we were in a brightly lit store, to be honest."

"And we don't want to summon them by accident."

I laugh, and then shiver. I still, very much, want to go upstairs, in a way that doesn't feel entirely...*me*.

"The powder room was in, uh, rough shape," I say.

"That powder room is straight out of *America's Cleanest Homes Digest* compared to what's upstairs," he replies. "You're not going to shower all week."

Oh God. I hadn't thought about this, but I refuse to concede the point. Maybe I'll sneak over to the hotel and pay to use their spa. "I'll be fine. I'll jump in the water if I feel especially gross."

"There are probably alligators in there."

"You're making that up."

He laughs. "Am I? We shall see. Imagine how much Harvey will blame you if you come back missing an arm."

He's laughing, but my stomach is in knots. He truly has no clue how far Harvey will go to blame me for a million tiny things.

"It was a joke, Maren," he says after a moment.

"Harvey wouldn't stay with me if I lost an arm."

He'd find a way to blame me for it, and then he'd move on to someone else.

"If you're married to a man who would leave you for suffering a tragic accident," Charlie says unhappily, "then maybe the alligator will have done you a favor."

I sigh as I roll away.

He might have a point.

It's a tap that wakes me. Three distinct taps to the shoulder, in quick succession—the way an airline attendant might wake you if you were still asleep as the plane is landing.

My eyes fly open in the moonlit room, and I roll toward Charlie, wondering why the hell he's woken me...except he's flat on his back and sound asleep. That's when something furry brushes against my arm.

I scream, scrambling atop the only point higher than me in the entire room.

Which is Charlie.

His arms band around me tight and alarm sharpens his features. His body braces and his arms tighten further. "Is someone in the house?"

"No, there's something in the *room*. Like, a rat or a mouse, or something. It just brushed against my arm."

His features relax, and a half-smile stretches across his face. "And you decided sex with me would take your mind off of it. I knew we'd get to this point eventually."

He's joking, obviously, but there's something large and firm pressed to my abdomen, which I shall politely ignore. "No, idiot. I want you to do something about it."

"Like what? Accuse it of trespassing? Threaten to sue if it doesn't leave?"

Skittering feet race past again near the top of our heads, and Charlie jolts at the sound, managing to headbutt me in the process.

"Ouch."

"Sorry," he says as he somehow climbs to his feet with me in his arms.

"Not so funny anymore now that you felt it too, huh?" I demand.

He starts walking toward the light switch, holding me aloft, with my legs around his waist. "I could put you down, you know, and let you walk on your own."

"You are brave and strong, and I won't even bring up the fact that you probably gave me a concussion just now."

He flips on the light and, after confirming that anything living in here has departed, sets me down and checks his watch. "It's three thirty. Probably not worth getting a hotel at this point.

So our options are sleep in the car or take our chances with the mouse."

Hardly even a decision.

Ten minutes later we've folded down the third-row seat of the car we rented and are huddled in the back. It would be an okay fit for small people, but neither of us are small people.

"It touched me," I whisper, once we're settled in. "Aren't rats what spread bubonic plague?"

"If it'll make this trip end faster," he replies, "I hope they're still spreading it."

His breathing evens out within a minute or two—the long, unconscious breaths of someone who's deeply asleep. It's only then that I remember that tap on my shoulder. It felt like a warning.

Even if Charlie was awake, I wouldn't tell him what I'm thinking. It's too crazy to say aloud.

9

———

MAREN

I wake surprisingly refreshed for someone who's just slept in the trunk of a car, had a rodent crawl over her, and was aggressively hit in the head by her stepbrother.

"I've been cured of my desire to camp," I tell Charlie as he opens his eyes.

His mouth curves. "I'll leave Elijah a note. You check on flights."

"It hasn't cured me of my love of the *house*," I reply. "Besides, I bet Elijah's not scared of rodents."

He rolls his eyes. "I wasn't *scared*, Maren. I just didn't fly down here with a bunch of rat traps in my carry-on. And I assure you that one last night was the first of many."

I shudder. I still love the house, but...it'll be a while before I sleep in there again, and that's not even factoring in that ghostly tap on the shoulder.

It was probably my imagination. But it sure didn't feel like it.

Charlie opens the trunk and climbs out. I follow him stiffly. Maybe I didn't have such a great night of sleep after all.

While he goes upstairs to brave the shower, something I'm

not quite ready to do, I open my larger suitcase and pull out the juicer I brought.

Yes, I brought a juicer. A top-of-the-line, ten-pound juicer. Charlie's eventual ridicule over this fact is inevitable.

I set it up on the kitchen counter. I used cleaning wipes in here last night, but there's no amount of cleaning that can salvage this place: the avocado green cabinets and laminate countertops are peak 1970s chic and I saw a huge roach running across the rust linoleum floor yesterday. Ignoring this, I grab the veggies I bought at the store last night, the ones Charlie insisted no one here would eat. It's one of many daily rituals at home that I manage to make stressful. I worry that all the produce comes in plastic. I worry about the green apple I add to make it palatable—is it too much sugar? If I truly cared about my health and that of my future offspring, wouldn't I skip it entirely? This is a conversation I have with myself every morning as I put the fruit through my thousand-dollar appliance. It's an endless process between the chopping, the grinding, the hand scrubbing of all of the components—all for a glass of juice that I will continue to feel somewhat guilty about.

And maybe that's the issue—that I can't seem to find anything in my life that I don't feel a little guilty about. Or maybe it's that I have so much time on my hands now that ruminating on stupid questions like this is the only way to fill the empty space.

Most people would say it's a good problem to have, but I was a lot happier back when I didn't have the time to think about any of it.

"Tell me you didn't bring a fucking juicer," grumbles Charlie, walking into the kitchen. I'm not sure why I was the model instead of him. His hair is damp, pushed off his face, he hasn't shaved, and he's wearing a T-shirt and shorts, but he still looks so good you'd buy anything he was selling just to feel as if you could be him or be *with* him one day.

He takes a seat at the cracked mustard-yellow table and I pour him a glass of juice. "I added extra green apple just for you. You already get so much sugar in your diet from alcohol that I probably shouldn't have added any at all."

He looks with dismay at the glass I've set in front of him. "Would it help matters if I told you that I'm probably not drinking it, with apple or without?"

"You're drinking it, Charles. I put in a lot of effort, and this will undo at least a week of your Manhattan lifestyle."

He crosses the kitchen and reaches for the bottle of vodka he purchased last night. "Fine, but I'm augmenting it."

"Charlie," I huff. "For God's sake, it's nine o'clock in the morning."

"You don't always need to tell me the time," he says. "My watch does that quite successfully. And with less disdain."

"But why?" I ask. "Can't you get through the day sober?"

"I could," he replies, "but I'd prefer not to."

He returns to his seat at the table with the vodka and holds his glass up to the light, as if deciding how much alcohol is required.

"I don't mean to judge—"

He sets the glass down and looks up at me with a single brow raised. "Prefacing judgment by saying 'I don't mean to judge' makes it no less irritating. And you're always judging me. Let's not pretend otherwise."

I ignore this. "If you have to drink to make your life bearable, there's probably something deeper going on."

"I stand corrected. Nothing judgmental about that at all."

My shoulders sag. He's not wrong. I *am* being judgmental, and no fun, and the green juice looks really unappetizing. Maybe I'm every bit as lame and uptight as he seems to think.

"Look," I say, sliding into the seat across from his, suddenly weary, "I'm not pretending for a minute that my own life is perfect, but do you see my point?"

Something slightly bleak flashes in his eyes, as if he's opened the shutters to show me what really lies underneath the attitude and the drinking and the one-night stands.

"I'm trying to get by, Maren. Same way you are."

My heart sinks.

All this time I'd somehow convinced myself he mostly enjoyed his life, the past month or two aside. That he knew something I didn't about how to make meaningless things pleasurable, about living in the present.

But no...he's just handling his sadness less secretly than I'm handling mine. And maybe mine's not the secret I thought it was either.

Charlie sure seems well aware of it.

10

CHARLIE

When Elijah rolls up to the house after breakfast and sits at the table to discuss costs, I'm faced with a dilemma. I already know I'm keeping the house—I emailed the property developer last night and gave him the news. But I don't need Maren here running the cost of the renovation up astronomically, so do I come up with a clever excuse to get rid of her for this conversation, or am I just blatantly rude?

I opt for rude. It's easier. She expects it of me anyway. "Maren, go for a walk while Elijah and I discuss costs."

She raises a brow, reminding me very much of Kit, except if Kit did that, I'd fear for my life. "*Excuse me?*"

I run a hand over my face. "Look, I don't need you telling him we need a roof made entirely of bulletproof glass or walls painted in liquid gold."

"That's ridiculous," she sniffs. "Bulletproof glass is too heavy for a roof and gold would clash with the brass fixtures."

Maren gives me the finger, and we both watch as she walks away. Elijah watches her just a moment too long, which might be because he's wondering what our deal is, but more likely is because Maren is incredibly hot and wearing shorts that barely cover her ass. *Again*. I'm tempted to tell him she's married, but I can't think of a way to do it without sounding like a jealous dick.

"She's married," I bark.

Well, that was subtly done, Charles. Well played.

He cocks his head. "Yeah, I figured when I saw the Hope Diamond on her hand."

Why the hell did I tell him, anyway? It's none of my concern if she gets hit on down here. It would actually be ideal. Maybe she'd realize how much happier she could be without Harvey. Either way, I've got more important shit to deal with than Maren and her relationships. "How soon can you get started?"

He frowns. "You really ought to bid this out, Charlie. It's a big job."

He might be right, but I just want it...behind me. And I don't want to babysit someone while it's going on. "I need to be in San Antonio for half the summer and probably most of the fall, so I want to trust that I'm not getting screwed over when I'm gone. I know you. I won't know anyone else who bids on this."

"I can get some guys out here by tomorrow morning to start underpinning the foundation, but you know..." He glances out to where Maren is now walking. "It's probably for the best if you're not sleeping here while there's work going on, at least until the structural stuff is done."

I laugh. "Some kind of animal brushed Maren's arm in the middle of the night. There's not a chance she's sleeping in the house again."

He nods. "You've got another five nights here, right? Closest decent hotels would still be a haul. I guess we could take a look at those cottages your mom had us build. You could sleep there and use the kitchen in the big house to eat."

I heave a sigh. Fuck. I've got no idea what my mom used

those cottages for, if she used them at all, but they're probably full of art supplies or garbage, and only one of them has plumbing. "I guess they can't be in worse shape than the house."

"So…" He glances toward Maren again. "Do you want to look at just one of the cottages or both?"

Why the fuck did she introduce herself as my sister? "She's my stepsister. We were in college when our parents got married," I tell him. And then I realize I've just made it sound as if sleeping with my stepsister is *okay*. "But we'd be better off with separate places if possible."

We find Maren on the path, and together, the three of us walk around to the other side of the cove to the first of the cottages. The wood steps Elijah and I built fourteen years ago have seen better days, but they're sturdy. I unlock the door, bracing for old lawnmowers on top of easels on top of discarded furniture…and find a furnished room instead. There's a bed with a quilt folded neatly at the mattress's end, a small nightstand with a lamp, a bookshelf stocked with mysteries and romances, a small desk with office supplies.

And a half bottle of the Chanel perfume I got my mom every year.

Fuck. I wince, hit by yet another wave of guilt, and then slide open the drawer of a small desk, hoping for another letter, some explanation for the fact that she never told me things had gotten so bad. "My mom must have been living out here. Why the fuck didn't she tell me she'd had to move out of the house?"

Maren crosses to where I stand and squeezes my hand. "We'll figure it out, Charlie, okay?"

I don't actually think we *will* figure it out, but something about Maren has always soothed me. She soothes everyone, which is why it pisses me off that her husband doesn't try to give that back to her. Someone should.

"I guess we've found you a rat-free home for the next five days," I tell her.

She laughs and puts her head on my shoulder, and Elijah glances between us once again.

We act more like a besotted couple than we do siblings, something Maren doesn't realize.

While it's something I've known since we met.

11

MAREN

The cottages are adorable. As much as I like the house, I can see why his mother would have preferred to sleep out here, if she was alone. They're cozy, first of all, but also set side by side into the hill, with an entire wall of windows facing the water, and each boasting a French door that leads to a small deck overlooking everything.

Charlie says I'm not allowed on the deck because the floorboards are sagging, but generously gives me the furnished cottage—which is the only one with its own bathroom—rather than the one that is currently so full of painting supplies and discarded lawn items that we can't stand fully inside it.

"You can't sleep in here," I tell Charlie.

"I'll empty it out," he says. "It'll be fine."

My mouth opens to tell him he can just stay with me, but I suppose that might sound a little weird to Elijah. And Charlie isn't exactly a shrinking violet. If he *wanted* to share a cottage with me, he'd have just told me he was going to.

Elijah leaves to go deal with permits and tells us to dump the stuff from the cottage on the grass and he'll have a crew get it tomorrow. Charlie walks him out, and I finally get around to returning my mother's call from the day before.

"How's your diet going?" she asks. "I've got some juice for you to try. It's lemon juice with cayenne pepper and agave syrup. We'll get that weight right off you."

My mother is, objectively, a terrible parent. She tried to talk both Kit and me out of going to college and has suggested to us both that bulimia would be the perfect solution if it didn't ruin your teeth (though, she added, veneers can fix that right up). This—her efforts to help me lose the whole ten pounds I packed onto my five-foot-eleven-inch frame once my modeling days ended—is as close as she's ever come to maternal.

"Oh, I actually, uh—" I look around me wildly. "I'm at a resort."

"A weight-loss resort?" she asks hopefully.

I wish I could just tell her the truth, but even if she knew about Charlie's mom's death and the house, I would not. She'd make it into a thing, probably a thing that would ruin the family entirely, a family I adore. I love our get-togethers—me, Roger, my mom, Kit, Charlie, and Henry—who's now best friends with Roger. We are six wildly dysfunctional people who somehow become normal around each other, and I can't imagine how depleted my life would feel without that.

"No, no weight loss," I reply, because otherwise she'll suggest joining me. "They're more focused on meditation."

The purr of an engine catches my attention. Charlie is, inexplicably, driving the rental car over the long grassy lawn. Why the hell he's driving when we're five minutes from the house is beyond me.

"Mom, I've got to go," I tell her.

"I hear a motor," she says. "Tell me you're at least walking around the resort and not taking a golf cart. Those pounds creep up fast when you're—"

"Sorry, Mom, silent meditation. They're taking the phone." I hang up before she can suggest ways I could lose weight while meditating too—*walking meditation works just as well as sitting! Fidgeting burns calories too!*—and head down to where Charlie is now parking the rental—right on the narrow trail and perilously close to the marsh.

"What the hell, Charlie?" I ask. "You couldn't walk?"

His shoulders are tense and he doesn't quite meet my eye. "I want to get this shit out of here. I don't want to wait for the crew."

Oh.

That's what's behind the tension. I think it bothers him, seeing these remnants of his mother's life disposed of, and he'd rather cut the emotion away than sit with it. I get that. How many times have I thrown myself into decorating something at the start of my period to keep from weeping over the fact that my period arrived at all?

"Okay," I reply, grabbing the keys from his hand and popping open the trunk, "but if that car slides into the marsh, you're the one telling the rental company."

"That's fine," he says. "Anyone who's seen you drive will still assume it was you."

It takes hours—and multiple trips to the dump—to get the little cottage emptied. I try to suggest to Charlie that he might eventually want the rakes and the lawnmower and fifteen bags of potting soil, but he just says no in that hard voice, and I decide not to push. As subpar as my relationship with my mother is, if she chose to die alone or never told me how hard her life had gotten, it would break my heart. And I think it's breaking Charlie's.

We stop in Oak Bluff on the final run to the dump. I grab some groceries and cleaning supplies while Charlie heads to the liquor store down the street. I guess our little talk this morning about his drinking didn't do a lot of good. I head to the only register in the whole store, staffed by Martha, the friendly woman who rang us up yesterday.

"You were in here last night," she comments, scanning the chicken broth.

I give her an awkward smile. "Yeah, forgot to get cleaning supplies."

"You know why I remember you?" she asks, and I brace myself. "I've never seen someone so muted. It's as if there are all these colors inside you, but they're covered by this dark cloak."

That's not where I'd thought she was going—people tend to either recognize me or suggest I look a lot like *that model from the 90s*, by which they mean my mother—and I have no idea how to respond. "I've been told that I don't look great in black," I tell her with a small laugh, glancing at my T-shirt. "I guess I should've listened."

She shakes her head. "It's not your clothes. It's your *aura*. Who or what is it that's cast this pall over you?"

My mouth falls open, but I've got no jokes, no response. "I don't know."

She shakes her head. "I bet you do. When you allow yourself to answer the question, you'll realize you already knew. That's always how it is."

I say nothing. And I'd like to dismiss what she says as crazy, but as I leave the store, I've got the uncomfortable feeling that she might be right. I already know.

WE CLEAN both cottages as best we can. It's slow going, as I'd never used a mop before, so I didn't realize I'd need a bucket too, though I probably should have.

When we're finally done, Charlie goes to the main house to shower and I go to the cottage, grateful to strip out of my sticky clothes and stand under the spray while I try to pinpoint the source of my good mood.

I have a spectacular home in Manhattan and my life is easy: I don't have to clean; I don't change my own sheets. I don't even wash my own clothes. I take care of the dogs, I see my family, I help plan various seasonal fundraisers. When I express any discontent with my life, when I mention being tired of the routine, Harvey tells me I'm a spoiled brat and he's probably right, but...I was happy today. Even though I've got blisters from carrying paint cans and my sneakers got trashed when I stepped into the marsh, the hours were full. I felt productive, useful. Maybe the problem at home isn't that my life is jam-packed, but that it's jam-packed with things that don't matter.

I emerge from the cottage bare-faced, with my wet hair twisted atop my head, feeling like a new version of myself. Or maybe an old version of myself, the girl I said goodbye to a long time ago.

Charlie, sitting on the back veranda, watches me approach with a small smile on his face and raises a bottle of wine. "Pizza is on the way. Celebratory drink in the meantime?"

I silence the voice that wants to say *pizza has a high glycemic index.*

"I don't drink," I reply, "and what would we be celebrating?"

"You've successfully talked me into spending all my money, in addition to money I don't have. It's quite a feat. And since when don't you drink? It's not as if you're already pregnant."

He didn't mean anything by it, but the reminder hurts. I've tried. I've tried and tried. I've employed every scientific way to induce fertility and every non-scientific way. I've eaten yams, I've worn a fertility goddess charm, I've remained in bed after sex with my legs straight up in the air...all to no avail while all around me, my friends are having their second kids and an accidental third. *He looks at me and I get pregnant,* they'll laugh-ingly complain, resting a hand on their swollen stomachs. I smile the widest of anyone so they don't know I'm bothered, my jaw grinding hard the whole time.

I hitch a shoulder. "I'm just trying to stay healthy, so I'm in good shape if IVF works."

"Maren," he sighs. "Not to sound like the bad kid in an afterschool special, but a little bit of wine isn't going to make a difference. You know that, right?"

He isn't wrong. But when I don't get pregnant, I will look back at each individual failure—taking this trip, the glass of wine he's talked me into—and have to assume I brought it on myself. "I guess."

"Give me a percentage. What percent chance is there that having half a glass of wine will somehow be bad for a baby you're not even carrying yet?"

"If it was arsenic-laced, it would be."

He laughs. "Sorry, I didn't realize I had to exclude the very real possibility that I'd poison you, which I now wish I'd thought of because it would have saved me money. Presuming the wine is totally normal, what percent chance?"

I sigh. "Extremely small."

"And," he continues, "what is the chance that being more relaxed will actually *help* you get pregnant?"

I see where he's going, and I wish I had an argument, but I don't. "Also small, but less small."

"By that logic, then, you are actively harming your chances of getting pregnant by not enjoying a glass of wine with me."

"While I'm positive this is incorrect, fine, whatever. I'll have half a glass."

He pours me an entire cup and I take a sip. "God, that's so good," I admit.

He laughs under his breath. "Welcome back to the dark side, Maren. There's so much in store for you here."

A pleasant shiver runs over my arms and there's a clench in

my core once again. *If I wasn't married and he wasn't my step-brother...*

I dismiss the thought before it can keep playing out in my head. I've actually had to discard this thought so many times I barely notice I'm doing it anymore.

The pizza arrives. Charlie carries it to the table on the back porch, and we wash it down with wine out of plastic cups as the light dies out over the water. Harvey and I honeymooned in Germany. We stayed at five-star hotels and dined at the best restaurants...but I like this more.

I wasn't happy there, something I wish I'd admitted sooner. And I'm happy here, which is something I sort of wish I could forget.

Once we've cleaned up all our trash, Charlie walks me to my cottage and brushes his teeth at my sink before he goes to the door.

"Lock this when I leave," he warns, "just in case some weirdo saw you in town. And do *not* go on the deck."

For someone who acts as if he doesn't care about anything at all, he seems to spend a lot of time worrying about me.

When I climb into bed, I kind of miss having him a foot or two away.

12

MAREN

Before I've even looked at my phone, I can tell it's early—the sun is up, but low in the sky still. I go to the French glass doors and step out onto the deck, though I promised Charlie I wouldn't. The water moves in gentle ripples from the soft breeze, the marsh grass waving. I close my eyes and take a deep breath. When they open, the first thing I spy is Charlie, running the path around the inlet.

He cleaned up his act here, once upon a time. If we were staying longer than a week, he might manage it again, simply because there's no one to drink to excess with, no one to sleep with, and nothing else to do.

He's running hard, drenched in sweat, and a surprising bubble of envy rises in my chest. I used to run. I'd be antsy on the days I couldn't do it, as if my body was overflowing with energy it needed to expend.

I don't know what happened to that version of myself. It's as if I've been holding perfectly still, scared to take a breath, while I wait for an outcome that never arrives.

I head to the kitchen. Juicing takes forever—I've only just

finished and am in the process of making him some eggs when he enters the kitchen, freshly showered.

"You made eggs?" he asks. "You hate eggs."

I shrug. "I made them for you."

His mouth lifts into a quiet smile as he takes a seat at the table. I set the plate of eggs and a glass of green juice before him. He drinks the entire thing with neither complaints nor vodka.

"We should stay," I blurt. We were supposed to go home next Thursday, the nineteenth. But there's really no reason we can't remain through the following weekend, is there?

He glances up from his plate. "Huh?"

"Through the following weekend. I won't be ready to leave on Thursday, and you can be gone a few more days, right?"

His fork lowers. "What about the dogs? And, less importantly, your spouse?"

"I checked on the dogs this morning and they're great, and Harvey—" I attempt a nonchalant shrug. "He'll be fine. He was only going to be home three days next week anyway."

This is a lie. Harvey will not be fine. In part because of his inexplicable jealousy of Charlie, in part because he'll view this as a dereliction of duty on my end, though all that duty consists of is patiently waiting to get impregnated and being at home when he calls.

"I don't know that there's going to be much for you to do, Maren," he warns. "Most of the cosmetic stuff is a long way away."

"That's okay," I tell him. "I just want to stay."

I'm doing it for him, but it wasn't a lie. I don't want to go anywhere yet.

We're still having breakfast when Elijah and his crew arrive. I pour Elijah a cup of coffee while he slaps a notice on the table —a warning that the house is scheduled for inspection.

"This was on the door," he says. "I don't know what triggered it. Maybe me pulling the permits yesterday. I wouldn't worry about it too much. We've made it clear we're fixing it up."

Charlie runs a hand over his face. "Or the property developer who wanted this place is pissed that I turned him down."

Elijah shrugs. "It's a formality, either way."

He pulls out an iPad and starts to review his plans for the renovation. They'll get started in the basement—underpinning the foundation will apparently take weeks—and he suggests that Charlie can get started replacing the rotting wood. Charlie was, I'm sure, hoping for a role that involved drinking and threesomes, but he hides this as he nods.

"Is there anything I can do?" I ask.

Elijah bites his lip. "It's still several months out, but I'll eventually need to know what you want to do with the kitchen, the light fixtures, the bathrooms…I'm assuming you'll want to overhaul a lot of that, but like I said, you've got months to decide. I guess if you want to help you could start stripping the wallpaper?"

Elijah's being kind, but it sort of leaves me feeling like a kid instructed to draw pictures just so she stays out of your hair.

I can be useful. I know I can. I just wish I knew how.

I spend fifteen minutes reading online about wallpaper removal, and then ask Charlie for the car keys, which he only provides after forcing me to share my location with him.

"In case you wind up in a ditch," he explains.

"So you can come save me?" I ask.

"Possibly," he replies. "But mostly so the funeral home will have coordinates to find your body."

I laugh. He's such a dick when he's trying to pretend he doesn't care.

I drive to the nearest hardware store, which is not near at all, for wallpaper spray, a scraping tool, and a wallpaper steamer.

When I return to the house and unpackage everything, the

real work begins. I start off hesitant but soon discover there's no reason to be careful. The walls will need to be touched up anyway, so there's not too much harm to be done.

Removing wallpaper is quiet and boring but also...peaceful. Once I stop thinking about how boring it is, my mind seems to float in a million different directions, some of them good, some of them bad. And in those moments when my head goes entirely blank, my gaze turns toward that looming split stair-case, where the sun flows through a stained-glass angel at its center.

I still haven't been up there—and Charlie asked me not to since he's worried about the attic ceiling caving in. But it still feels, just as it did the first day, that the house really wants me to go take a look.

In the afternoon, I take a quick shower and drive to the store.

I can't remember the last time I left the house with wet hair and no makeup, wearing flip-flops. At home I'm too worried about running into someone I know to go anywhere like this. Too worried about the way they'll gossip later that I looked *sad* or *tired* or *rough*, the sort of words you use when discussing someone in decline...or headed for a divorce. No one looks aghast when I step out of the car here, though. They smile or they ignore me and both those reactions are a relief. A gentle easing of some weight I didn't even know I carried.

Charlie's in the kitchen, freshly showered, when I return with the groceries.

"Do we still have a rental car, or do I need to call a tow truck?" he asks, pouring me a cup of wine.

"Ha ha," I reply, though I did actually run it up onto the curb while parking. I pull chicken out of the bag and grab the cutting board I bought yesterday. "I'm making coconut curry soup for dinner, by the way. Loads of protein, turmeric, very healthy."

"Just to be clear, the phrase 'very healthy' is not a selling point for me," he replies, "but put me to work."

I blink. "With cooking?" Not in a million years would Harvey have offered to help.

Charlie shoots me a leering gaze. "Unless there was something *else* you wanted me to work on. I'm incredibly good with my hands. Other parts too."

I laugh as I return to the chicken. "No, Charles, there's nothing else I want you to work on. I guess you can chop the onion?"

"We need music for this," he says, pulling out his phone and choosing a playlist.

I'm about to argue. I'm about to say, *"You don't actually need music in order to chop onions."*

I stop myself because...why not? When did I become someone who thinks you shouldn't listen to music while you cook? *Probably around the same time I stopped having a glass of wine at dinner and began worrying excessively about the glycemic index of pizza crust.*

Charlie's just finished with the onion when Florence + the Machine comes on. My head nods in response to the beat almost unwillingly. He grins at me and turns the volume up as loud as it will go.

"Isn't it too loud?" I ask.

"For whom? There's no one but us for miles."

He crosses the kitchen and removes the knife from my hand before spinning me in a circle. A part of me wants to object to all of it—to the volume, to the dancing, to the fact that I have raw chicken on my hands, which means he now does too. But he is spinning me and I do love this song, and there's no reason we shouldn't be dancing or listening to music as loudly as we are.

The real issue is that I don't want to start loving things I'm going to have to give back in a few days. I don't want to start loving things Harvey will immediately snatch from my hands.

And in a few months, I might have my fondest wish—a pregnancy—but it will mean being stuck with Harvey, to one extent or another, for life.

I guess I'm giving up an awful lot. I wonder if it might be too much.

13

MAREN

The next morning, I'm in my cottage, looking out the windows and bickering with Harvey when Charlie comes into view, running hard along the trail.

"I just don't see why it matters if I stay a few more days," I tell him as Charlie nears. He's removed his shirt and is carrying it balled up in his hand now. Charlie, shirtless, is a thing of beauty—all sinew and flashing muscles, his skin gleaming with sweat.

If there were a calendar of Charlie, shirtless and sweating, I would buy every copy and paper the walls of my home with it.

If I was still single, that is.

And if he wasn't a relative.

"For starters, because my wife shouldn't be sleeping under the same roof as another man."

"I'm not. I'm sleeping in this little cottage on the shore by myself." Ten feet from Charlie, but Harvey doesn't need to know that part.

Charlie slows as he nears the house and then drops down to the grass to do push-ups. I press my face to the glass to get a better view.

"Maren," Harvey says, "if you care this little about getting pregnant, I don't know why I'm blowing twenty grand on in vitro."

I blink, refocused on the conversation. He doesn't give a shit about twenty grand. I've seen him lose that in a couple hours in Vegas. But of course the money isn't the point. Reminding me I can still be *punished* is the point.

"If money's an issue, I'm sure Henry would be willing to pay," I reply, innocent as spun sugar, knowing it will silence him. Harvey seems to want to get in a dick-measuring contest with the men of my family, so asking them for help would be a blow he couldn't recover from.

"I don't need Henry's fucking money," Harvey explodes. "You seem to be missing the point, which is that you're not acting like someone who's really invested in starting a family, and maybe that's why we don't have a fucking kid yet."

Tears sting my eyes. I've given up everything for this, and he knows it. I gave up my career, and when we'd gone a full year with no pregnancy, Harvey started blaming everything else— running, coffee, alcohol, sugar, simple carbs—and one by one, I relinquished each. Everyone else laughs about how boring I am, but nothing is enough for Harvey.

"I've got to go," I whisper, hanging up the phone. He calls again but I ignore it and walk out on the deck, trying to pull myself together.

The waves lap gently against the shore. The marsh grass and Spanish moss wave in the slight breeze while seagulls swoop overhead. Charlie is still doing push-ups and my God, I don't know how many he's done, but he may be breaking a record.

I'd forgotten what a beautiful place the world was until I arrived here.

Charlie agreed to postpone leaving until a week from

Monday. If it wasn't for the dogs, I wouldn't want to leave then either.

~

I SPEND another day removing wallpaper. It's slow going, and all the while, I can feel the upstairs tugging at me, the way a child tugs at your hand when she wants to leave a store.

It's exhausting. My shoulders ache from the hours spent fighting that pull. Charlie told me not to go up there, but I think the real reason I'm fighting it is...when in my life has a house ever exerted *anything* on me?

Especially a house that's already tapped me on the shoulder.

"How's it going?" asks Charlie, emerging from the powder room.

"You're covered in mud, so I don't feel like I've got the right to complain, but...how much of the upstairs is wallpapered? Because this is taking a really long time."

He laughs. "You don't want to know. Regretting this yet?"

My arms ache, I'm sweating and filthy, and...no. Weirdly, I don't regret it at all so far.

"Only if I contract bubonic plague over the course of the week," I reply.

"You probably already have it," he says with a blithe smile, and I laugh. Charlie Dalton is the only person alive who could make me laugh over contracting a fatal illness.

I make a simple dinner that night while Charlie showers in my cottage. We eat out on the back deck—I bought a little machine at the store to run off the mosquitos—and I am slightly tipsy though I've only had one glass of wine.

Charlie's telling me about this woman he took home once who wanted him to rate each of her parts on a one-to-ten scale. He was—typical of Charlie—slightly too honest.

I swirl the remnants of the wine in my glass as I turn toward him. "Can I ask you something?"

He raises a brow. "The fact that you think you need permission to ask means this must be incredibly invasive. Fine. Yes, I've jerked off to a photo of your mom. Are you happy? It was way before my dad married her."

"Charlie!" I scream. "Jesus. No. That is not what I was going to ask. For fuck's sake. My *mom*?"

He shrugs, entirely without guilt. "She was in *Sports Illustrated* and I was, like, twelve. I mean, if it helps, I was kind of thumbing through the magazine, so it was maybe only twenty-five percent Ulrika. Okay, thirty percent. Thirty to forty."

I push my plate away. He's destroyed my appetite—probably forever. "Does your dad know?"

"My father is a man," he says, "and as a man, he recognizes that any straight male with access to a picture of your mom straddling a beach ball has jerked off to a photo of her straddling a beach ball. It's like asking if I've ever coughed. Of course I've fucking coughed. I'm human and my lungs function."

Ugh. I really wish I didn't know this. "You don't still...?"

He flinches. "God, no. I mean, don't get me wrong, your mother is still attractive. But to know Ulrika is to see below the surface and...no offense, but it's pretty murky down there."

I rise, stacking his plate atop my own. "I can't tell if you're referring to her soul or something sexual."

"I was referring to her need for attention and her constant self-focus, but given how many men she's been with, she strikes me as being somewhat murky in other regards as well."

"Nice double standard, Whore of Manhattan."

He laughs, following me with the wineglasses as I head into the kitchen. "That's fair. Now, what did you want to ask?"

"Never mind."

"Oh Maren, how little you know me after all these years." He bumps me out of the way at the sink and begins washing the dishes, as we've discovered that though the dishwasher works, it doesn't work *well*. "Surely you realize that I'm going to continue suggesting disturbing things until you tell me? Do I think my father has ever peed on your mother? Perhaps, but by accident. Are they into role-play? I guarantee your mother has a schoolgirl uniform. Do I think they have anal? There's a ton of lube in their bathroom. More than two people could ever require. At least three times a—"

"I'm begging you to stop."

"Then ask me your question."

I grab a dish towel and start drying. "You need to be honest."

"Brutal honesty is all I'm good for, as you well know."

"Do I need a boob job?" I ask, releasing the breath I'd held a moment too long. "I know you probably feel like you've got to say no, but I just want an honest—"

"Yes," he says firmly.

My heart sinks. "Really?"

"If you're asking me, that must mean that you're insecure about them. If you're insecure about them, nothing I or anyone else says is going to change that. So do what will make you feel best. If you've got to go shoot some silicone in those puppies to feel good about yourself, then knock yourself out."

They don't *shoot* the silicone, but that isn't what matters right now.

I shake my head. "I...I'm okay with them. I mean, they're not huge, but I think they're a decent size for my frame."

"Then why are you asking?" He turns toward me with narrowed eyes, as if he already knows the answer and is waiting for me to confirm it.

"Harvey gave me a boob job for Christmas."

"What? He's not even a doctor."

I laugh. "He didn't *perform* one. He paid for the surgery and gave me a gift certificate."

Charlie sets a pan down with a thud. "Had you told him you wanted one?"

I shake my head. "No. I mean...I know he likes them big. Bigger than mine. But—" I shrug. "I assumed mine were okay and now I'm not sure. Kit will tell me they're fine if I ask, and any surgeon is going to tell me the choice is mine. You're sort of the only unbiased source I have."

His nostrils flare. "Let me make sure I'm understanding this correctly. You never expressed any dissatisfaction with your breasts, and he bought you a boob job. As a *gift*."

I told Harvey to get a refund because I wasn't interested, but hearing Charlie state it the way he just has makes me wonder if I underreacted. "Yes, pretty much."

"Why the fuck do you care about anything this man thinks?" Charlie asks, grabbing the pot I just dried and shoving it in a cabinet with unnecessary force. "Fuck Harvey. Not literally. Literally *don't* fuck Harvey ever again. He needs a lifetime of fucking therapy."

"But...what if he's right?" I ask. "I mean. I know, I know, beauty is relative or whatever, but...if he had snot running down his face, I might be a little repelled, so..."

His jaw gapes. "You're comparing your breasts to *snot*? Are you serious right now?"

"It was just a metaphor or analogy or whatever. You see my point. It's entirely possible they're...not their best."

"Let me see," he demands.

I cough. "What?"

"Let me see them. I promise to tell you if they look like two sad deflated balloons."

"Forget it."

"You want an honest opinion, yes? You know you won't receive one from Kit or your friends—I've seen the way you comment on each other's shit on Instagram. Post a single terrible picture and a hundred women will say, 'Literally a goddess.' So let me see them, and I will kindly but firmly tell you if they are a bit repulsive."

I'm waiting for the punchline. I'm waiting for him to say he's going to jerk off to the image later, the way he did to my mom's. But he looks more bored than anything else, and this is Charlie, who's seen most of the breasts in Manhattan, so of course it's boring.

He might be the one straight man I know who's capable of making this call with utter detachment. Maybe it's the wine, or maybe it's just that I spent so much time being observed and judged by strangers during my modeling days, but it doesn't feel like a big deal.

I shrug. "Okay. But this stays between us," I tell him, and somehow, keeping this our little secret makes it all feel...a little dirtier than it did before.

I pull my tee up to my collarbone, swallowing down my discomfort. I'm still mostly dressed, but I'm also standing in front of my stepbrother in a bra.

"Remove the bra, Maren," he says, rolling his eyes. "You know those things hide a variety of sins."

He's completely uninvested in the process, which makes this all a little easier. I unhook the back and slide it off before forcing myself to meet his gaze.

He pours the last of the wine into the sink and glances over. "They're fine."

I roll my eyes as I tug my tee back down. "They're 'fine?'" I demand, crouching to the floor to grab my bra. "That means they're *not* fine. Just say it. You promised you'd be honest with me."

He sighs. "You want honesty?" He turns and nods toward his crotch...where I can clearly see the shape of his cock in a way I couldn't moments earlier. Given the size, it's unmissable. "There's your honesty. Your tits are astonishing and if I were Harvey, I'd have been too busy attempting to fuck them to wonder about how I could perfect them."

He starts washing our glasses and I turn away, trying to fight off the image of Charlie...doing what he just said he'd do. "Okay, thanks. And this stays between us, right?"

He frowns over his shoulder, as if the question is ridiculous. "I'm not about to run off telling everyone I got rock hard by accident like a teenage boy with the hot math teacher."

I grab a sponge to clean off the table but turn back toward him before I walk out the door. "Did that really happen with your math teacher?"

"It did."

"Did she see it? What did she say?" I gasp.

"You just got an eyeful," he says with a grin over his shoulder. "Obviously she asked me to stay after class."

14

MAREN

I stand on the porch, my morning routine, watching Charlie do his post-run push-ups and burpees in the grass.

He's ripped. Tan. That trail of hair beneath his belly button drags my gaze like a car crash. I wish I hadn't noticed and also wish I'd brought binoculars.

I turn to go inside for another call with Harvey that's certain to be as tense as the last. He's furious that he couldn't bully me into returning to Manhattan.

It wasn't always like this. When we first dated, Harvey was a prince. He was smitten. It was only after he proposed that I started to see that other side of him, the way he can shift on a dime from wooing you to slamming the door in your face. It's gotten worse from there, but I want children more than I want a husband I can trust and adore, and I'm *so close* to getting them. A friend of Harvey's is this amazing fertility doctor. He moved us off the wait list, ahead of hundreds of other families. A year from now I could be holding a baby of my own, the one thing I've ever truly wanted.

I hate that I have to relinquish my backbone to get it, however.

"I need you back," he says immediately. "There's a client thing next Saturday."

Not my problem. Isn't that what he said to me when I told him we needed to leave Aspen for Kit's engagement party? Of course, if I bring this up now, he'll remind me that Kit didn't even show up for that party and ran off with my ex-boyfriend instead.

"I'll let you know," I reply.

"You'll *let me know*?" he repeats, enraged. "You seem to have forgotten which one of us actually cares about you, so allow me to remind you: it's not your fucking stepbrother."

I step back on the porch. Charlie's still doing push-ups. His back gleams with sweat.

"I haven't forgotten," I reply, more to myself than him.

IN THE MIDDLE of the day I go to the cottage to use the bathroom because the entire crew now uses the first-floor powder room, so it's caked in mud. To my surprise, Charlie's on my deck, his shirt damp with sweat, looking oddly at home in his jeans and tool belt.

"What are you doing to my deck?" I cry.

He raises a brow. "You mean the deck I told you not to walk on? I'm fixing it so that you survive the week."

The words are grumbled and cranky, but I smile anyway. Charlie never wants to admit that he cares, but that's...pretty freaking sweet.

"I never dreamed you'd look so natural with a hammer in your hands."

"I'm more accustomed than you might think," he says with a smirk, "to handling a *big hammer*."

"Yes, I'm sure you're handling that big hammer all the time these days."

"You have no idea," he says with a laugh, and suddenly I'm picturing...*Stop picturing that, Maren.*

"I wish you could see how red you just turned," he says as I turn away.

My phone buzzes in my pocket as I head to the bathroom—it's Harvey's ringtone.

I'll call him later because I don't care what he says.

I'm staying.

~

I STRETCH out atop my bed to phone Lori for my daily video time with the puppies just before dinner. Her brow is furrowed when she answers. "Hey...I didn't expect to hear from you. What's up?"

I sit up. I've called her every day since we arrived. Why wouldn't she expect it? "I was just checking on the puppies. How did today go?"

Her eyes widen. "Harvey sent someone over to pick them up. He didn't tell you?"

My stomach sinks. Harvey is mostly irritated by the dogs and has never lifted a finger to help me with them. He wouldn't voluntarily take on the work of watching them while I'm gone. And even if he did like the dogs...he's supposed to leave town again, so what will happen then?

I tell her there must have been a *miscommunication*. It's a word I don't think I ever used once prior to marrying Harvey, and now find myself using frequently. It's the polite way adults cover their rough edges, and Harvey and I have a lot of rough edges.

> Hey. I just talked to Lori, and she said you had someone pick up the dogs?

HARVEY

At least I know how to get your attention now.
Why didn't you call me back?

> I was going to call you tonight. I didn't want to bother you at work.

But once the dogs come into the picture, you don't mind bothering me, apparently.

> I just wanted to make sure there wasn't some kind of mistake. Because I know that you don't want to take care of them.

No, I really don't want to take care of them, but it seems pretty fucking cruel to leave them with a stranger, don't you think? You're not planning to do this with our future children, are you?

> Lori isn't a stranger. And they like playing with the other dogs.

Part of being a responsible parent—to dogs or to humans—is making some sacrifices so that you are there for them.

My jaw grinds. Harvey isn't concerned about the dogs—this is his way of punishing me for staying here and kudos to him, because it worked. I'd rather they stay with Lori than him. He won't even remember to feed them.

> I thought you were planning to leave town again?

If I have to go, I'll just leave them with Elodie.

I like that even less. Maybe it's simply that I don't know

much about little boys, but watching his sister's kid stab a wounded bird with a stick when we were all in St. Barth's last winter sent a chill up my spine.

What kind of kid wants to inflict damage like that? Probably the kind of kid who'd feed a puppy chocolate to make it sick or kick it if no one was looking.

And what kind of parent doesn't stop him? Because Elodie saw it and shrugged.

So I tell Charlie I have to go home on Thursday after all, and when he asks why, I tell him that Harvey has a client thing. Because otherwise I'd have to admit that I'm planning to have children with someone I can't trust with a pet.

And it would sound pretty fucked up if I said that aloud.

15

MAREN

I stand on my newly reinforced deck the following morning, looking for Charlie.

It rained overnight and the air is cool, the world soaked in soft pastels. Sunlight sparkles across the damp grass and the trees that shade the path around the inlet hang low, heavy with moisture.

He appears in the distance, running hard, and jealousy pangs in my chest. I miss jogging. I never pushed myself the way he does, but I was once someone who could easily knock out a few miles without thinking about it and who'd spend the rest of the morning luxuriating in the extra endorphins.

Why'd I give it up? Why'd I give everything up?

A few ounces of wine won't impact my fertility. Same with the occasional piece of pizza or a morning jog.

And some part of me knew this. I wasn't doing it in order to build us a family—I was doing it to avoid Harvey blaming me, while knowing he'd blame me anyway. Whenever he doesn't get what he wants, he finds a way to pin it on me, and I generally wind up agreeing with him.

I'm tired of hating myself for my failure to get pregnant, but if it's going to happen no matter what I do, I might as well make myself happy now.

I go back into the cottage and begin shucking off my pajamas before I can change my mind. I didn't bring real running clothes, but something about this moment feels too important to be put off. So I slide on cut-off jean shorts and a T-shirt, paired with the ruined sneakers—flat soled, only meant to be fashionable—and jog down to the trail.

In my head, I am still that same girl who could knock out several miles without even thinking about it.

I discover within *seconds* that I'm no longer that girl. My lungs burn, my thighs tremble, and when I finally stop to walk, I'm still close enough to hit my cottage with a rock if I had a good arm.

What else have I lost over these years with Harvey? And are they things I'll be able to recover when I finally realize I've lost them?

In the afternoon, Charlie leaves to go to the lumberyard. I continue scraping the walls, but the upstairs starts calling to me again.

It can't be that dangerous. Elijah and Charlie have been up several times, and Charlie showers there when he doesn't use mine. I throw my tools to the ground before I can even think it through.

The stairs leading to the second floor creak but have a firmness to them that modern stairways don't. From the landing, I see what must have been the primary bedroom on the left side, but it's the room farthest down the hall to the right that I'm drawn to. My feet are moving toward it before I've even commanded them in that direction.

It's not like something out of a horror film—I'm not pulled

there against my will. It's more like spying your favorite person across a crowded room...*of course* you're heading that way.

And as soon as I enter...I feel at rest. For the first time since we entered this house, I'm not fighting any pull at all. It's as if I've finally come home after a long trip.

The room is small and feminine. Tiny violets dot the ancient wallpaper. The only piece of furniture is an ancient mirror opposite the windows. I walk into the room's center, and this sensation begins sliding over me, climbing from feet to legs to chest.

Giddiness.

It's the excitement of a teenage girl when she's just been asked out for the first time. The excitement of a college admissions letter, or the way I've imagined I'd feel seeing a positive pregnancy test. It's ecstatic, delighted, bubbling over with hope. When was the last time I felt like this? It's been years—so many years that I'd forgotten I could feel it. The sensation washes over me—one wave after the next—until my legs shake under the onslaught and I finally have to slide to the floor. I scoot to the wall and let my eyes fall closed, remembering high school and the way my friends and I would gather in someone's bedroom, giggling and borrowing makeup. We had the whole world in front of us, and anything was possible, but where is that world now?

After another moment the memory shifts. I'm no longer thinking of those nights with my friends, but something different, when I was about the same age—strolling down a road under the shade of live oaks and discussing some dance being held, one I was desperate to attend.

"You can't miss it," one of my friends had said, wide-eyed.

"Papa will never let me go," I'd replied. "Not until my brothers get home."

A name is shouted from very far away. I turn to look down

the lane behind us, but there's nothing, and no, the voice isn't even here. It's...

My eyes open slowly, heavily, as if weighted.

"Maren?" calls Charlie.

I stare blindly at the opposite wall of an unfamiliar room.

What the hell was that?

Papa will never let me go, I'd told them. *Not until my brothers get home.*

Except, I don't call anyone Papa. The closest thing I've got to a father is Henry, who I've always called by his first name.

I also don't have brothers.

"Maren?" calls Charlie again.

"Up here!" My voice isn't as loud as I'd intended it to be, as if I'm coming from very far away.

His footsteps echo along the hall and then he's standing in the frame of the door, with his brow furrowed. "What are you doing?" he asks. It sounds less accusatory than concerned.

I bite my lip. I can't tell him this, right? No, of course not. It's too weird. Maybe the mold issue is worse than Elijah had thought. "Nothing," I reply. "Just closed my eyes for a second. Why are you back? I thought you were leaving for the lumberyard."

His mouth opens, then closes. He crosses the room and crouches beside me, placing his hand to my forehead. "Maren, I was gone for two hours. I texted to see if I should pick up dinner and you never replied."

Two hours. That's just not possible.

I've been up here five minutes at most.

But a glance out the window confirms that the light is dimmer than it was. Too dim by far to be mid-afternoon, so, again, what the hell just happened?

Charlie is still crouching in front of me, frowning. His thumb brushes my face, and for the strangest half second, I picture kissing him. I picture the softness of his lips and how

I'd get a little whiff of his shampoo as I leaned in—and I long for that: his mouth on mine, his acquiescence, in a way I've never craved it from *anyone*.

My gaze meets his. For a half second, I suspect he'd let me do it, and the thought sends all the air rushing from my lungs.

What the hell is this house doing to me? To us both?

16

CHARLIE

I convince Maren to grab dinner in town with me. The restaurant is not great by any means—the flatware sticks to the table and half the patrons are yelling at the TV—but it will suffice. She tries to order a salad, and I make her eat a steak as well. I order us each a glass of red wine, though she didn't ask for one.

I'm still worried. She seems fine now, but for long minutes after I found her, she behaved like someone coming out of a trance: her movements slow, uncertain.

And how do you fall asleep and then have no awareness of it when you awaken? She says it's probably because she went for a run this morning, but a short run shouldn't knock anyone out *that* much.

As much as I've belittled her concerns about the house—though I think they're actually Harvey's concerns—I now wonder if there was some truth to them. Is there too much carbon dioxide up there? Is she allergic to something? If she doesn't wind up pregnant when they start IVF, she'll never forgive me or herself.

"Are you okay?" I finally ask.

She forces a smile. "The bartender has been watching you all night."

I look over my shoulder, and the bartender in question gives me a flirty little smile. Under other circumstances, I'd consider it, but she doesn't hold much appeal with Maren sitting right in front of me.

"Pretty bold of her," I tell Maren. "For all she knows, you're my wife."

Maren's lovely eyes darken. "There are a lot of women for whom that would only make you more appealing."

I watch her face carefully, wondering if I can ask the question that sits on the tip of my tongue: *Is Harvey cheating? And if so, why the fuck are you putting up with it?* She won't tell me the truth, though. She knows I'd kick his ass and she probably knows I've been eagerly waiting for the chance.

Harvey doesn't understand what he has. He's never gotten her, although I'm not sure he's the type of guy who'd treat anyone well for long.

"Why are you with him?" I ask. "He's sort of an asshole, especially to you. I suspect you know this."

She presses her napkin to her lips. "Because I'm thirty-two."

"That old? I hope you've set up end-of-life instructions. There's a nice new graveyard they're putting in over on—"

She balls up her napkin and tosses it at me. "Shut up. It's different for you. You can have children forever."

Indeed. I'll never be free of that fear. Even vasectomies—I've investigated—can fail. Genitalia: the double-edged sword.

I push my plate back. "Then have them with someone else."

She glances at her lap. Those model cheekbones look sharp in the bar's dim light. "I should have married someone else," she says, "but—"

"Miller?" I cut in, my voice harsher than it should be.

"No," she scolds. "I told you...I'm absolutely over that. No, Harvey has this friend who is such a sweetheart. He and his wife got married around the same time we did, and he's dying to have kids, but I don't think she wants them. Every time we've ever gone to dinner I think, 'I should have married someone like him.' But if I left Harvey, first I'd have to find someone else, then I'd have to date him for a year or two and somehow convince him to marry me in spite of the fact that I've got these fertility issues—"

"I see that as winning the lottery, just so we're clear."

She smiles. "Shut up, Charlie. Anyway, I convince him to marry me. At this point I'm thirty-six or thirty-seven at the absolute youngest, and it's even harder to get pregnant. And that's only if *every single thing* goes the way I want it to go."

She's clearly thought this through, which is good, but she's come to the wrong fucking conclusion, which is less good. "You're giving up an awful lot to have kids. Are you sure it's worth it?"

Her eyes shine with conviction as she looks up at me. "I am. Becoming a mother is the only thing I've ever wanted. I don't even know what's left without it."

I hate her response. I don't know why. It's not as if I'd be enough for her, no matter how she answered.

17

MAREN

I dream that night about my wedding day. I'm at my mother's house—still in a robe but with my hair and makeup done. All that's left, really, is to put on the dress. My mother is doing her usual thing, panicking unnecessarily, flapping her hands and yelling at me to go upstairs and get ready just like she did on my real wedding day. I pass Charlie in the hallway on the way up—delicious in a tux, minus the jacket—and he must see something in my face. When I get to my room he's there, behind me. "Let's have a chat," he says, following me inside. He shuts the door behind him and flips the lock.

I don't think he's ever been in here before. He's certainly never been in here with me alone, behind a locked door.

I have a single, crazy thought: *and now he never will be.*

And that thought makes my throat tighten, as if I'm losing something that matters.

It's just cold feet. It must be.

He puts his hands on my shoulders and pushes me to sit on the little ottoman beside my vanity, and then he crouches in front of me. "What's wrong?" he demands.

I'm sad that the two of us will never be alone like this again, not in the way I suddenly want to be, and that's way too crazy to ever give voice to.

"Nothing." My voice is faint. I force a smile to make up for it. "Just pre-wedding jitters."

A muscle flickers in his jaw. "You don't have to do this, Maren. I can sneak you out the back. We can go anywhere you want."

He doesn't suggest he'd be doing this as anything but my stepbrother, as anything but my friend. But the possibility that we are something more is there, isn't it? His eyes burn in a way that says more than a volume of poetry ever could.

I picture myself jumping onto a plane with Charlie, taking him to my favorite island in the Azores. I picture some brief debate about whether we'll need one room or two, and we'll end up in one. I picture his hands—still on my shoulders—pushing the robe off to reveal me.

Except I'm the daughter of two reckless people—a woman who has cycled through boyfriends and husbands, and a man who took off before I was born and later knocked up a student two decades his junior. I want a normal family, a normal life. Things I can have with Harvey. Leaving now—it's the kind of shit my mother would do. But is making the mature choice supposed to feel like dying inside?

"Okay," I tell Charlie, untying the robe. "Let's go."

I wake in the darkness, my heart hammering. It happened. Aside from that last bit, the part where I agreed to go, it happened just the way it did in my dream. How could I have forgotten?

Maybe I read too much into what he was saying. Maybe I read into that look on his face.

I must have. We're family. There's no way he wanted me to run away with him like *that*, in a romantic sense.

Only now, in the dark, will I admit something to myself, something I'm never going to think about again: he might not have wanted it that way, but I did.

I'M MAKING breakfast with my left hand and scrolling through tile samples with my right when Charlie calls my name from the foyer. He sounds amused. "You got a delivery," he says, arching a brow and nodding toward the oak nearest the house, against which two bikes are leaning.

My stomach sinks. I'd pictured staying here longer. I'd pictured spending Sunday—the day Elijah and his guys aren't working—exploring the area with him.

"I bought bikes."

"Yes, I actually deduced that part myself. *Why* did you buy bikes, Maren?"

Suddenly my reasoning sounds incredibly childlike. *I thought it would be fun. I thought we could have a picnic.*

"It's a good form of exercise. And I thought I'd have more time here."

"Since when do you care about exercise?"

"Fine. I thought it would be fun. Never mind! I didn't expect the Spanish Inquisition."

A slow, sweet smile spreads across Charlie's face. "You thought it would be fun. That's all you had to say."

A shiver races over my skin, and it's both bad and good.

It's a shiver that says *this is what life could be like with someone who actually cares about you, someone who cares about your happiness. This is what you're giving up, remaining with Harvey, and why would you ever be willing to live without it?*

I walk away, pulling out my phone to text Harvey as I go.

> Hey, I'm not coming home tomorrow after all, but I'll be back on Saturday in time for your event.

Even if it only gives me two extra days here, I'll take them.

Harvey sends an array of rage-filled responses—implying that I'm sleeping with Charlie, that I'm just like my mom, that I'm not looking like a good candidate for motherhood—and I just swipe my finger over each, deleting them as if they're notifications from an app I never meant to download. Beyond meaningless—simply an imposition.

Charlie cuts out early and we go into town to gather supplies for our bike outing. There's this cute store in Oak Bluff that actually has an adorable wicker picnic basket in the window—the inspiration for this idea in the first place—but Charlie says his testosterone level has already dropped dangerously low in agreeing to ride on the "girly" bikes I bought and he's putting his foot down.

So we end up at the Stop-n-Shop instead. Martha and I are friendly now. I enjoy my near-daily chats with her as she rings my groceries up.

Today, while Charlie runs back to grab one more thing for our bike trip, she grins at me.

"You've shrugged it off," she says. "That pall you had over you when you first came? I can see all your colors again."

I smile. "I guess a week out of the city was all I needed."

"It's not being out of the city." She nods at Charlie. "It's him. He's what brings your colors out."

Once again, I have no idea how to respond. "I mean, I guess maybe I'm just more comfortable around him since he's family."

She laughs. "It's not because he's family."

∽

By mid-afternoon we're setting out, and it's a perfect day for it: slightly overcast, breezier than normal. Not a single car passes us as we ride on a paved road that should, eventually, lead us to the beach.

I was on a road sort of like this in my dream. And I don't know if I'm embellishing things now or not, but I remember details I didn't notice when it was happening: the swirl of skirts around my feet. My friends wearing broad-brimmed hats.

I've been accused of having a vivid imagination before, but this is extreme even for me.

The trees get sparser and eventually turn to brush, and suddenly we're crossing a bridge with dunes on the other side. We dump our bikes when we reach them and climb over to reach the long sand beach. It's the perfect time of day—still light, but the sun has lowered, and the sky is now cast in bright blues and muted orange. Charlie spreads the blanket while I get out our snacks, and then the two of us settle back to look around.

The tide is out, the water calm. Gulls swoop over the placid water, hunting for their dinner.

"I wish I could stay here forever," I tell him, turning my face toward the sun as it breaks through the clouds.

"I'm glad you came with me," he replies, "even if you cost me a million dollars."

I fight a smile. "I paid for the bikes."

He laughs. "I was referring to the *house*."

Oh, right. I do feel bad about the cost. I'd have covered it, if he'd allowed me, although Charlie was full of crap. There's a big difference between not having money and not wanting to *spend* your money, and he was doing the latter. I know he's sunk a lot of money into this arena football team he's funding in Texas, but he's a venture capitalist. They always have extra on hand, just in case a new opportunity presents itself.

"You agree now, though? That you ought to keep it? I mean, mostly because it's amazing but also because your mom asked you to?"

"It's not that amazing, Maren, and I've got no fucking use for this place, but yes, I agree I should have kept it for my mom's sake. It's the bare minimum of what I should have done."

I wish I had a tool to excise that shame from his voice. "What do you mean?"

"I was a shitty son," he says quietly. "She came up to visit me last winter, and I barely made time for her. She wanted to go to MOMA, and I took her, but I spent half of the trip on my phone replying to emails."

I shake my head in silent argument. I wasn't there, but I know him, and this can't be true.

"I once read that we never truly remember anything...we simply remember the last time we remembered it. Don't let this story you're telling yourself be the way you recall those last days. Tell me a moment that you actually enjoyed, because I know there was one, and I want to make sure you remember it."

He frowns, watching the gentle waves near us collapse into foam. "I got up, on one of the days that I'd taken off, and she made breakfast. A big breakfast, like the kind she used to make here. And it was ridiculous...I don't even eat breakfast at home, but we sat down, and we ate together, and she was just smiling the entire time, watching me. She used to do that..." His voice cracks. And he stops talking.

I squeeze his hand. "She used to do what?"

"She used to like to watch me eat. She loved me so much that it just made her happy to watch me eat. It took so fucking little to make her happy, and I didn't even try."

I place my head on his shoulder, my gaze trained on the gently curling waves. "Charlie, you did try. I bet you remembered her birthday every year, and Christmas and Mother's

Day. I bet that anytime she ran into a financial issue down here, you offered to swoop in and save her, and anytime you heard about someone being a dick to her, you tried to fix it, the same way you do for all of us. And if I ever have a child, all I will want is to sit back and watch him eat his breakfast, nothing more required, as long as he's happy and fulfilled."

His smile falters. "I'm not sure my mom ever saw me happy and fulfilled."

"Maybe she's watching to see it happen now."

A low laugh rumbles out of his chest. "I know you're trying to console me, but if I thought my mom was watching twenty-four hours a day from beyond the grave, it would put a real damper on my private life."

I sort of think his private life could *use* a bit of a damper, but I'll keep that to myself.

"She had more faith in you than you have in yourself," I say, pressing my lips to his cheek and enjoying the tickle of his scruff against my mouth more than I should. "That's the real reason she asked you to come."

He smiles. "What she should have had faith in is that you'd convince me to do the right thing. But I'm glad you did. I think I'm going to stay."

My head lifts from his shoulder. *Stay?* For entirely selfish reasons, I hope I've misheard him. "Wait. What?"

He stares at his lap. "If someone had asked me how I was a couple weeks ago, I'd have told them things are great. I'd have rated my life a seven, at least. But...I'm happier here. I wouldn't rate this a ten either, though. Nowhere close. Which means in New York, I was maybe at a three or a four and lying to myself. I think maybe my mom knew it, and that's why she wanted me down here. So I'm gonna stay for a bit. Until the inspection, anyway, but probably longer. I don't have to be in Texas until mid-summer."

Mid-summer? I'd barely see him over the next month anyway—only at a family dinner or something to celebrate Kit's engagement. There's no reason at all to feel as if the ground is swallowing me whole.

So maybe it's for the best that I'm leaving in a few days after all.

18

CHARLIE

Elijah saunters into the kitchen and takes a seat at the table.

Maren pours him some of her awful juice. I don't know why that annoys me. I guess I just thought it was sort of *our* thing.

Annoyance over the green juice aside, I made the right decision in hiring him. He's just as hard-working and upfront as he was when we were teenagers. If I'm forced to leave before this place is done—and I absolutely will be—I'll know it's in good hands.

He goes over the schedule for today and then turns to Maren. "How's the wallpaper coming?" he asks. "You got started on the second floor, right?"

My gaze shoots to hers. She didn't go upstairs yesterday. I didn't want her up there and I still don't, because what the fuck was that? Even now there's something worried in her eyes, something she's not telling me about.

"I don't want her up there," I announce. "Not until the HVAC is in. It'll be sweltering by noon."

Elijah tips back in his chair, observing me for a long

moment. Maybe he knows this excuse is bullshit since he's up there all the time. "She'll be fine as long as she keeps the windows open. This house was built before A/C existed, so it's got good airflow."

"I'll be fine, Charlie," she says.

We exchange another glance. I've got no arguments left.

She sort of looks like she wishes I had another one, though.

"BUNCH OF FURNITURE IN THE ATTIC," Elijah says a few hours later, when I emerge from the basement. "You want to take a look? Otherwise, I can just get it carted to the dump."

I wish he hadn't asked. If it belonged to the original owners, I'll have no emotional attachment to it and therefore I won't want it. If it belonged to my mother, it's still going to the dump, but I'll feel guilty as hell about it.

I set my toolbelt on the kitchen counter and shrug. "Ditch it," I tell him, heading for the sink. And then I think of Maren. Maren, with her stories about a family playing croquet, having a billion children. Last night she was talking about the cotillion they might have hosted here.

I suspect her stories are an amalgam of everything she knows about the South after the war and every movie she's ever seen about the 1920s. So basically, it's post-war *Gone with the Wind* meets *The Great Gatsby*, but knowing Maren, it'd only be the good parts of those books: it'd be the croquet they played on the lawn dressed in head-to-toe white, earnest couples courting, wild parties where everyone sloshed champagne across a ballroom floor while waving cigarettes in long holders.

No one's going off to war or running someone over with their car.

"Actually, let me check," I reply, wiping off my hands. It'll give me an excuse to go make sure Maren's okay anyhow.

He just nods, but I sense, once again, what he's thinking as he walks away, which is that sometimes Maren and I sound more like husband and wife than we do stepsiblings.

I go upstairs. A peek in the first bedroom to the right shows Maren's been hard at work: it's buried in shredded wallpaper.

She's in the second room, standing on a ladder to grab a strip near the wainscotting. The curve of her bare ass is visible as I move to hold the ladder. Over a week without sex has reduced me to a man who'd give his entire fortune to palm that ass once, but who am I kidding? I've always been a man willing to hand over his fortune where she's concerned, whether I was getting anything out of it or not.

"Hey," she says, "I'm glad you're here. You've got to look at this."

"If it's a creepy doll that keeps moving around the room when your head is turned, we're on the next plane home."

"The doll ordered me not to tell you about our friendship," she replies, climbing down the ladder. "She said you'd try to turn us against each other. No, look."

She points out something written on the wall where she's removed the paper.

Sam shouldn't get the biggest room.

"Isn't it cute?" she demands. "This must be Walter because Sam complained about him on his wall."

"Proving that children have been little pains in the ass who fight over fucking nothing century after century. But speaking of the dead ghost children, Elijah found some stuff in the attic and wanted to know if he should dump it."

She inhales as if she's been slapped. "Dump it? Without us even looking first?"

I figured she'd say that. She turns, heading down the hall

toward the attic, and she's reaching for the pull before I can warn her not to.

I wrap my arm around her waist and snatch her backward just before the ladder comes sliding down.

For a moment she's sandwiched against me, the soft curve of her breast pressed to my arm. *Jesus*. I'm not sure why I'm being tested like this, but I clearly did something really fucked up in a past life.

"Thanks," she whispers. "I didn't know that was gonna happen."

I release her and pull the ladder the rest of the way down before allowing her to climb up, with me in her wake.

The attic is mostly an empty room full of rotting joists and crooked beams. Elijah thinks it's safe enough, but I still tense as Maren heads toward the furniture in its center. I'm sure it was considered quality stuff a century ago, and the fact that it's still in one piece, though somewhat weather damaged thanks to the leaky roof, attests to its craftsmanship. But...I still don't want a bunch of dark, mahogany furniture, so I sure wish Maren wasn't already pulling drawers open the way she currently is, which will inevitably lead to *oh, Charlie, look...little Sam threatened someone's life here. It's so cute, you can't throw it away.*

"This is really good furniture," she says, "but it's pretty ugly."

Thank Christ.

"Agreed," I reply. "I'll tell Elijah to dump it."

"Hang on now," she warns me. "We haven't looked at everything yet."

"I'm pretty sure I'm looking at it as we speak."

She nods toward two boxes sitting side by side on the rotting floorboards and crosses the room to them.

She opens the one on her right and withdraws a book. "Weren't you just saying you wish you had a *Farmer's Almanac* from 1941?" she asks with a grin.

Reluctantly, I join her and open the second box. There are a lot of old law journals and books from the turn of the century —*Commentaries on the Laws of England, Constitutional Limitations*. They're probably valuable because of their age, which is precisely the reason I shouldn't have opened this box in the first place. I'm going to feel bad sending it straight to the dump, but I'm already a little maxed out on guilt, so to the dump it goes.

"Charlie!" she squeals. "Look! There's a photo album."

She sprawls out on the dusty floor with her back against the wall and pats the space beside her, commanding me to sit. Like a whipped idiot, I do it.

The album must have belonged to the family who built the place. There's a photo of the house under construction, horses tied to the nearest tree. A woman in a long dress, holding a baby on her hip. The next photo shows a family on the front porch once the home's been completed: that same woman, who stands with a different baby and three very small boys.

"Look at how cute they are in their little suspenders," Maren murmurs longingly, running her index finger lightly over the photo. "Oh my God. I wish you could still dress little boys like that."

"I mean...you can. They'll just get beaten up."

She ignores me, continuing to flip the pages. "They had another baby," she says.

She flips ahead, reading the cursive caption aloud. "Margaret and Papa," she whispers.

I'm not sure why she sounds so troubled.

Elijah stays late, so Maren invites him for dinner.

I spend more than enough time with Elijah during the day. I sort of like having our dinners on the back porch alone, just me and Maren, and she's only got two nights left here, but I can't exactly rescind the invitation.

Maren makes roast chicken and potatoes and grills Elijah for stories about the summer I spent here. She seems certain it was more exciting than we've let on.

"So there were no girls here? Not that entire summer?"

"Well, we did have your sister and her friend out here that one night," I remind Elijah. "That was pretty exciting."

Elijah laughs as he takes the potatoes from Maren. "Charlie's full of shit. It was my little sister and her friend, and they were, like, thirteen at the time."

Maren's eyes widen. "Weren't you, like, eighteen?"

"Nobody hooked up," I promise her. "We told them there was a ghost—"

"I think we actually *believed* there was a ghost," Elijah counters. "So we waited until it was late, and then we climbed on the roof and lowered this sheer fabric from overhead. My sister *literally* pissed herself."

"And then her friend punched you," I add with a laugh. "Whatever happened to that kid? Some pretentious name. Kestley or Eastwick or something."

"Easton," Elijah says, his smile fading. "She moved away. She comes back at the holidays sometimes, but that's about it."

I've struck a nerve. It almost feels like I should apologize for bringing her up. There's a moment of strained silence and Maren's gaze flickers between us.

"I want to do a sleep out, Charlie," Maren says, gamely changing the subject.

"I promise, you don't. You realize how humid it is, right?"

"It won't be that bad now that the sun's down," she replies.

"And you love the mosquitoes, too, so there's that."

"I'll run our little machine. It'll be fine. Why do you keep shitting on my plan?"

Because your plan hasn't been thought through and that mosquito device doesn't work for shit.

I lean back in my chair. "You're going to be sweating your ass off and getting eaten alive while sleeping on a rickety deck."

"Correction," she replies. "*We're* going to be sweating our asses off and getting eaten alive while sleeping on a rickety deck."

"Now I know you haven't thought this through," I reply, "because there is no way in hell you can offer me anything worth enduring that."

And she just smiles at me in that way that says she's already won.

Which she has.

Hot girls are a menace. Especially this one.

"Have fun with that campout," Elijah says to me as he leaves.

JUST AFTER NINE, we drag her mattress out onto the deck.

"Should we tell ghost stories?" she asks, smiling at me in the moonlight.

I'm being suffocated to death by the humidity, but I grin anyway. "Someone did die out here, by the way."

"You mean...in this section of South Carolina?"

I laugh. "No, I mean, literally where these cottages sit."

She swats my arm. "And you're just waiting to tell me now?"

"I didn't want you going full Professor Trelawney on me and start channeling the dead."

"So who died?"

I shake my head, rolling on my back. The crickets and cicadas are making such a fucking racket tonight I can barely hear my own voice. "I don't know. There was a shack here. Elijah and I tore it down before we put up the cottages. But apparently whoever owned the house at the time came out here and died in her sleep."

Maren's eyes go wide. "She died in her sleep? Are they sure? I mean, sometimes there are gasses in the ground that—"

"Which is exactly the sort of shit I knew you'd worry about. She was super old."

"How old?"

I smile at her. "Like...your age. Natural causes."

She hits me again. "We're the same age, Charles."

"Males and females age differently, like dogs. What's thirty-two times seven? That's your real age." I meant it as a joke, but she isn't laughing. "I was kidding, Maren. She was legitimately old."

She rolls onto her back and stares at the sky. "I know."

I'm on the cusp of reassuring her that she's not old and her fertility is fine when she rolls toward me. "You said your mom got this place dirt cheap, but I don't understand how it didn't stay in the family or sell for a billion dollars."

I'm just relieved she isn't choking back tears about her declining fertility.

"My mom bought it from the bank," I reply, "so I assume it was foreclosed on. It was in rough shape even then, and the area wasn't booming. I imagine no one wanted to deal with it."

She bites her lip. "But they had so many kids. You'd think their descendants would pitch in to save it."

It's sort of endearing how naïve she is about the way the world works—she and Kit grew up with too much money. "Maren, the majority of families probably can't *pitch in* to buy a mansion."

"But this is a family who started off *here*," she argues. "They had money."

"It was over a hundred years ago. There've been three major wars since then. A lot has changed."

"What are the odds all those boys survived World War One?" she asks quietly. "They were just about the right age."

"All of them?" I ask. "Not good. Reason number one to not have kids, beyond the hundred ways they ruin your life."

She elbows me. "You'd like kids, if you had them."

"I know," I reply. "That's why I don't want them. Look at what happened to my parents and tell me why any reasonable person would assume that risk."

We lapse into silence. It's too hot to sleep, so it looks like I'm gonna lie awake all night, thinking about how I wish things were different. Wishing she didn't want the things she wants and that there was just a fucking way to...

"Charlie," she whispers tentatively.

A viciously hopeful part of myself, one I have tried to beat back for years, suggests that she might say, *"There's something going on between us, isn't there? There's always been something going on between us."*

"Yeah?"

"It's so hot out here. And that mosquito thing isn't working at all."

I laugh, stifling a hint of disappointment. "That's not what I thought you were going to say."

"What did you think I was going to say?"

If my life was on the line, I wouldn't admit the truth. "That you'd murdered someone," I reply. "Maybe you were drunk driving as a teen and weren't sure if you'd killed a kid. Your sober driving is sufficiently dangerous, if we're being perfectly honest."

She laughs. "Okay, back to the subject at hand... Are we in agreement that this is miserable, and we should go back to our beds?"

"I think it's perfectly lovely outside," I reply. "But if you want to quit, go right ahead."

"There is no way that you think it is *perfectly lovely* outside right now," she says. "You're sweating anytime I try to raise the air conditioning above sixty-five."

I laugh. "Yes, it's fucking miserable, Maren, just like I told you it would be. And we can go in as soon as you've said, 'Charlie, you were right about this the same way you were right about everything because you are wiser and more logical than me. Probably because I have a weak female brain.'"

She sits up. "You realize that I could just go in regardless of whether or not you agree?"

My hand presses to her stomach. "I could always pin you in place."

Our eyes catch. Hers are wide, surprised. Even in the darkness I can see the flush crawling over her face. And I'm suddenly picturing her calling my bluff. Saying, *"Try it and see, Charlie."*

I *would* try it. And goddamn, would she see.

"Charlie," she says, "you were right about everything, and you were always super smart and logical, and whatever else I was supposed to say."

"Because you have a weak female brain."

"Fuck that," she says, and I laugh again.

She's finally standing up to someone. Even if it is, regrettably, me. Even if it means I don't get to pin her to this mattress.

Which she wants me to do.

She'd never admit it, but she wants it too.

19

———————

MAREN

Charlie helps me drag the mattress back inside and then returns to his own cottage, though I wish he'd just stay with me.

I could always pin you in place.

He said it with his hand pressed flat to my stomach, as if he was ready to act. The memory of it is enough to make my core squeeze tight. I picture that hand sliding lower, beneath the elastic of my shorts.

Think about something else, Maren. Please think about anything else.

It's not as if I don't have anything else to focus on. That photo album has been freaking me out all day. *Margaret and Papa.*

I tried really hard all night not to make it into a thing. Not to be *crazy Maren with the overactive imagination,* but when I dreamed I was walking down the road, lamenting that I couldn't go to the dance...was that *my* dream or was it someone else's *memory*? Perhaps a memory belonging to the girl in those family photos, a girl standing beside her handsome brothers. In the final photo, they were grown but still young. Teens or early twenties at most. *Samuel, Walter, Leonard, Raymond, and Margaret* someone wrote beneath it in careful, curling script.

They must be dead by now, all of them. But how on earth, with all those children and probably a ton of grandchildren, did this house wind up for sale?

I could always pin you in place.

Jesus. I'm never going to get that out of my head.

Only Charlie Dalton could have a girl more focused on *him* than the fact that she was recently possessed by a ghost.

I WAKE on my last full day in Oak Bluff, determined to finish up Walter and Sam's rooms…and avoid Margaret's.

Today, though, the call from the room is harder than ever to resist. And I absolutely should resist because of the way being in there seemed to bend my brain: the sight of Charlie crouching in front of me, the urge to lean forward and press my mouth to his…I can't seem to get it out of my head.

But when will I ever come back here? What possible excuse will I ever have to fly down to my stepbrother's strange, haunted mansion once I return to Manhattan?

So I go. I walk into her room and reach toward the curling paper on the wall with its tiny lavender violets. When I give it a small tug, I'm half-braced for a scream from the room, a popping lightbulb, a shattering window, but nothing happens.

"Sorry, Margaret," I whisper to the wall. "I don't mean to destroy your room. I'm sure it was really pretty in your day."

There's a smell in the air, suddenly, though the windows are shut. I close my eyes to place it. Roses—not the way they smell in a hand lotion but the way they smell fresh from the garden. And that's when I feel it again. That giddy, adolescent thrill, as if I'm about to hit the high point of a roller coaster, as if I'm Cinderella climbing the stairs to meet Prince Charming for the first time, as if my entire life lies ahead of me and I know it's going to be perfect.

And then it doesn't just fade…it bottoms out. I drop to my knees, racked by sorrow. A tidal wave of grief, unlike anything I've ever known.

When my eyes open, my hands are pressed flat to the wall. There are tears sliding down my face, and I don't know if the tears are mine or Margaret's. Perhaps she was sad, but I'm sad too.

I don't want to leave the house.

More than that, I don't want to leave Charlie, and it's never going to be like this again.

I crawl from the room on my hands and knees, gasping, and sit in the hallway until my hands stop shaking.

Grief is instructive in mythology. Demeter's grief creates the seasons. Achilles' grief over Patroclus's death is what makes him recognize his pride and stubbornness.

This grief…it's meant to teach me something. I don't know what it is, but I'm not leaving until I've figured it out.

I text Harvey with shaking hands.

> Hey, something's come up here. I'm not going to make my flight. Sorry about the party, but I'll be back Monday.

Under normal circumstances, I'd be terrified. I'd be holding my stomach, waiting for him to explode.

But it's as if I've emerged from the room a little wiser than I was when I entered: nothing Harvey can do to me comes close to what I just went through. If he left me, if he died…it wouldn't approach the sorrow I just felt.

And it probably should, shouldn't it? Maybe that's what I was meant to learn…that I don't feel enough to stay with him. I suspect I already knew that, but I can't leave Harvey now. Not when Kit's on Everest getting engaged, perhaps at this very moment. This is her summer, and it needs to remain her summer, rather than having it overshadowed by my divorce.

I rise on weak legs, yawning. Tears always tire me, but this is excessive—I need to lie down. I stumble out of the house, gripping the rail to maintain my balance just as Charlie emerges from the basement.

"You okay?" he asks.

I nod, suppressing a yawn. "Yep, just feeling a little off. I'm staying until Monday, by the way."

He bites his lower lip, cautious as he meets my gaze. "What changed?"

I can't tell him about the room. He'll never let me go in there again. And while a part of me doesn't *want* to go in there again after what happened, I suspect I'll go anyway. Maybe it's Margaret or maybe it's just a wiser part of my subconscious, but if it wants to teach me something this much—it's something I need to hear.

"If I attended every party where Harvey wanted to make an impression, I'd be attending parties every night of every year. I've paid my dues. It's enough."

His tongue prods his cheek. "I'm glad you found your backbone," he says softly, his brow furrowed as he studies my face. "I'm just not quite sure why it took you thirty-two years."

Yeah, me either.

HARVEY RAGE-TEXTS for most of the afternoon. The further I get from the weird thing I went through upstairs, the more my guilt starts to bother me until I finally tell him I'm turning off my phone.

In the evening there's a party Elijah invited us to, on what was supposed to be my final night here. It's a rare night out for Elijah, whose mom has been sick, and it sounded nice enough at the time—some deck overlooking the water, a live band. I beg off at the last minute, telling Charlie I still don't feel great, which is true enough. Even though I napped, I'm drooping with exhaustion.

He suggests that maybe he should stay home with me, but I send him off. "I'm going straight to sleep," I promise. "Honestly, I'm fine. I just need some rest."

Once he's gone, I take a shower and climb into bed. I'm dying to sleep, but I told Harvey I'd call, and if he doesn't hear from me after the day we've had, God knows what he'll do.

"Hey," he says when he answers. His tone is almost cordial, a pleasant surprise.

Perhaps my show of backbone actually helped. Maybe he finally saw exactly how far he could push and yell before I just stopped listening.

"Hi," I reply. "Sorry about the party."

"I'll get over it," he says.

I don't even know who this calm man is, the one who isn't telling me a thousand ways I'm a disappointment.

"So you're in town tonight and tomorrow, and then you're gone again?" I ask.

I hear the clatter of keys dropping onto a counter. "Yeah," he says. "I'm going to LA for most of next week."

I wince. A better wife would have come home to see him before he left.

How many times, though, has he left when he didn't need to? How many times could he have invited me along and didn't? A million.

"Are you going to take the dogs back to Lori?" I ask. There's a regrettable note of worry in my voice, wheedling. I just can't help it. "I can arrange to have them brought out to Brooklyn if that helps."

"It's not an issue," he says firmly.

It's not an issue...*how*?

"What do you mean?" I ask, sitting up, because I know he's not taking them with him.

"Look," he says, "I didn't want to get into this tonight, but those dogs have caused us nothing but arguments for the past year and we don't have time for them. So I gave them to Elodie's kids. Belated birthday presents. Hadley was fucking over the moon. She thinks you're the best aunt ever now."

"That's a joke, right?" A hysterical laugh burbles out of me, but I'm already clutching my chest as if I know it's true.

"No. If you actually cared about them, you wouldn't have fucking left. They named them Buddy and Lolly. Everyone's very happy."

My stomach has dropped so far I'm not sure it can be found. It has to be a joke.

"You didn't," I whisper.

"Come on, Maren, those were fucked up names. Echo and Narcissus? You named *siblings* after mythological characters who were in love. Little incestuous, don't you think? Then again, maybe that's what you intended, given how you and Charlie act around each other."

I can't even address that. It's so ridiculous and irrelevant. I press a hand to my chest. My God. How disastrously wrong I was when I went through with the wedding.

"How could you have done that to me?" I ask. "You know how much I love them."

"Yeah, so much that you left them at a kennel for a full week."

It wasn't a kennel. They were with Lori, who they know and adore and—

"You got too complacent with them," he continues. "They made you feel like you were already a mother, so you took your eyes off the prize. Now you can fully focus on IVF."

There's a buzzing in my ears. Fully focus? He wants me fully focused? I've been so goddamned focused that I gave up my job and my independence. So focused that I let him mock me in public, implying I was too spoiled to work.

I stopped running.

I gave up drinking and coffee and nights with my friends.

I turned myself into a fucking wreck over whether my green juice had too much sugar.

What has he given up? Not a fucking thing. This wasn't even about the dogs. It was about wanting to pull one more thing from me, a punishment for going to Oak Bluff in the first place.

Well, fuck Harvey. Fuck Harvey for constantly suggesting things about me I could change without ever changing himself. Fuck Harvey for suggesting that travel was the issue so that I would quit working, that running was the issue so I would quit running, that the one cup of coffee I allowed myself was the issue so I'd give that up too. Fuck Harvey for doing his level best to take everything away from me without taking a single thing away from himself.

I want children more than I want anything in the world, but not if it means raising them with a monster like him.

"Fuck you, Harvey," I tell him. "I want a divorce."

And then I hang up the phone and start to wail.

20

CHARLIE

I'm at a beach bar with Elijah and a couple guys on the crew—lots of decks, picnic tables, beer in pitchers—but I'm enjoying myself less than I'd expected.

Some girls have wound up at our table. One of them is all over Elijah; another is all over me. I guess I'll be taking her home, and I don't know why I'm not more excited about that... It's been over a week, after all. That's a decade in Charlie years.

"So you're from New York?" the girl shouts over the band. "I went there once on a school field trip."

She starts telling me all about some guy grabbing her purse in Times Square, and I'm barely listening. I'm not sure why I lack the energy to act interested. I wish I'd just stayed back with Maren. I have a bad feeling, and I don't know why.

I shoot her a text while the girl beside me is *still* talking about Times Square. We could have flown to New York in the length of time she's spent telling this story.

You okay?

MAREN

Not really.

When the fuck does Maren *ever* admit things aren't perfect?

"I'm sorry," I tell the girl. "I need to make a call."

I'm already walking outside as I hit Maren's number.

"What's up?" I demand the second she answers.

"I'm just—" Her voice wavers, then cracks.

"What happened?" I hiss.

Her swallow is audible. "He gave away the dogs," she whispers, and then she lets out this wail, a sound that rips my heart from my chest. I've seen Maren tear up. I've never heard her cry like *this*.

I blink, not understanding. "He did *what*?"

"My dogs," she sobs. "Echo and Narcy. Harvey gave them to his sister's kids."

"Mare," I say, looking at the smokers around me as if they might help make sense of this, "I don't understand. You mean they're *watching* the dogs?"

"No," she chokes out. "He gave one to each of the kids as a belated birthday gift. He said I needed to focus on IVF. That they'd made me too complacent."

What the fuck?

Anyone who has seen Maren with those dogs for five seconds knows she's obsessed with them, that she carries them in her arms and coos to them, and thinks every single thing they do is adorable when it isn't.

I don't even like dogs. But only a monster would have done something like this.

"Go to bed," I tell her. "If Harvey calls, don't answer. We'll figure this out in the morning."

"Okay." She sounds like she doesn't believe me, but why would she? She's under the impression that there's nothing to figure out because Maren can't conceive of demanding her dogs back from two little kids.

Fortunately for her, I like kids even less than I like dogs.

I go back inside the bar, ignoring the girls while I tell Elijah I'm taking off.

"Everything okay?" he asks.

I give him a small shake of my head. "I've got to get back to New York. I'm going to see if Maren's stepfather can hook me up with a ride, but otherwise there's a six AM flight out in the morning."

"What's so urgent, though?"

I'm so furious I want to flip a table in lieu of answering. "Maren's husband needs to be punched in the face, repeatedly. That's what's so urgent."

Elijah raises a brow. "Somehow I knew this would have to do with Maren."

"Her husband gave away her *fucking dogs*. What do you expect me to do?"

He laughs. "Exactly what you're doing right now."

Four hours later, I'm on a private plane out of Hilton Head, too furious to sleep. I've hated Harvey from the instant Maren brought him home. I hated him long before he ever gave me a reason to and hated him more once he did.

I've restrained myself for her sake. Now, the gloves are off at last.

21

MAREN

God, I've made such a mess of my life. I guess I'll need to go stay with my mother, but she really focuses on the wrong things in moments like this. She'll put me on a diet and start setting me up with Roger's sixty-year-old friends an hour after I've arrived.

I lie in bed, weeping, trying to solve an unsolvable problem. I want my puppies back. I don't want them anywhere near Elodie's horrible son. But her daughter is sweet, and how do I tell two children I'm taking away their birthday presents? I could buy them new dogs instead, but then I'm just setting up two different dogs to suffer in their hands.

I guess most people would say the bigger problem is that I've blown up my entire life. I married a man who turned awful while we were still on our honeymoon, and I *stayed*. I don't even know why I stayed. Was it because we'd just had this massive, seven-figure wedding and I couldn't imagine admitting my mistake? Or was it because I was so accustomed to scrambling for approval that scrambling for *his* just felt familiar?

I don't have a job, I don't have hobbies, I don't have fun. I also don't have a husband or kids.

I've got nothing, and that's still better than being with a man who'd treat me the way Harvey did today.

I just wish I'd figured it out a lot sooner than I did.

NORMALLY, the sound of Charlie's cottage door shutting is my morning alarm, but when I wake the next day, the sun is high in the sky.

I go to the balcony, but there's no sign of him on the trail around the cove and he wouldn't work out this late anyway.

Apparently, he had a lot more fun than I did last night. I've got no business being bothered by that, but I at least expected a shoulder to cry on.

When I go to the kitchen, the missing car keys confirm it.

He didn't fucking come home.

What the fuck? He knew what happened to me and he just...went home with someone else?

I press my face into my palms, more hurt than I have a right to be.

Why am I here? What am I even doing? Of course he stayed out all night and if my head was in the right place, I wouldn't care about that at all.

Maybe he didn't actually want me to stay. I've been cramping his style for over a week. Of course he didn't want me to—

There's a long creak as the front door swings open. And then...tiny feet scamper across the tiled foyer.

I move toward the sound and have just stepped into the dining room when Echo and Narcy come rushing toward me.

Oh my God. What?

I start crying as I drop to my knees, hugging them to me, stunned and shaken.

Charlie stands in the frame of the door with circles under his eyes and the sweetest, most pleased grin on his face.

"How did you get them back?" I whisper, crying too hard to speak normally. I set them down but they're so excited they just keep jumping on me so I pick them back up. I missed them even more than I realized.

Charlie runs a hand through his hair. "I made your dickhead husband call his sister and tell her to put them in a car and send them back."

I shake my head. "*How*, though?"

That's when I notice his knuckles. The skin is cracked. "Oh my God, you didn't punch him, did you?"

"Define *punch*."

"Charlie, you know what *punch* means."

He grins. "Okay, then yes, I did. But the bloodshed was just for my own entertainment. He's still alive, in case you're worried. Henry only let me get in two good hits."

I laugh and dry my eyes on the corner of my T-shirt. "Henry?"

He shrugs. "I had him call Harvey and explain that he'd employ every available resource and every dollar he possesses to ruin him if we didn't have them back by morning. I'd have done it on my own, but that sort of thing is a little more threatening when it comes from a billionaire. He met me at your condo early this morning just to make sure Harvey knew how serious he was."

And now I'm crying again. It's the kind of thing I'd expect Henry to do for Kit—not me. "I can't believe he was willing to do that. I can't believe *you* were willing to do that. You don't even like dogs."

"People love you a lot more than you realize, Mare. And the fact that you love those dogs is the only thing that should've mattered to your husband."

"Ex-husband." I've said it before, yes, but this time, I know

I'm not going back. Because the man who's supposed to care about me above all else can't hold a candle to the one in front of me, who does his best to pretend he doesn't care at all. "I have no idea what to do with my life from here forward, but it won't be with Harvey."

His gaze holds mine a moment too long, his lips opening as if to speak. For a half second, I think of my wedding day, of Charlie saying *we can go anywhere you want*. If I'd done it, where would we be right now? I'd have avoided all these years with Harvey, but it's not as if Charlie and I would have stayed together, if we'd gotten together at all. He'd probably have broken my heart, and our entire friendship would be ruined.

Whatever I saw in his face disappears entirely and his mouth curves. "So I guess that means you've got nowhere to be?"

I blink up at him. "Huh?"

He lifts a shoulder. "I'm just saying...that wallpaper's not removing itself and I'm staying til mid-July. So maybe you could stick around until you've got a reason to go home."

This euphoria I'm feeling could just be the house again, or these squirming puppies in my arms.

But I'm pretty sure it's Charlie. I'm pretty sure I'm simply thrilled that he wants me to stay.

My relationship with Henry has long been...awkward. I'm grateful for the role he's played in my life, but there's no way to hide the fact that his relationship with Kit is very different. She wouldn't blink an eye at calling to yell at him because she knows her position is secure. I've never quite felt that way. But by that same token, I'm immensely grateful for the things he does on my behalf, things Kit would barely even notice.

> Thank you so much for helping Charlie get the dogs back. I will never forget it.

HENRY

> I'm your father. You don't have to thank me for that. You should have told me the second it happened.

> Well, anyway, I'm very appreciative. And you won't have to deal with Harvey again. I told him I want a divorce.

> Of course you do. My attorney is already drawing up your separation agreement.

I smile. I guess the benefit of being raised by people who can't stay married for long is that they know exactly how to get you out of your marriage when the time comes.

Unfortunately, now that Henry knows we're in South Carolina, his best bud Roger will too...and therefore my mother. Charlie calls his dad to get ahead of it, but I put off calling my mom until later in the day, because it's not going to go well. She won't be upset that I'm leaving Harvey—she adores breakup drama, which is probably the reason she threatens to leave Roger as often as she does—but she's going to have an issue with the fact that I'm in South Carolina with her stepson.

I wait for a bit after Charlie phones his dad, then I call her from the back deck, while Echo and Narcy tear around the yard, and deliver the news about the divorce first.

"I'm going to set you up," she says. "Roger has a friend who's going through a divorce and his youngest is leaving for college, so he'll be looking for someone to fill the void. I'll have you over for dinner. Although, speaking of dinner, you know if you want to model again, you're going to have to drop about ten pounds. But anyway, let's shoot for Thursday. Roger!" she shouts, fully prepared to set me up with this guy whose kids are grown adults.

"Mom, stop. I'm not in New York. I'm in South Carolina. Helping Charlie."

"Helping *Charlie*?" she repeats, as if Charlie is some random guy out on parole, one we can't trust. "With *what*?"

Charlie's inside, but I look around anyhow before I proceed. "With the house, Mom. I've been removing wallpaper, and I think I'm going to start redoing bathroom tiles soon."

There's a tick of silence, one that sets my heart beating in my throat. "But why?"

There's so much embedded in that *why*.

She's saying *Why does he suddenly matter to you? I sense drama, and this is something I could get upset about!*

"Mom, it's not a big deal. I like house renovations, and he needed help."

"Where are you *sleeping*?" she asks, and this question isn't innocent either. Her tone implies that I'm not simply in the same bed with Charlie but actively sleeping *on* him, with his penis wedged inside me all night long.

I sigh heavily. "Jesus, Mom," I hiss, glancing over my shoulder to confirm that Charlie's still not in the vicinity. "I have my own cottage. Charlie has his own too."

"Keep it that way," she warns. "You could ruin everything if you..."

She trails off without specifying, but I'm pretty sure I can figure out the rest of the sentence on my own. "I know, Mom. I know. God, what do you think of me? I just told my husband I want a divorce twelve hours ago."

"I think you're single and so is he," she replies, "and that leads nowhere good. That's what I think. You shouldn't be down there. You need to come up here and get your career back on track."

She's probably right. I've got nothing now. No home and no idea what happens after South Carolina, and the timing of it is really not great, with Kit's upcoming engagement. I know her—

she's going to feel guilty and there'll be nothing I can say that will entirely erase it.

And yet, despite all this, I'm sort of...happy? I think perhaps it's just a break from all the worry—about ticking biological clocks, and where my future is headed, and angering a man who couldn't be pleased. Most of those things are *still* a concern. But for right now, I've got my puppies and I've got Charlie, and the whole world just feels as if it's finally been set right.

22

———

MAREN

I'm woken by Echo and Narcy yipping at the window. Charlie's outside, tying his shoes as he prepares to run along the path.

I open the French door and step onto the little deck. "I think the puppies want to come with you."

"Hard pass, unless you've had them on an intensive cardio regimen for at least a year."

"They're barely a year old *now*."

"I guess that's a no then," he says, putting in his AirPods and vanishing down the path. He'll come around to them eventually, I'm sure.

"I guess it's just us, guys," I tell them. "You want to go for a run?"

I change into jogging clothes and head in the same direction Charlie went a few moments prior. The puppies crap out before we're ten minutes from the house, but I'm sort of relieved because I was exhausted five minutes in.

I need to get back into shape. I need to do a whole lot of things—get my career on track, remember what it's like to enjoy myself, get to the point where I can run a few miles without wanting to die.

But the most pressing voice, the one I'm fighting myself to ignore, tells me to find a replacement for Harvey as soon as possible.

Sure, I could pursue IVF on my own, or adopt, but I watched my mother raise kids solo and it isn't ideal. Which leaves me stuck finding someone new, the sooner the better, and it's haste like that which can lead to disastrous choices. I almost wound up with Harvey, a man who'd give away my dogs to punish me, and I wasn't even *hasty* when I chose him.

I shower and meet Charlie in the kitchen for breakfast. I love these mornings with him, drinking coffee, watching him eat, bathing in that quiet smile of his when he glances up from his empty plate.

My phone buzzes on the table and I ignore it, lifting my mug instead. Harvey's been relentless for the past day. Sometimes he sort of apologizes. Most of the time he calls me a whore and details the pornographic things he assumes I'm doing with Charlie down here. I thought *I* was the one of us with an imagination, but Harvey's puts mine to shame.

When my phone and Charlie's buzz with a text at the same time, I'm terrified to even look. It's one thing to read it myself. It'll be another entirely if Charlie knows what's being said.

But it isn't a message from Harvey. It's from Kit.

> KIT
>
> I'm engaged! And I didn't even run away this time!

This is followed by a picture of her beside Miller at Everest, holding up the ring to the light. Charlie's gaze darts to me, as if he's assessing how this information hit.

"I'm thrilled for her," I tell him before he's had a chance to ask.

I groan, because this is what I'm in for now: months and months of people assessing my reaction and looking for distress. "You don't seem surprised."

"I helped Miller pick the ring and you don't seem surprised either. We all knew this was coming."

Charlie still doesn't look convinced, perhaps because I'm not being all that convincing. I *am* thrilled for Kit, but it's hard not to feel as if my star is dimming while hers is on the rise, like an aging actress gently being shoved aside in her recurring role by some younger, hotter ingenue. Kit's getting *congrats* texts and I'm getting ones that say, "*So how many times a day do you suck Charlie's dick?*"

Her whole life is ahead of her, and if I don't find someone soon, it's going to feel like mine is in the past. It can't be over for me, right? *I can still meet someone. I can still have a family. I've just got to get my ass in gear and—*

No. Not like that. I'm not going to look for someone because I'm panicking. I'm not.

"I'm going on a cleanse," I tell Charlie, setting my juice down.

He groans. "Maren, your whole fucking life is a cleanse. What's left to even give up? You barely drink. You don't eat sugar. Or carbs. You appear to have given up sex, although you were married to Harvey, so I don't blame you there, but what the fuck is even left?"

"If you're entirely through, I'll tell you. It's not that kind of cleanse. I'm going to give up all the stuff about getting pregnant."

He blinks. There's a long pause before he finally speaks. "That seems like a pretty sudden change. I haven't heard you express an interest in anything *but* getting pregnant for years."

"I know," I say, "and I'm not writing it off. I just think I need a break from all the worry. And I need to start wanting something else."

He tips back in his chair. "So what's the new pastime going to be? Gambling? Sex addiction? I can probably help you with both."

I laugh. "I'm not planning to get addicted to anything. I just want to spend a little time being open to what life brings me. Not panicked about fertility."

"That is an incredibly boring cleanse," he says, "but not as boring as I assumed it would be."

My mother calls not long after breakfast, excited about Kit, already planning some surprise engagement party in the Hamptons a few weeks hence.

"Miller's taking her to Turks and Caicos as soon as they return from Everest," my mother informs me. I don't mention that I already knew this, that I packed the suitcase, just like I didn't mention that I helped choose the ring. My mother would be testy for weeks that I was given the inside scoop, and she was not.

"That's great," I reply mildly.

My mother's tongue clicks. "I know the situation is tough, but you're going to have to try a little harder than that while we're setting up for the party."

I groan audibly, plucking Echo from the marsh. "Mom, I'm *fine. Happy.* But I don't know that I can get there early. I'll still be down here helping Charlie."

"No offense, but nothing you're doing down there can be all that vital. What skills do you even have?" Her point is hurtful, but accurate. I have no skills, and I'm sure one of Elijah's guys could tackle every job I've done since I got here and complete them in a day's time.

"You should be up here on go-sees anyway," she continues. "You'll need to get back down to a sample size two, but I think you can still recover, though honestly, you're pushing it at thirty-two."

Wow. She just managed to take a hit at both my age and

weight. *Impressive.* "Let me look at the calendar and get back to you," I reply before I hang up.

Because it's a Sunday, no one's working at the house. We bike down to the beach, each of us carrying one puppy in our bike's basket, which Charlie says is the least manly moment of his life, "including infancy."

Echo and Narcy exhaust themselves and lie at our feet as we spread out a blanket and lie down side-by-side. I grab the book I pilfered from Charlie's mom's collection—one in which the vampire hero will *literally* die if he doesn't mate with his other half, who can't accept his *"massive cock, twice the size of a human's"* until she's fully *ripened.*

"What's that?" Charlie asks, and before I can stop him, he's snatched the book up and has begun to read. *"The time is nigh, little witch. I'll plunder ye until'*—oh, wait. He's Scottish? Apologies. Let me start over, with the accent. *'The time is nigh, little witch. I'll plunder ye until yer belly is full of my seed. And when you drip with—"*

I snatch at the book. "Stop. Sidenote: your accent is terrible. You sound like a leprechaun."

His accent is perfect. I'm so turned on right now I could die from it.

"Then apparently you're turned on by leprechauns because I can see your nipples straight through that shirt." He grabs the book back. "What a filthy little girl you are. I had no idea. I can just read the rest for you while you finish yourself off. Go ahead. No one's looking. Where were we? Belly full of seed. Right. Dripping. There we are. *'And when you drip with gallons of my come.'* Gallons? I hope he's speaking metaphorically because Jesus. Gallons, *multiple*? That could probably kill someone."

I huff out an exhale. Sweat's begun to drip from my hairline. "You realize this was your *mother's* book, right? And let me tell you...the pages were *worn.* She read this book repeatedly. Do you want to read the passage where he describes *how* they'll mate, once it happens? It involves several holes. And his brother."

Charlie stiffens and throws the book back to me. "I'm not sure why you had to ruin everything by bringing up my dead mom. I mean, you didn't *entirely* ruin it. I'm still going to jerk off to this, and I really hope she's not watching."

"Do you want to borrow the book?"

"Nipples, I wasn't turned on by the *book*," he replies as he rolls onto his stomach.

Which means...he was turned on by me? I like the idea of that way more than I should.

In the evening, we go into town for dinner. There are two bartenders working, including the one with a crush on Charlie. Not that I blame her—Charlie would stand out almost anywhere, and this restaurant is a sea of balding, middle-aged men gone soft aside from him.

"That toothsome bartender is staring at you again."

He raises a brow. "*Toothsome*? Have you suddenly turned into one of the Bronte sisters?"

"I meant...the girl with the teeth."

"Toothsome means attractive, I believe."

"Eh," I say with a shrug. "I don't know if I'd go that far in describing her. Let's stick with my definition."

He turns to glance over his shoulder. "Maren, perhaps she's never been the face of a Tom Ford campaign, but that girl is definitely attractive. Or maybe it's just that I haven't had sex in over a week, and she looks more attractive than my right hand."

I glance at Charlie's right hand reflexively. His lovely, large hand. I picture it grasping his lovely, large...*stop Maren*.

"You should ask her out then," I say, picking up my fork, focusing on my plate, as if the suggestion means less to me than my next bite.

He raises a brow. "Is that what's going to happen here, now that you're single? Are we going to be each other's wingmen?"

"No, because I don't need a wingman. What would be the point of me dating someone here? I'm not staying."

Which again has me thinking I shouldn't be on a cleanse at all. I should be back in Manhattan, being introduced to better men than Harvey.

"Maren, have you ever dated anyone *without* hoping it would lead to marriage and children?"

"Why would I?" I demand. "What else is in it for me? I don't need some guy's money."

He shoves his plate away, laughing. "Companionship? Sex?"

"I have my family for companionship and sex is—" I shrug. "Not all it's cracked up to be. Unnecessarily stressful."

That brow of his raises again. I swear to God I'm going to Botox it in his sleep if he keeps it up. "How the fuck is it stressful?" he demands. "Then again, I'm speaking to a woman who's admitted to freaking out about the healthfulness of her green juice, so if there's a way to make it stressful, I'm sure you'll find it."

I shrug. I could blame Harvey—he certainly didn't improve the situation—but that stress existed long before him.

"You never know what someone's going to think. If he's comparing you to his ex; if he's decided he prefers someone curvier than you or less curvy. Or he wants someone louder. Or quieter. There's no standard. No way of knowing what any guy wants or if he's happy with you. And I just don't like it that much."

Harvey was so consistently unhappy with me—not just in bed but everywhere—that it's almost impossible to imagine anyone could feel otherwise.

Charlie runs a hand through his hair. "Of course you don't like it much if that's what you're thinking the whole time, and if you're this insecure, my heart breaks for all the women who weren't models at some point. Maren, if a guy wants to sleep with you in the first place, consider the challenge won."

"But you need him to enjoy it enough that he wants to stay," I argue. "Something no female has managed to pull off with you, apparently."

He finishes his beer. "Exactly. Because it's not about whether or not you've succeeded in some way…Some men, like myself, don't want a commitment, so there's no chance of success. You sleep with them just for the fun of it—no other reason. Before you start looking for husband number two, why not attempt to enjoy sex, just for what it is?"

Charlie clearly has no understanding of how deeply I want the things I want. I've never felt like a full-fledged member of my family. I've woken each day of my sentient life craving a family of my own—a group of people I could love unreservedly without fear that they'd shut me out.

"I don't think I'm capable of it. If I like someone enough to sleep with him, then no matter what the guy said about commitment, I'd be hoping to change his mind."

He gives me that cocky half-smile of his, high on one side, full of mocking doubt. "So you're saying you think you could change me?"

"You might be the only person I know who's douchey enough that I'd *never* think I could change."

Charlie's smile spreads to both sides of his face. Dimples emerge. The bartender would piss herself if she could see it. "Well, that presents us with an interesting predicament."

I laugh. "I don't think it does."

But for just a moment, his gaze catches mine, and neither of us are laughing.

It's sort of a joke.

But also sort of not one.

"I guess that means you're going home with the bartender," I say, forcing myself to smile. It takes way too much effort.

His tongue glides over his upper lip before he casually glances over his shoulder toward the bar. "Nah. You can't wave top-shelf whiskey in my face and ask me to settle for light beer instead."

I could argue that I wasn't waving it in his face and that I don't love being compared to something known for its age, but I don't. I'm too damn happy he's coming back home with me.

23

———

MAREN

Elijah enters the kitchen on Monday looking grimmer than normal. He takes a seat at the table and waves me off when I hold up the coffee pot.

"I've got some potentially bad news," he announces. "They moved the inspection up—it's now happening Wednesday."

Charlie's jaw drops. "That's two days from now. How is that possibly legal?"

Elijah shrugs. "I doubt that it is, but in the time it would take to get our complaint heard by anyone, the inspection will already have been done. I'm still assuming the whole thing's a formality—I mean, they know we're in the middle of a renovation—but I've contracted with a roofing crew out of Beaufort to start repairing the joists and then the roof. As long as we can prove that we've got it all in process, we'll be fine."

Charlie pinches the bridge of his nose, stressed out even though Elijah's telling him not to be. It's a surprising side to a guy who gives the impression, at home, of always being slightly too relaxed. "So you want me back in the basement?" he asks.

Elijah tips back in his chair. "I think we've got to spread out so by the time this inspector arrives, he can see that every hazard is in the process of being repaired. I've got an electrician coming in to look at the wiring, so you can help me redo the porch and I'll leave a small team finishing up in the basement. And Maren...wallpaper?"

I nod, laughing at my uselessness. *Can't pass inspection without wallpaper removal. Everyone knows that.*

I clean up breakfast, then grab the wallpaper steamer, with the puppies at my feet. I've barely got one foot on the steps to the second floor before Echo and Narcy both start crying. They follow me to the third step before Echo turns and races back to the first floor with Narcy in her wake.

"What's going on?" Charlie asks.

"They're scared to go up," I tell him. I'm trying not to be freaked out by this. They're scared of lots of things they shouldn't be—the robotic vacuum was so distressing to them that I finally gave it away. "But, you know, we don't have stairs at the condo, so they're not used to them."

Charlie gives me a side-eye. "They ran up the porch stairs just fine."

"I hate when you apply logic."

"Yes, I've noticed," he says. "So are we in agreement that the house is haunted, and we should be getting the hell out?"

I grin. "You don't want that any more than I do. You like it here. Admit it."

His smile matches my own. "It's okay. Not crazy about the *Amityville Horror* situation currently unfolding, however."

I shake my head. "If there's a ghost, it's a good ghost."

"You know who says that? The first person to die in a horror film." He lifts Echo and Narcy, one under each arm. "Your mother is about to be possessed by spirits of the undead, so I guess it's gonna be the three of us from now on."

I'm smiling as I watch him walk outside, still talking to them. He's already come around to them, and he doesn't even realize it.

I start upstairs again, a little more unsettled than I was before. And though I'm determined to avoid Margaret's room for the time being, when I reach the landing, it's as if...my feet are accustomed to turning in that direction, like one of those paths you've taken so many times that you can arrive at its end with no memory of how you got there.

I walk in, and nothing happens. No giddiness, no grief. But just as I'm leaving the room, I catch a glance of myself in the mirror, and it's as if...I see her, and I see me too. Both of us young and hopeful. It's gone before I'm even sure it was there, and what am I supposed to make of it if it was? I keep waiting for Margaret to write me some big message, telling me clearly what I'm meant to do with myself, and it doesn't happen.

I head to the primary suite. I love this room too, but in a different way. I love Margaret's room the way you might love your childhood home. I love the primary suite simply because it's glorious, with two full sets of French doors and a wide balcony overlooking the backyard and the cove.

I picture this room with its carpet pulled up, the gleaming hardwood beneath it refinished. I picture it with a canopy bed piled high with blankets and a dog bed at its foot for the puppies. *Not that the puppies will sleep here.* Obviously, it will be Charlie's room one day.

It's strange that I keep forgetting it won't be mine too.

THAT NIGHT, I dream about a desk I had as a kid, one that belonged to my mother as a girl. I pull out the chair and feel beneath the desk's top drawer for my journal, hidden in the open space between the drawer's frame and the cross post.

I am bursting with news that I can share with no one but this book in front of me. It feels as if my life is changing by the minute, growing more exciting and more troubling all at the same time.

What's strange is that when I look at the hands holding the pen, they are mine and yet they are not mine. I try to focus on the words spilling onto the page, but I can't quite make them out. I only know that I can barely contain my excitement and that they are absolutely one hundred percent about *him*.

My eyes fly open. It's barely dawn, and the puppies are sound asleep at the foot of the bed. The desk in that dream... did I see it in the attic last week? I'm positive it's just my imagination running away from me again, but...the hands. I noticed my hands, and even at the time, I thought that they looked different.

And the handwriting, too. I tend to print more than anything else, but those words in the dream were in perfect, rounded cursive...almost like calligraphy.

It's definitely my imagination, the whole thing.

But what if it isn't? I saw Elijah's guys carrying the furniture out of the house yesterday...Did they take it to the dump already? And if the furniture is gone will I actually drive to the dump like a lunatic, crying that I dreamed about a journal?

I climb from the bed, waking the dogs as I slip on shorts and flip-flops. I exit the studio with them at my heels, and I've just passed Charlie's door when he emerges in nothing but boxers, running a hand over his face—a motion that sends a dozen muscles rippling across his stomach. "Maren, why the fuck are you up and making a racket at five-thirty in the morning?"

"Sorry," I whisper, wincing.

"You know, you whispering *now* doesn't help me much. Why are you up and...inappropriately dressed?"

I frown at him. "Inappropriately dressed?" I demand, looking at my outfit. "Sorry, Winston Churchill. I didn't know we had a dress code."

"I'm pretty sure you know you ought to be wearing a bra when we've got thirty strangers working on the property."

I glance down again, and like clockwork, my nipples decide to stand at attention. "Oh. Well, no one's here right now. I just wanted to see if the furniture from the attic was still in front."

He scrubs his hand over his face again. "It is. Mystery solved. And we're not keeping it, so go back to fucking bed."

Thank God I don't have to drive out to the dump, because I absolutely would have. "The dogs are up, so I'm just going to check on some stuff. Go back to sleep. Sorry I woke you."

"Put on some clothes first," he barks as he returns inside, letting the door slam shut behind him.

I ignore him—the crew won't be here for hours—and continue on to the front of the house, where the oaks block the early morning sun and the furniture remains stacked in a big pile—tables atop shelves, bed frames disassembled and leaning haphazardly against the surrounding trees. Fortunately the little desk is only on top of a credenza. I'm in the process of dragging a bookcase over so I can climb up when Charlie walks around the house, now in a T-shirt and shorts.

I flush. I'd rather he not be out here to witness my insanity. "I thought you were going back to bed."

"Yeah, that was the plan, but I had a sudden image of you climbing on sixteen poorly balanced pieces of furniture to get something and here you are. *Why?*"

My exhale is half embarrassed and half exasperated. I wish he'd stayed in bed—then I wouldn't have had to explain this thing that might sound a little quirky. Possibly worse than quirky. "You've got to promise you won't make fun of me."

"That's...a really tall order."

"Fine," I reply, beginning to scale the bookcase, which sways slightly beneath my weight. "Then you don't need to know."

He was ten feet away, but I've barely climbed up one shelf

before his hands are around my waist and he's setting me back on the ground. For a single moment, I'm wildly conscious of those hands of his, in a way I shouldn't be. "I won't make fun of you," he says, letting me go. "Tell me."

I don't actually believe him, but it'll all come out eventually. "You remember our first night here?"

"Of course. It's the closest we've ever come to having sex. I'm not about to forget that anytime soon."

I roll my eyes. "We were *not* about to have sex. But anyway, it wasn't the mouse that woke me up. I was tapped."

"Tapped."

I reach out and tap his shoulder three times in a row. "Like that. I thought it was you."

He regards me with wary eyes. "What the fuck, Maren? And you didn't *mention* it?"

"I thought it would sound crazy if I said some ghost was warning us about the mouse, so I—"

"What if it wasn't a ghost? What if there was someone actually in the house?"

Oh. I hadn't thought of that. Still... "There wasn't. I'd have heard footsteps. Anyway, you remember that day you found me in the room upstairs, and I didn't realize all that time had passed?"

"Yeah..." he says with a hint of dread.

I reach down to pick up Echo, who's whining beside my left leg. "It wasn't like I was dreaming. I didn't think I'd fallen asleep, though I guess I did. But I had this huge burst of excitement, out of nowhere, and I was thinking about high school and then suddenly I was remembering something else, something about going to a dance and telling someone Papa wouldn't let me attend until my brothers got home from college. Except I don't call anyone *Papa*. And I don't have brothers."

His jaw locks. "This is why you were weird about the photo album."

"I wasn't *weird*," I reply, setting Echo down again. "It was just...I'd had this dream that I was a young girl who had several older brothers, and it turns out that the girl who probably lived in that room...had older brothers."

"You realize that doesn't mean anything, right? Lots of people have older brothers. It's not...rare."

"I know. That's why I didn't say anything. But then this morning I had this dream about that little desk, and I'd hidden a journal under one of the drawers, so—"

"So you came running out here without a bra at dawn to see if you might acquire the magic journal."

My nipples stand at attention again. It's as if they perk up any time they're being discussed. His gaze drops quickly, then shoots back to my face. "For someone who routinely has multiple girls naked in his apartment, you're making a really big deal out of the bra. But yes. I just wanted to check, and I know it sounds crazy, but...wouldn't you want to look if you were me?"

His raised brow says quite clearly that no, he would not want to look. "Maren, honey, you're starting to freak me out a little bit. I'm worried I'm about to find you crawling on the ceiling or speaking in tongues."

I shake my head. "I know it's strange, and I know I haven't always made the most rational decisions, but this is different. It feels like the house is trying to tell me something."

"You realize that's the kind of thing a girl would say in a movie right before she started crawling on the ceiling?"

"If I start crawling on the ceiling, you have my permission to remove me from the house."

"If you start crawling on the ceiling, I'll be too busy running toward town screaming to get you out of here."

I laugh. "That seems fair."

He nods toward the desk. "I don't want you climbing. Tell me what drawer."

If I'd checked on my own and found nothing, I'd have felt a little silly. If Charlie checks and there's nothing, I'm going to feel like a fucking idiot, but it's pretty clear he's not going to just leave me alone here if I request it. "The main one," I tell him. "Like, if you were sitting, it's right above your knees. She wasn't keeping it in the drawer, though. She was hiding it underneath."

He leans toward it, resting a hand on the credenza as he glances up. "Maren, I can see beneath it right now. There's nothing there."

"Oh," I say. "Okay."

He turns, looks me over, and gives me a weary smile. "Would you like me to look under the other drawers?"

My whole face must brighten because he laughs.

"You're going to have me dismantling this desk if it doesn't turn up, aren't you?" he asks, reaching toward the desk again. He pulls the bottom drawer out and finds nothing, pulls the middle drawer out and finds nothing, pulls the top drawer and finds—

"Huh," he says, almost inaudibly.

He slides his hand beneath it...and withdraws a book.

I take an automatic step backward in my shock. It doesn't look *exactly* like the diary I dreamed about, and it wasn't under the correct drawer, but...

"This is weird, right?" I ask.

He climbs down the bookshelf. "A ghost is possibly trying to overtake your body and is directing you to clues now, so yes, it's pretty fucking weird."

"She's not trying to overtake my body," I argue. "I'm just remembering these moments of her life."

He runs a hand over his face and into his hair, bicep flexing. "Great, and now you're *defending* the ghost trying to overtake your body, which is pretty much how I'd have predicted this would go."

I laugh. "Stop. Okay, so assuming the weirdest interpretation here is the correct one, why would a ghost be directing me toward clues?"

"Obviously, to solve the mystery of her untimely death at the hands of a murderer who will somehow become *aware* that you're onto him and go on a killing rampage to stop you."

I shrug, glancing over my shoulder at the house, now framed in gold by the rising sun. "Based on my knowledge of horror movies, all of you guys will die, but I'll survive and that's what matters."

Charlie frowns, glancing at the journal one last time. "It's probably just some crap girls do. Like you all read the same Nancy Drew book as kids." I never read a single Nancy Drew book and I'm pretty sure they didn't exist when Margaret was a child, but I get the sense Charlie's trying to normalize all this for himself. I wish I could do the same.

"Maybe," I conclude. "Go get your run in. I'm going to feed these guys."

With one final, uncertain glance at me, Charlie gives in and heads to his cottage while I take the puppies into the kitchen. I fill their bowls and take a seat at the table, opening the diary with more anticipation than I should feel over a century-old book. "It would serve me right if it just turns out to be grocery shopping lists," I tell the dogs.

Even *they* seem embarrassed for me. Even they seem to be saying *Maren, you've really gone too far*, as they focus on their food.

I open the book. And there, in that neat, precise cursive, is Margaret's journal.

May 10, 1916

There's a party this weekend at Grayville Manor, and

George Graves asked if I'd save him a dance, and he didn't ask anyone else to save him a dance, and I'm dying inside because Papa is never going to allow me to attend, not until the boys are home from school. There will be other dances, and Walter will be back from USC in a week, but I'm so heartbroken that I won't be there.

I wince. Should I be reading this? Because I doubt I'd want anyone to find my highs and lows as a young adult, particularly as so many of them involved my sister's fiancé. But no, this girl —Margaret, I assume—wanted me to read it.

I think.

May 12, 1916

I'm going to the dance! Sam is coming down with his friend William Howard, who's doing work for Papa this summer. Ruby Wilson says William is a thousand times more handsome than George, but I remember William from when I was small before he moved away—and I don't think he was all that handsome. She's just bitter that George said I was the prettiest girl in school. I'm wearing the yellow chiffon dress Mama ordered for me from Atlanta if it arrives in time. Otherwise, I suppose I'll just have to wear the blue lawn.

May 16, 1916

Sam arrived with William today. He _is_ handsome, unfortunately. More handsome than George. More handsome than anyone, really. Ruby will gloat if I admit it, so I intend to lie when she asks. Mama is making him stay in that shack down by the water, though she calls it a "cottage" to William's face, as if that makes it better. I think it's cruel, but Mama says it would be inappropriate to have him sleeping on the same floor as me. I found that rather thrilling, the idea that I could be so endangered by William Howard.

Mama is letting me wear her ruby broach to the dance! I've been asking to wear it my entire life!

May 18, 1916

What an incredible disappointment. The ball did not go at all as I had hoped. George and I danced, but someone stepped on my foot and I was in such agony. And I have no idea why anyone calls William charming. He is far too aware of his looks. The girls fell all over themselves to get his attention, which is, no doubt, what's made him so arrogant. He also made a rude joke about my dress. I was sorry for him because his father died when he was small and he and his mother had to go live with an aunt, but I no longer am.

May 20, 1916

William is doing exercise drills in the yard right now. He does them every morning because he believes the US will enter the war soon, now that Canada has. He looks ridiculous doing his sprints and his push-ups. Well, I'll admit he appears exceedingly strong, but it's still ridiculous. So ridiculous I can scarcely stop watching.

May 22, 1916

Why does William have to be so handsome? If he was simply amusing, I could overlook it. I'm shallow enough. But no, he has to be handsome as well. His face is a glorious thing. I'd stare at it through all of dinner if the boys wouldn't ridicule me for it later.

May 24, 1916

Today George asked me for a token of my affection. I

thought he was perhaps asking for a kiss, but he actually wanted a memento—something to remind him of me when he was taking his exams in Columbia. I said I had nothing and he asked for Mama's brooch, which I was wearing to impress him when I should have given it back to her.

Oh, why didn't I just return it after the dance? I didn't want to admit it wasn't mine...so I let him take it, and now I'm sick with fear Mama will ask for it while he's gone.

May 25, 1916

A group of us took a picnic onto the Bluff. Sam came, which was lovely, but William showed up for the latter half and just laid there in the grass, smirking, as if he was smarter than all of us. It's possible he _is_ smarter than all of us—Sam said he had the highest marks of anyone in their class—but he doesn't have to be so smug about it.

George said he hoped to marry soon, looking at me, and William said he was too young to have decent judgment. I hate him.

George still hasn't returned Mama's broach. I'm worried he means to keep it. She'll never forgive me if she finds out.

May 27, 1916

Well, a day that began catastrophically has ended all right. It was my worst fear come true: Mama asked for her broach, but it was still with George, and I couldn't exactly walk up to his door and demand it, could I? So I told Mama I would go upstairs to get it and then went down by the water and cried instead. That's how William found me: curled up in the gazebo near his cottage, crying my eyes out. He asked what was wrong, and I have no idea why I told him the truth. He laughed and I was so angry, but an hour later, he returned—I was inside by then, on the cusp of telling Mama the truth, and he slipped it into my pocket. When I felt its weight there, I could barely believe it. I'm not sure what he said to George, and I don't even care. Maybe William isn't so awful after all.

Oddly, William makes me think of Charlie: Charlie, doing push-ups in the grass, Charlie rushing back to New York to retrieve the puppies.

I shut the journal and go upstairs to Margaret's room, staring at myself hard in the mirror hanging there.

It feels as if my life and Margaret's are combining, somehow. As if I'm now half me and half her. It's got to be her influence, making me think of Charlie in the way I have been.

"Stop, Margaret," I warn. "I'm my own person. You don't get to decide who I like."

For once, the room is silent. There's no euphoria and no grief.

There's only me, admitting that it's possible Margaret has nothing to do with it, and that these feelings for Charlie may have been there all along.

CHARLIE AND ELIJAH are stuck in the basement for most of the day, fixing some new area that's letting water in. I begin stripping wallpaper in the rooms that must have belonged to Leo and Ray, but I can't stop thinking about the journal...despite the fact that I'm not sure it's in my best interest to keep reading.

I look up the house online, but find very little aside from the fact that it was "built by a wealthy judge for his wife and five children." The father's name was Richard Ames, but even when I go into ancestry databases, I find nothing. There are plenty of Richard Ameses, but none who fit the profile—and how is that possible? He had five kids. How can there not be a *million* family trees emanating from this branch? Perhaps Charlie's joke about untimely deaths wasn't so funny after all.

Charlie doesn't need the car that afternoon. I drive into Oak Bluff and ask Martha where I might find historical info about the town. Oak Bluff is too small for a library, she says, but there's a little history section in the town's administrative office.

I follow the directions she's given me down the street and the receptionist points toward a small shelf to the left. It mostly seems to hold awards for things like "best small-town parade," but there are also a handful of books.

"Look for *A History of Oak Bluff* by HM Fletcher," she says. "But I can't let you borrow it since it's our only copy."

I find the book easily and take a seat in the lobby as I begin to thumb through.

The author seems more enamored of the pre-Civil War history than the post-Civil War history. There's an entire chapter about the town's winter ball in 1860, but the decade following the war's end is summed up in a single sentence: *Devastated by the war's toll, Oak Bluff fell into despair.*

It picks up again in the late 1800s, when families began moving here from Charlotte. A school was built in 1890, and *"banker Edmund Graves moved here, to great acclaim, with other well-off families taking a cue from him."*

The father of George, the broach thief, I imagine.

The only mention of Riverbend is again a discussion of Richard, the patriarch—a successful lawyer back in Charlotte before he was elected a judge in Oak Bluff. Obviously, his daughter wouldn't have been encouraged to take up a career, but it's a little surprising that none of the sons are referenced. And I don't think anyone was murdered in the house, either. If "Mary Leavitt's famed blueberry pie" warrants a full page in this book, a murder would at least get a mention. But then, what the hell happened to them all?

I return the book to its shelves and walk to the receptionist's desk. "Does the town have a graveyard?" I ask. "Like...with older graves?" Knowing when they all died might answer some of my questions, if not all of them.

She nods. "There's one in back of the church on Magnolia Street, although any family with a property the size of yours was buried on the grounds. That's typically the way it was done."

Except do I even want to know if that's the case? A grave is always bad news, always sad, even if Margaret's tells me she died a proud widow and a mother of ten. I think I'd rather try my luck with the journal instead.

June 2, 1916

Today was the last day of school. The boys are all home, which means the house is very lively but also very full. Sam has been offered a job in Greenville, and I hope he doesn't take it. Greenville is very far away. We'll never see him. And what happens if he goes? William is working for Papa, but he's here as Sam's friend. He might decide to go as well.

June 3, 1916

Today, the President issued a new act doubling the size of the army, and now all the boys are talking about joining up. George said he's not going to fight if we end up in the war, and William called him a coward. I hate to say it, but I rather agree with William.

June 5, 1916

Sam is not taking the job in Greenville. Mama put her foot down. I've never been so glad.

June 9, 1916

I was walking home from town today when the skies opened up and you will never believe who pulled up beside me in his Model T. William Howard. He offered me a ride, and I was on the cusp of refusing when lightning cracked directly overhead and he shouted at me to get in the car using words I am too much of a lady to repeat.

I told him a gentleman would not have used words like that in front of a lady and he replied that I wasn't a lady until I had enough sense not to walk home during a lightning storm. We said nothing to each other for the duration of the ride, although when I was shivering, he reached in the back and got a blanket for me, which I guess was sort of nice. I thanked him when we got to the house and he said "thank me by being more careful" so I slammed the door as hard as I could and ran inside. I don't know why he has to be so awful even when he's being nice.

June 13, 1916

George asked me to go for a walk last night and William said he would walk with us. My jaw dropped. He stayed with us the entire time, just to be a pest. And what's worse is that somehow everything George said sounded a bit dim with William there, listening in. I wish William had never come to Riverbend. He's ruining my entire summer.

"Obviously, she's falling for William Howard and doesn't have a clue," I tell Charlie as we make dinner side-by-side. I'm making a red wine reduction while Charlie's handling the potatoes on his own—which should be interesting. "I bet they got married, but why didn't their children save this place?"

"You do realize you're not reading some book with a vampire on the cover?" he asks, shaking some salt into the potatoes. "These are real people, so it's possible they won't follow your little rules for their story."

"Of course they will, Charles. By the way, I might need you to take me grave hunting at some point."

He gives me a side-eye. "Is that your idea or Casper's?"

I scoop a taste of Charlie's potatoes on my finger, and he taps my hand with a spoon.

"More salt," I tell him. "I'm still trying to figure out why there's not a trace of information about any of them. The woman in town said they were probably buried on the property, though I'm also not sure I want to know."

"It floods here a lot, so they tend to bury people high. If they're anywhere, they're probably on the bluff about a half mile down the cove. And I think you're messing that sauce up." He sticks his finger into the pot, and I attempt to tap his hand with the spoon, the way he did mine, but just end up splattering sauce all over my T-shirt. "More salt," he says, just to be annoying.

I grab the salt and add it to his potatoes before I return to my sauce. But when I reach over and dip my finger into the potatoes again, he grabs my wrist and wraps his mouth around my index finger. He meant it to be silly, a way to get me back, but there's a rush of heat at the contact.

My gaze meets his, and for a half second...there's something more going on. His eyes are molten. My nipples are pinched so tight they hurt.

I wrench my finger away from his warm tongue as fast as I possibly can. "Charlie, gross," I say, marching to the sink to wash my hands as if those two seconds of contact haven't left me soaked.

He shrugs as if I'm being ridiculous, but I don't miss the odd way his left hand clenches before he continues with the potatoes.

We eat dinner and clean up. He brushes his teeth in my bathroom and tells me to lock the door behind him, the way he always does. I climb into the shower, desperately trying to think of anything but his tongue against my finger and it doesn't work. It's all I've thought of since it happened.

Think about Margaret and William. Think about anything else. Please.

When I climb into bed, I grab my phone and type the name Margaret Howard into ancestry websites, but none are the correct Margaret Howard. Fortunately, there are no Margaret Graves either.

I pick up the diary again when I slide between my sheets, and even though, as Charlie pointed out, these are real people who might not live out the romance I've created for them in my head. I'll take their disappointing romance over the things my brain wants to make of that incident in the kitchen any day.

June 17, 1916

Today, I went to the second ball of the season. William was talking to all the girls but particularly to Melanie's older sister, Rose, who's just back from the teacher's college. Everyone says Rose has hair like spun silk. No one's ever said that about mine. George and I danced three times and he said I was the prettiest girl there, but somehow it wasn't as thrilling as it was the first time. George is a very nice boy, but I do worry sometimes that nice boys don't make the most interesting husbands.

June 23, 1916

The dance was at George's home, but George was off taking his second set of entrance exams. Everett Meyer spilled punch on my dress and William was talking to Rose again and I was so dispirited that I just went out to the porch rather than endure another second of it. I'd barely sat for a minute before William came out after me and asked why I wasn't dancing. I said I was tired and he said, "I guess that means I'm not getting a dance."

"Why would you want a dance?" I asked. "You don't even like me."

And he pulled me to my feet! My heart hammered in the queerest way. It's doing it now too. And then he spun me around the porch as if I were a queen, and I swear, for a moment, he intended to kiss me. I don't know what to make of it, but I haven't been able to think of anything but him since.

My eyes fall closed as I picture this unfolding. William's nostrils flaring as he grabs my wrist and puts my finger against his hot tongue and—

My eyes fly open.

Ever since I started reading, I've been picturing myself as this unnamed girl falling hard for William Howard. That makes sense.

But I didn't realize until now that it was Charlie I was picturing as the hero. It was Charlie's tongue against the pad of my finger, and it was Charlie's nostrils that flared for a half second, like a predator scenting prey—and I guess those things did happen, but they're getting so confused in my head.

Am I falling for William Howard? Am I falling for Charlie?

Falling for either of them is definitely a lost cause.

24

———————

CHARLIE

I 've just come around the cove's corner, at the tail end of my run, when Maren appears from the opposite direction, blonde ponytail and perky tits bouncing equally, the sun glancing off her shoulders and the crown of her head. Her eyes widen at the sight of me, suddenly wary.

It's the finger thing, from last night. I meant it as a joke. I was just going to *pretend* to do it. But my palm circled her wrist and someone else entirely took over. I was still telling myself it was funny, but I knew it wasn't, and the minute her finger was in my mouth...fuck. The things I wanted to do to that finger would make a porn star blush. And apparently, she knew.

The evening went back to normal after that, aside from the fact that I had a semi all through dinner. Which actually isn't all that abnormal either, now that Maren's gotten so casual with her bra use.

But it looks like I've got to fix things.

"Hey," I say, jogging to a halt on the gravel path and leaning against a tree to stretch. "How far are you going?"

She wipes her brow and looks at her watch. "I was going to do another half mile, then turn around."

"Learn anything new from your journal last night?" Her eyes widen and something guilty flashes across her face.

She blushes and shakes her head. "I'm not going to read it anymore. I'm gonna leave the whole thing alone."

"That's a sudden change."

She doesn't quite meet my eye. "You were right, last night. It isn't a novel. It's real life. And if it doesn't end happily, I'd rather not know."

THE INSPECTOR ARRIVES SHORTLY after breakfast.

He's approaching retirement age and surly from the get-go. Even Maren can't get a smile out of him, when she emerges from the house in all her long-legged glory to offer him a cup of coffee.

"Don't know how you thought this place was gonna pass," he says, spitting on the ground as he approaches the porch stairs. "I can already tell you right now it's not."

"Well, if the state hadn't moved the inspection date up by two weeks with almost no warning," I snap, "maybe it would be different."

Elijah gives me a look...the kind that says *settle the fuck down*. And he's right. I'm not going to win this guy over by arguing with him, but it's also pretty clear he can't be won over.

"We've got a crew starting work on the roof tomorrow," Elijah says, "and we'll have the porch done by the week's end."

The inspector rolls his eyes. "Thanks for telling me what I already knew, which is that this is a goddamn waste of my time."

He stomps around the house, scowling, marking things down, and eventually I just let Elijah follow him because I'm too angry to deal with even one more of his bitter, laughing, "yeah, that's not up to code" comments beneath his breath.

"What happens if we don't pass?" Maren asks, wide-eyed.

"I have no idea. I assume we appeal." I scrub a hand over my face. I'm not from the South, but I have a decent idea of how the law and due process work, and this entire thing feels shady —the inspection that came in as soon as I turned down the property developer, the timing of it, and the way this guy's had it in for us from the minute he stepped out of his truck.

Something underhanded is going on, so the normal rules might not apply. And I don't know what the hell we do then.

THAT AFTERNOON, someone tapes a sign on the window while we're in back saying the property is condemned. The letter they've slid through the mail slot informs us that any inhabitants must vacate the premises immediately.

We'll appeal, but if that fails, the state will be demolishing the house in the next thirty to sixty days...at my expense.

"It's that fucking developer," I hiss, sitting at the table on the back porch with Maren and Elijah—technically, I guess, we should no longer be sitting out here or using the kitchen, but fuck that. "If this guy is gunning for us, he'll find a way to condemn us no matter what we do between now and then."

Maren pours us each a glass of wine—I know a situation is stressful when *she's* the one suggesting alcohol.

"There's also a strong possibility that whoever wants your land this badly will just go ahead and get a crew out here to tear the house down in thirty days' time and claim it was a miscommunication, regardless of whether or not you've gotten your extension. You could sue for it, obviously, but that won't be worth much, given the shape the house is in now."

"Fuck that guy," reaching for the bottle to top off my glass. "I don't care if they tear the house down. I'm still not selling. I'll buy an RV and call it a vacation home."

Elijah bites his lip. "And then the state will declare eminent domain and take it from you anyway, Charlie. I think we need help."

"I have an idea," Maren says, lighting up suddenly.

She's impossible to say no to when she's like this, so rosy-cheeked and hopeful, but then again, when do I ever say *no* to her?

"Harvey has this friend—"

"*No*." Okay, it's possible after all.

She clicks her tongue to scold me. "You don't even know what I was going to say."

"It doesn't matter what you were going to say. I want nothing to do with Harvey and more importantly, I want *you* having nothing to do with Harvey."

She huffs an impatient breath. "I said *friend*, but Andrew's more an acquaintance he's friendly with. We had dinner with him and his wife a few times. But anyway, he's originally from South Carolina, I think, and he also does a lot of real estate law —he might know people at a state level who will shut this down. They'll *have* to back off if someone from the governor's office is insisting on it."

Wasn't she telling me about some guy they used to go to dinner with, the one she thought would make a perfect husband? I'm sure they go out with lots of couples. It's still suspect.

She sends out a text, and within a minute she's got the call set up for this evening. I'm not sure how great a lawyer Andrew can be if his schedule is this empty.

She returns to her cottage, Elijah leaves, and I sit on the steps, stewing. I don't like anything about this. I don't like that this shady developer has the power to get us condemned this fast and I don't like that this guy *Andrew* might be the one to swoop in and save the day.

Maren returns just before the call begins, and I like the situation even less. I've grown accustomed to Oak Bluff Maren, bare-faced and hair in a ponytail. Now she's Manhattan Maren —mascara, hair falling around her shoulders.

"You put on *makeup* for this?" I ask flatly.

She hitches a shoulder. "I mean...the people we know at home sort of expect it. And I figured I ought to look presentable."

"You looked presentable enough without it." I grunt, unhappy as she opens her phone and hits the meeting link.

There's a two-second delay, and then Andrew appears. He's maybe in his early forties—and though his hair is flecked with gray, it doesn't make him look old. He smiles broadly at Maren, as if he's thrilled to be on this call when he's doing *her* a favor.

I'm liking this less by the fucking minute.

"Long time no see, Maren," he says. "How are you?"

She flushes. "It's been a busy couple of weeks. Oh, and do you know my stepbrother? Charlie Dalton."

"I don't think we've met," Andrew says, civil and nothing more before he returns to Maren. "I heard about you and Harvey. I'm so sorry. You always deserved better than that guy. Kristen and I both said so."

It's pretty weird that he's referencing his wife while he's looking at Maren with that intimate smile, like he's already undressing her. And that's what was ringing a bell before...is this the guy? The one Maren mentioned who'd be the best husband?

"Thanks," she says. "I'm happy to be out."

"Not sure if you heard but Kristen and I separated too."

That's why he's fucking looking at her like that.

Maren's mouth forms a small *O*. "No, I'm so sorry. I've been out of the loop for a while. I hadn't heard."

"I really wanted kids; she didn't," he says. "She'd kind of left it up in the air for a while, but we were getting to that age, and she still couldn't pull the trigger."

This asshole knows good and well that statement is the way to Maren's heart. Already, her blue eyes have gone velvet soft.

"I'm sorry. That had to be a hard decision."

"It was and it also wasn't," he says. "She's married to her job. I wanted someone who was actually interested in being married to *me*."

Someone like Maren, clearly. This dick is two seconds from asking her what her ring size is.

"Anyway," I cut in, ignoring Maren's sharp glance, "this developer wants the place, and he must be paying people off because we were condemned immediately, and they've only given us thirty days, which is barely enough time for an appeal."

Maren kicks my foot and smiles at Andrew. "I just thought since you're from down here and this is what you do for a living, you might have some thoughts."

Andrew shrugs. "I'm actually from North Carolina, but I do have some thoughts on how to proceed. Why don't I come see the place, and we go from there? I'll file the injunction immediately, but it'll be easier for me to go to bat for you if I can say I've seen it with my own eyes."

Bullshit. It's not the fucking property he wants to see with his own eyes.

"That would be fantastic," says Maren, "if you can spare the time."

"I've got some friends golfing in Hilton Head this week, and I was thinking about coming down for a few days anyway. What if I swing by Friday, and then I'll head there after? And you might want to ask around, in the meantime, to see who in town is benefitting. The Junior League/country club crowd would be a good place to start if you have an in."

"I'll get right on it," Maren says. "Friday is perfect."

Andrew is grinning ear to ear. "It's a date," he says.

No, it fucking isn't.

We end the call, and she bounces off the step and throws her hands in the air. "It worked!" she shouts. "Charlie, he's totally going to solve this for us. I know he is. I can't believe he's coming down here."

I squeeze the bridge of my nose. "Did we just sit through the same call, Maren?"

Her mouth falls. "What are you talking about? You heard him say point blank that he has thoughts, and he's even coming to see the place. I mean, I know it's not in the greatest shape, but that's sort of the whole point...we're working on it and—"

"He's coming down here to fuck you," I say between my teeth. "Helping us with the house is just an excuse."

She stares for a moment, then laughs. "*What?* That's crazy."

"Maren, he didn't look at me once through the entire call."

"He was on video! You couldn't even tell who he was looking at!"

"I could fucking tell," I growl, gripping the step beneath me. "He ended the conversation with *it's a date*, for God's sake."

"That's just an expression, Charlie. People use it all the time."

"Yeah, especially when they're flying several hours south to fuck the girl they've just said it to."

"Stop saying that," she scolds. "It's so crude."

"Oh, I'm sorry, Maren. He's coming to make love to you. Is that better? He's coming to initiate the biological processes that lead to reproduction."

"Charlie, he did not say a single thing like that on a call during which he was speaking to both of us."

I climb to my feet and walk down the stairs to where she stands. I'm too close to her, too angry. "Ah, so the part where he's crying about how bad he wants kids was for my benefit, was it? That's a perfectly normal thing to share with a dude you met five seconds prior."

Her arms fold, pushing her gorgeous, way-more-than-a-handful rack up to its full advantage. The sight alone would have Andrew waiving the prenup. It could make *me* waive a prenup, and I don't even want to get married.

"I have no idea what's wrong with you," she says. "He was lovely, he's obviously going through a hard time, and he's going to help us out. That's all you should be taking from the conversation."

"He's the guy you mentioned, isn't he? The one you thought you should have married?"

She blushes. "Yes, but...I had no idea he was separated. That's not why I thought of him."

I walk inside before I say the words bubbling up within me. Words that go something like this: *I saved this house for you. But I'll burn it to the ground to keep you from winding up with someone else.*

25

MAREN

I was Andrew's hall pass, the one person he was allowed to step out of his marriage to sleep with should the opportunity present itself.

His wife told me. She'd thought it was funny. I'd pointed out that a hall pass was supposed to be someone famous, and she'd countered that I *was* relatively famous.

So I'm not all that surprised when Andrew texts a few hours after the Zoom call.

ANDREW

Do you have time to get dinner after I see the house?

Of course. There really isn't a lot in Oak Bluff, however.

I was thinking we could have dinner in Beaufort? I got a hotel room there, just for Friday. Heading out to Hilton Head the next day.

It doesn't make much sense. Beaufort is farther from Oak

Bluff than Hilton Head is. And it also places me with my subpar driving on dark country roads.

> I'm actually not the best driver. Oak Bluff might be better.

> I'm happy to drive you back if that's the issue.

Internally, I groan. It's been a few years, but I've played this game before. The one where it's late and a guy wants you to come upstairs for a drink, and then he's suggesting you could just stay over.

It's never, ever as PG-rated as he makes it sound when he's talking you into it. And you feel like an absolute shrew for insisting on being taken home when all you're asking is that he stick to the damn plan.

But then again, this is Andrew, who I know.

Andrew, the exact guy I always thought I should have married in the first place. It makes absolute sense that he wouldn't want to eat in one of Oak Bluff's two unappealing diners. Even if I'm not entirely comfortable with it...this seems like the sort of thing I should do if I want my life to move forward.

This is not going to fly with Charlie, though I'm not entirely sure why he cares whether Andrew has ulterior motives for coming down here. Andrew's a good guy. A more supportive sibling would be *encouraging* Andrew's ulterior motives if they kept me away from Harvey.

You sure weren't thinking of him as a sibling the other night, though, were you Maren?

"Shut up," I warn my internal voice.

I don't know what the hell that was in the kitchen. Maybe I'm lonely. Maybe it's just been so long since someone touched me that I forgot who I was with. Maybe Margaret is infiltrating my thoughts until I don't know which way is up.

All the more reason to go on a date with someone else.

"No," Charlie says flatly over breakfast.

I've just informed him of the plan. It's not even a plan I'm interested in necessarily, but that doesn't mean Charlie gets to say *no* as if he's in charge.

I set down my fork. "Excuse me?"

"You're not going on a date with this guy just because he's helping with the house. You're sure as fuck not relying on him to get you home from Beaufort. We both know how *that* turns out."

"Just because you play those tricks doesn't mean everyone does, Charles."

"I'm the only man you know who doesn't *have* to resort to those tricks, Maren, but I assure you, that's exactly what's happening."

He walks out without another word, leaving me to wash the plates by myself.

Sighing, I return to the cottage to get ready for my visit to Palmetto Reserve, the local country club: floral dress, curled hair, lots of makeup.

I carefully step onto the porch—the guys are working on the far end, but there are boards missing everywhere—and Charlie gives me a once-over. "What's with the outfit?" he snarls. "Got another call with Andrew?"

I'm not one to fight in front of other people, but I don't care who's listening right now because this is nuts.

"What's with the attitude?" I demand. "I'm pulling every string I can pull to fix this, and you're kind of being a dick."

"No one asked you to pull those strings," he grunts.

I'm used to Charlie being a jerk to me in harmless, funny ways, but this isn't harmless or funny. And he's doing it with an audience. The guys beside him cease hammering, watching the argument unfold, and Elijah, carrying planks of wood over his shoulder, freezes. Great—every eye is on me as my anger turns into tears. "I'm going to the country club," I say, my voice rough, "because I'm trying to help."

I haven't even reached the bottom of the stairs before Charlie's there, extending a hand to help me down the last step.

"I'm sorry," he says quietly, not releasing my hand. "And I would hug you right now but I'm filthy and you look beautiful. I appreciate it, Maren. I do. I don't know what's gotten into me. Tell me you're not mad."

It sort of seems like you're jealous.

It would do no good to say it aloud. "I'm not mad. But can you give it a rest with the Andrew stuff? He's just trying to help."

"No," Charlie says, pressing his lips to my forehead, "because I still think Andrew's a worthless dick."

I want to cry, but I also sort of want to laugh as I climb in the car.

I drive through Oak Bluff and then another two miles to Palmetto Reserve, with its stately white mansion, rolling golf course, and ten glorious tennis courts occupied by blonde women with lots of Botox.

I'm taken on a tour of the facility by Kara, the membership director, who is vaguely aware of my career but particularly aware of my mother's—for better or for worse.

"Is it true that she dated Shepherd Lawrence?" she asks.

I wince. My mother is very diligent when it comes to her weight, but less diligent about *not* fucking other people's husbands. Yes, it's true, but I'm fairly certain Shepherd Lawrence was a newlywed when it took place.

"I really don't know," I tell her. "She's been with my stepfather for so long. I barely remember who came before him."

"Do you think your mother would have any interest in joining?" she asks.

Would the members consider that a boon or a liability? Would they love having a famous supermodel as a member, or would they deem it *tawdry*?

Both, I suspect.

"I'm sure she'll come down to visit—as well as my father."

She bites her lip. "Your father? Is that Jacob Duncan?"

No, Jacob Duncan was the rock star boyfriend who gave my mom a black eye, the guy Kit ended up fighting off with a golf club. He came before the boyfriend who stole a hundred grand of my mom's money, but after the boyfriend who said I could have his Porsche if I let him spank me.

I shake my head. "My biological father is Yves Marchand, the artist? But I was adopted by Henry Fisher. You know, Fisher Harris Media?"

Her eyes widen ever so slightly. There is nothing tawdry about having a billionaire who owns half the magazines in the country on your membership rolls.

"Oh, I had no idea," she says. "You know, we're having a big summer dance next Thursday. It might be a good chance for you to get to know our members."

It also might be a good chance for me to make the contacts I need and bypass joining this club entirely—which is the reason I nod enthusiastically.

It has nothing, *nothing*, to do with wanting to attend a dance with Charlie.

The invitation she sends me home with is as heavy as a thin book and incredibly fancy.

Charlie is still working on the porch when I pull up, on his knees, muscles flexed as he hammers in a four-by-four. I'm grinning as I make my way over to him, unable to help myself.

He raises a brow. "You're too excited, Maren," he says, holding a nail between his lips. "That never bodes well."

"We got an invitation to a ball!" I cry, too excited to contain my glee. "And it's *Bridgerton* themed and being held in someone's mansion."

He sets the hammer down and removes the nail. "This is getting better and better," he says dryly.

"We're saying yes, right?"

He moves a two-by-four and sets it in front of him. "As if you were ever going to let me decide."

That is accurate, because I was not. "I'd have allowed you to weigh in if you had some vital information to share. If there'd been a bunch of murders there, maybe. Or if it was haunted."

He grins. "Maren, we both know that would just make you want to go more."

I laugh. That's also totally correct.

It's funny how well he knows me. And how much I like being known.

26

MAREN

"So today's the day," Charlie says glumly over breakfast on Friday. "You sure you don't want to run into town for a last-minute bikini wax?"

I'm not playing this little game with him. He already seems to hate Andrew as much as he did Harvey and they've never even met in person.

"I had it all lasered off ages ago," I reply with my most withering look. "Smooth as a baby's bottom."

A muscle flexes in his jaw. "That was probably more than I needed to know."

"It was more than you needed to know when you asked me the question," I reply. "Let's not pretend *I* was the one who crossed the line."

I spend the day itching to open Margaret's journal again, as if it might tell me what I'm in for tonight, but Andrew is no George Graves. He's not pompous; he's not a coward. And Charlie is no William Howard, though perhaps that's simply because I assume William Howard didn't have threesomes or claim fatherhood is worse than being murdered.

It's late afternoon when Andrew's rented G wagon pulls into

the circular drive. Elijah and the guys are gone for the day, and Charlie has made himself blessedly scarce—to my surprise.

Andrew is exactly the guy I remember: fit, handsome, responsible, genuine. The kind of guy I should have married in the first place. He will not try to push me into sleeping with him tonight in Beaufort—I have no idea why I was worried.

With the puppies frolicking underfoot, I show him around the house—the views, the trail, the crazy old root cellar, all the rooms upstairs, and the century-old graffiti from Walter and his brother.

I tell him about the family and the mystery surrounding what happened to them, minus the bit where I dreamed of the journal's location. He's probably the kind of guy who'd think my wacky paranormal encounters are cute, but you can never be too sure.

"Seems like the kind of place that ought to hold a family again," he ventures, and there's something in his gaze that has me wondering if he's referring to *us*.

I swore I was on a cleanse from thinking about my marital situation and my ticking clock, but it's impossible not to consider the possibility.

Falling for Andrew could certainly solve a lot of my problems at once.

"So, what do you think?" I ask, forcing myself to focus on the task at hand.

"Clearly this place didn't deserve to be condemned. It might even qualify for a historical designation if there was time to apply for one."

"So there's not time?"

He frowns. "If this developer is as connected as you think he is, he's going to make sure this happens fast. But we can discuss over dinner."

I nod, reluctantly. I'm not sure why I'm dragging my heels but I suspect it's simply that I'm sad about missing a night in with Charlie. And speaking of...where the hell is he? We've toured the entire property, and there's been no sign of him.

"Okay," I reply. "Let me just see if Charlie can watch the dogs."

I leave Andrew on the back deck and walk toward the cottages. I'm nearly there when Charlie emerges, freshly showered, in khakis and a button-down. So handsome he takes my breath away.

Actually, he's always that handsome. I'd just gotten sort of accustomed to the version of him in jeans and a T-shirt.

"Are you going *out*?" It sounds angrier than I'd intended it to.

His smile is the tiniest bit cruel. "You're not the only one of us who can make plans, Maren."

"I was going to see if you could watch the puppies," I say, shoving my hands in my pockets. "If you'll just be in Oak Bluff, you'll be home before me. Can you please let them out when you get home?"

"I'll be in Beaufort," he replies, "and it's the kind of situation where you don't come home 'til the next day."

It shouldn't be the gut punch that it is.

I rack my brain for a way to object to this and come up short. I could argue that he shouldn't be meeting a stranger for sex—simply in terms of safety—but unless she's six-foot-five or armed, he's probably fine, and he wouldn't listen to me anyway.

"Be safe," I warn, my jaw locked as I proceed to the cottage.

I set Echo and Narcy up with food and water inside, then apologize to Andrew once I've returned. "I'm so sorry, but I can't be gone long because of the dogs. Charlie's apparently staying out all night."

Andrew laughs. "I guess his reputation serves, then. I know nothing about the guy, but I've heard the rumors."

I find it far less amusing than he does.

Andrew still wants to go to dinner in Beaufort, despite the

time restriction, which I guess is pretty sweet. On the way there, we talk about his divorce, which sounds far more amicable than mine.

"I'd like to come out of this thing still friends," he says. "I'll be running into her for the rest of my life, after all."

A few months ago, before I came down here, a statement like this would have made him seem like the perfect man. The opposite of Harvey, who'd be out to ruin me right now if he wasn't terrified of Henry.

Tonight, though, I'm fighting the fear that he's perhaps slightly too nice? That I sort of like someone with a tiny bit of an edge?

Stop. Andrew is perfect, and it's a pleasant change after Charlie.

Except I *love* all the ways Charlie isn't nice, aside from the one where he stays out all night with a woman he's just met.

That one isn't my favorite.

"I'm hogging the conversation," he says. "Sorry. How is your stuff coming along? Do you want to talk about it?"

My mouth opens, then closes.

Harvey's accusing me of sleeping with Charlie might sound as crazy to him as it is, or he might think *where there's smoke, there's fire*—especially given how hostile Charlie was to Andrew during their phone call.

"We had a prenup," I say simply. "My lawyer says I'll be free by next spring."

"That's good," he says with a half-smile.

Maybe I'm reading too much into everything—I've certainly been known to do so—or maybe Andrew's thoughts are traveling in the precise direction mine would have been even a few months ago: that we want the same things and might make a good team. It wouldn't be thrilling, but is any marriage thrilling once you've been in it long enough?

Over dinner, Andrew continues to impress me. He manages to discuss the failings in his relationship without making

Kristen out to be the villain. He is interested in what he does for a living but not obsessed with it. "I work long hours," he says, "but that's mostly because I don't have anyone to come home to."

As far as the house goes, he's got a couple old friends who are very well connected. He's placing some calls tomorrow. "I think the other angle we should consider is whether this property developer has done this elsewhere," he says. "If we can threaten him with bad publicity, he might back off."

It sounds as if there's almost no need to go to the *Bridgerton*-themed ball. Except that I really *want* to.

Our plates are cleared. Andrew's talking about golfing at Pebble Beach and for some reason, this makes me think of Charlie. I don't know why—Charlie doesn't even golf. But all I want in the whole world is to get back to Riverbend and sit on the porch with him, to tell him about my night and all my fears, and the fact that I'd like to be more excited about Andrew than I am.

Kit calls Charlie "the douchiest man in Manhattan" and he hasn't done a whole lot to disprove the name, but...there's no one else in the whole world I want to tell everything to. There's no one else I want to be around. If only he was going to be there tonight. And he's not, which ought to be all the proof I need that my interests are better served elsewhere.

"Look," Andrew says, setting the dessert menu off to the side. His face is open and genuine. "I'm going to be blunt. Probably too blunt. I've been interested in you since the moment Harvey introduced us. I was married, and I wouldn't have acted on it, but Maren...I liked you five years ago, and I've liked you a little more every time I've seen you since, so when you're ready to start dating again, I want to be first in line. I know you guys were having issues getting pregnant, but I'm ready to be a father, even if the kid isn't mine. I'm not entirely clear on how in vitro works, but if you've got those eggs ready to go and need someone there to raise a child with, I would like to be that guy. If you want to adopt, I'm okay with that too."

I guess I don't have to sit around guessing what tonight was about. He couldn't have been clearer, and it's everything I could have asked for. I should be bursting at the seams, but I'm not.

"Wow." My laughter is gentle, awkward. How do you reply to a guy who's just put all that on the table? "That's not where I thought tonight was heading."

His head tilts. "No? Kristen told me she'd shared the hall pass thing with you. I was so fucking embarrassed, but...I assumed you knew I was interested."

I love that he's so open. I love that he's not acting diffident, not keeping his cards close to his chest. I wish I could tell him that all this sounded great to me, and it *does* sound great. It just doesn't *feel* great.

"Harvey and I are not even officially separated yet, so I hadn't even begun to think about dating." It's not true, but it's easier than saying *give me some time to convince myself.* "I just need a little time to get myself together?"

"Of course," he replies, reaching across the table to squeeze my hand.

He pays the bill, and we begin to move through the restaurant. We're nearly to the door when my phone buzzes.

CHARLIE

I'm outside. I'll give you a ride home.

How does he even know I'm here? It doesn't matter. My whole body is weak with relief. He isn't going home with someone else.

"Charlie's date went badly," I announce. "He's waiting outside."

Andrew's brow furrows at that, but he says nothing. He walks me to the door. "I'll investigate the house situation a little," he says. "And you'll let me know when you're ready to date?"

"I will," I say, kissing his cheek before I head toward Charlie's idling car and climb inside.

"Kiss on the cheek," Charlie scoffs. "Sad end to a sad night."

I click my seat belt. "It was a lovely night, actually. And you're one to talk about sad nights. What happened?"

He pulls onto the oak-lined road that will lead us to the highway. "She had a magnet on her fridge that made me lose all respect for her."

I turn toward him, grinning. "You ended it over a fridge magnet. Was this magnet...pro Hitler? A Confederate flag? I'm really struggling to imagine what magnet could offend you to this extent."

"It said *Live, laugh, love*," he replies, as if this is an entirely reasonable answer. "What is that supposed to do? Does she assume I was not planning to live, laugh, or love, but now that I've seen it on her refrigerator, I'll think twice? Does she forget to do those things and simply need a reminder?"

"You're being incredibly picky, Charles."

"This from a woman now dating Andrew, a man whose only redeeming quality is that he's not Harvey."

I let my head rest against the window as I turn toward him again. "I'm not dating him, and he has other qualities."

"Name one."

I sigh. "He's nice. He has a good job. He's being decent to his ex as they divorce and he's helping us with the house. He—" I pause because I'm struggling to think of anything else.

"You can't come up with a goddamn thing you like about this guy other than the fact that he doesn't belittle you the way Harvey did," Charlie says. "Not a single goddamn thing. Is he attractive? Is he interesting? Is he charming? Is he powerful?"

"He's attractive enough."

He sneers. "That's a no, then, to all of it."

"Why do you care?" I demand, and he blinks, as if he's been caught at something, just as the light turns green.

"Maybe because you've got terrible taste in men, and I don't want to see you making another mistake."

"That's rich, Charlie," I snap. "You were just about to fuck a girl you'd never met and got turned off by her *fridge magnet*, while my 'terrible taste' led to dinner with a guy who said he's ready to settle down and have kids."

"And you want children so badly that you would essentially prostitute yourself to get them," he accuses.

"I wouldn't be prostituting myself," I argue. "He's a great guy."

"You're way happier with me," he replies.

Maybe he's right, but how's that even relevant? We both know nothing with Charlie can last forever.

27

MAREN

"When do you land?" my mother asks. "If you're arriving early enough, we can get lunch at Pierre's."

I'm still in bed, now sleepily throwing off the covers and opening the door for the dogs. And the engagement party is still a week away...*what the fuck?* "Mom, I'm not arriving a *week early* to help you with the party. I told you...I'm helping Charlie with the house. There's stuff going on."

"And as I told *you*," she retorts, "there's absolutely nothing you can do that will substantially help with that house."

"He needs moral support," I argue, putting the phone on speaker so I can dress while we talk. "And there's this big country club event Thursday night where we might meet some people who can assist with our appeal."

"You're talking as if it's *your* house," she says pointedly. "And I don't know why you can't be happy for your sister."

"I *am* happy for her!" I say with a heavy sigh. "But you seem to have no understanding of how awkward this is going to be for me. I dated Miller and now I'm getting divorced, and all your friends will be dissecting every look on my face, every sigh, and reading into all of it. It's going to be like the day after the Oscars, where they claim some actress was mad just because they've got a single photo of her not smiling. I can't win."

"Maren," she tsks. "If you think they're going to be examining your face to see if you are upset, just imagine what they will be saying if you haven't shown up at the party at all."

Jesus. "I never said I wasn't going. But let's stop acting like this is going to be super fun for me. All I can do is minimize damage, so I'm not arriving five days early to let all your friends get a head start gossiping about how upset I appear."

"You could remedy that by not appearing to be upset," she says.

"If even Oscar-nominated actresses can't appear happy every second of a three-hour event, I probably can't appear happy every moment over the course of several days."

"You're hiding out down there," she says. "Plain and simple. It's time to tear the Band-Aid off and return to real life."

It's possible she's correct. It's also possible that the longer I go without having to face all the fake-concerned looks from people about my divorce, the more daunting it will seem. "I'll be there Friday."

"With a smile on your face," she warns as I hang up, and my stomach knots.

Even *she's* doing it. Even she is acting as if I'm upset about Kit's engagement, as if I have to *hide* my feelings, when what's upsetting is that people will *assume* I'm hiding my feelings and are sort of hoping to see the cracks.

Charlie and I haven't discussed the party. I'd assumed he'd go, but with the house being condemned, maybe that's changed.

"Hey, you're planning to go to that party for Kit next weekend, right?" I venture over breakfast.

He finishes his green juice as if it's a shot before he answers. "I told your mom I couldn't make it. There's too much going on here."

I bite down on my lip. I know it's busy. So busy. And he's not even the one who wanted this house. But I need him there. He's always been the first to notice when I'm upset, when I'm cornered, when I'm in need of backup. If one of my mother's friends started in about how hard the situation must be, Charlie would ask some abominably rude question of the person giving me trouble, pull me onto the dance floor, or throw a drink if the situation was really dire.

"Are you sure you can't come?" I ask.

He frowns. "Maren, Kit's not even going to notice I'm missing."

I'll notice he's missing, but maybe that's part of the problem. Maybe my mother was right—that it's time to tear the Band-Aid off. If my life was a house, Charlie used to be a single brick, but now he's the entire foundation. Except he's not interested in being anyone's foundation. Which means that, eventually, he's going to crumble.

ON THURSDAY AFTERNOON, I cut out early to get ready for the ball. There's no one in Oak Bluff I'd trust to do my hair and makeup, but I got pretty accustomed to doing it myself when I was modeling. Once it's done to my satisfaction, I step into the red satin ballgown and shoes I rush-shipped down here at ridiculous expense.

The shoes are a full size too small, but I can stand them for a few hours, and as I take in my reflection, I'm barely noticing the pain.

Will Charlie like it? Will he give me one of those long, slow looks of his?

I shouldn't want it, but I do.

I tell myself that all this effort is on behalf of the house, on behalf of some mysterious town council member to be swayed or a shady developer to be brought into line. But it sort of feels like I just want to be a pretty girl in a dress, attending a fancy ball in an old mansion with the most handsome man I know.

Charlie is waiting as I emerge from the cottage. He wears a tux as if he was born in one.

"That's one hell of a dress," he says, his voice gravelly.

I fight a blush. "Anything for the cause."

"What cause was that again?" he asks, reaching for me as I come down the last two stairs.

I forget. It's something. It's the house or the developer...I'm not sure why I'm struggling to remember the answer.

He drives us to Oak Haven, the mansion where the ball is being held. Broad porches surround the house on both the first and second floors. Every light is on, and classical music spills through the windows.

It feels oddly familiar, but maybe it's just that I've seen too many movies about the old South.

We walk up the stairs side by side. As excited as I am to attend this thing, a part of me suddenly dreads having to share Charlie's time and attention.

"You do look nice," he says as we step through the door. "You look really nice."

He's so genuine sometimes, in moments like this. I don't know what to make of it. "So do you."

"Actually," he says, spinning me toward him in the nearly empty foyer, under the glow of a massive chandelier, "you look—"

"Maren!" calls a voice and we turn to find Kara, the membership director, sprinting toward us, hampered by her long gown. *Wow, her timing is so bad.*

"You must be Maren's brother," she gushes.

"Stepbrother," he amends smoothly.

Her blink is apologetic, as if the error was hers when *I'm* the one who said he was my brother. I'm not sure why I keep doing that. It's not as if Charlie feels like a sibling...He entered our lives far too late. It's possible that I'm just trying to remind myself that he's off limits, though it's not as if I could forget it, could I?

She introduces us to the wife of the club's president, who deftly steers Charlie away before I've even had a chance to shake her hand. "Let me introduce you to everyone," says Kara, leading me in the opposite direction. I take one glance over my shoulder, hoping to catch Charlie's eye, but he's now surrounded by a cluster of beautiful women and has likely forgotten I exist.

I'm introduced to the president of the board, and then— more interestingly—the widow of one of the club's founding members. "Welcome to Oak Haven," she says grandly, "the former home of George Graves, who led Oak Bluff's renaissance in the 1890s."

A shiver runs up my arms. *This* is where the ball was held, the one where Margaret and William danced together. I knew it felt familiar.

"Did you know any of the family?" I ask, and she shakes her head.

"I didn't grow up here. I met my husband at USC in the fifties and he brought me down. We bought the place in the seventies, long after the Graves' descendants had moved on."

She's still talking about her husband while my gaze is on Charlie, who's currently focusing all his charm on a pretty girl in a sleeveless, body-con floral dress. It hardly suits the *Bridgerton* theme, but suddenly I feel old-fashioned and dowdy in the red satin I was so pleased with an hour before.

"Back then, going to college was considered a waste to most men," the widow continues. "You're so lucky to be young when you are."

I'm not that young. Not like the girl in the body-con dress. But I'm guessing that youth, like old age, is entirely relative—to a child, anyone over the age of forty is old and to an octogenarian, anyone under the age of sixty is young.

"I didn't actually go to college," I tell her. "Well, I started, but then I left."

She nods. "You're the model. That's right." She pats my hand as if to console me. "No matter how things change, a pretty face matters more than smarts if you're female."

I'd like to be that rarest of things, a woman who's considered equal parts lovely and intelligent. Like Kit. Charlie's one of the few men who's ever made me feel as if I was.

But now he's off with some kid in an inappropriate dress. So maybe he just never found me all that lovely in the first place.

For the next hour, I'm led around to older board members, most of them male, who want to hear about my mother, and all the while Charlie is with that same girl, so I guess I know how tonight is ending—with me in my bed, listening to the rhythmic thump of a headboard next door while this girl shouts, "Oh Charlie, oh, fuck" again and again and again.

It was aggravating the night I stayed in his apartment. Now, it would be enraging.

"Maren, allow me to introduce you to Steve DeChen, Oak Bluff's mayor," says Kara and I somehow shirk off my sad thoughts and replace them with my broadest smile. Because even if tonight has been an absolute waste, having a friend on the town council can't hurt and having that friend be the head of the town council *definitely* can't hurt.

"Kara tells me you're living out at Riverbend, the old Ames place," he says.

I thought I was going to have to feign interest in this man, but now it's entirely genuine. Maybe he can tell me how it all turned out. I want to know if they were happy. If all those kids had kids of their own and brought them back to play croquet on that lawn while their parents looked on.

"Yes, my stepbrother Charlie is the new owner, but I'm so curious about the Ames family. Did you know them?"

He shakes his head. "I didn't really. The parents died when I was very young, and then it was just old Miss Ames. We were terrified of her." He laughs. "Poor woman probably was no older than I am now, but we assumed she had to be a witch, out in that big mansion by herself. My mom used to visit her."

My heart sinks. "So she never married?"

He shakes his head. "I have no idea, to be honest. Like I said, I was really young back then. She probably did. Most women married in those days." His gaze drops to my bare ring finger as if it's a deformity.

"Well, we just love it here," I tell him, since he clearly has no answers about Margaret Ames. "I'm sure you've heard we're having some issues with the inspections, but we're working as hard as we can to get the house in shape."

There's suddenly something guarded and distant in his eyes. "I'm certain you don't actually plan to *stay*."

I tilt my head. "Why else would we be doing so much work on the house?"

"Negotiating tactic," he says. "You convince the developer it's your dream home just to drive up the price."

Out of the corner of my eye, I see Charlie leading the pretty girl toward the dance floor.

"It's not a tactic," I reply, my voice harder. For the first time in my life I sound like Kit, as if I'm eager to go to battle. "It was Charlie's mother's dying wish that he *keep* the house, so he's *keeping* the house."

I'm not sure what's gotten into me but it's all...wrong. The night's just wrong.

DeChen's eyes widen slightly. "Well, I certainly wish you luck in that endeavor," he says, but his tone implies the opposite—as if we're up against an insurmountable force and he's glad it will prevail.

So he's probably getting kickbacks from the developer, as is everyone else, and all this effort was completely wasted. I was so hopeful when I was getting ready, too and I have no idea why. It was that giddy, besotted feeling I remember from adolescence, which is not typically associated with...meeting the town's mayor.

All I want now is to go home and probably have a good cry. I excuse myself, searching the room for Charlie, but he's on the dance floor with the inappropriately dressed girl.

She's lovely and probably a decade younger than me. She has her whole life, all her reproductive years, ahead of her—not that the latter would be an asset in Charlie's book.

Except I think he's full of shit. He says he doesn't want kids, but one day, when he's fucked every single female in Manhattan and several in Oak Bluff, he'll tire of the thrill. That's when he'll marry some girl decades younger and he'll have kids under duress only to discover, just as he has with the puppies, how much he enjoys them.

My father didn't want children either. I'm not entirely sure why he bothered to marry my mother, under the circumstances, except that she was beautiful, and he was smitten. But anyway, he was one of those guys, like Charlie, who think children are a fate worse than death, and when she got pregnant, he left. And what's really annoying about it all is the fact that he later changed his mind. It took fifteen years, but eventually he married some student of his, barely any older than me, and they had two children of their own, two children who appear with him in magazines, his "proudest accomplishment."

Perhaps that's why, when Charlie insists that he never wants children, I doubt him. Because the day will come when his incredibly young wife, for whom he will do anything, insists, and he'll be happy he gave in.

I'm done with this entire endeavor. I stalk out, near tears, and stand on the porch, which is dark aside from the light shining through the windows.

My feet are killing me, so walking home is out of the question. I take a seat on the swing, hoping to pull myself together.

Charlie's porch could use a swing like this once it's finished. *Yes, Maren, rush-order that swing the way you rush-ordered your dress, just to have Charlie enjoy it with someone else.*

Inside, a new song is beginning and Charlie's probably dancing to it. I'm never fucking get out of here. Frustrated, I dig into my purse for my phone.

> If you can take a break from hitting on the brunette, I need the car keys. I can come back to get you if you need a ride, though it appears you aren't planning to come home.

I reread the text before I hit send. It's too bitter, too jealous. I erase it and start over.

> I'm tired and ready to head home. You can stay, but can I get the car keys when you have a minute? I'll come back to pick you up whenever you're ready.

"Mare," says a quiet voice coming up behind me. I turn and there is Charlie with a quizzical smile on his face. "I was looking for you. Why aren't you inside?"

Because I saw you with someone else. Because I'm so jealous that I'm sick over it. "I don't know."

"You were so excited to dance," he says. "But I didn't see you on the floor once."

I shrug. "Unlike you, I'm not really interested in hitting on someone half my age."

His laughter is quiet. "Ouch."

"Speaking of which, where is your new friend?"

"She isn't my *friend*. She's the daughter of the property developer. I was trying to get some intel, but she seems to know even less than I do, so I told her I needed to look for you."

Do I believe him? I'm not sure.

Does it matter? Probably not. I don't know what's wrong with me tonight. "You can go back to her," I reply. "I can't dance anyway. These shoes are killing me."

He extends a hand. "Take them off, Maren."

"I can't. Once I take them off, I'll—"

He reaches down and plucks one off before the sentence is complete. I sigh in relief and the other one is removed too. He tosses both toward the porch railing.

"Come on," he says. "We're dancing."

He's pulled me to my feet before I've had time to object and closes the distance between us, placing one arm around me while his right hand clasps my left.

I blush as I smile up at him. "Are we waltzing? I'm not sure I know how."

"Me neither," he grins. "But I bet we can fake it pretty well."

I laugh. "I know you have a joke about Harvey in there somewhere."

He begins to move me over the smooth, painted wood porch, but there's no smirk as his eyes meet mine. "I'm not thinking about Harvey right now."

My heart thunders in my chest. This version of Charlie—the one who only has eyes for me—feels like the real version.

And this version of me—the one who'd die happy if he was the only thing she could see—is the realest version of me.

I love my family. I love my friends. I love the dogs.

But none of them are precious to me the way he is.

We move to the song as if we intuitively know how to do this. I close my eyes and stop thinking entirely, allowing myself to soak up everything about this moment: floating across this porch as if I'm weightless, my skirt swirling and airborne. The heavy press of the honeysuckle climbing up the trellis. The kiss of balmy air. Charlie's hand on my back.

He and I could exist in any time, and it would still be exactly like this: inappropriate and yet entirely right. I picture his hand around my jaw, the way he'd look just before he kissed me, and my eyes open to find that's exactly the way he is looking at me, with his nostrils flaring and his eyes on my mouth, and—

A door slams in the distance and we immediately stop dancing, as if that door was an alarm waking us from a dream we shouldn't have been having. His hands fall away, guilty, and he takes a single step back. "There," he says, running a hand through his hair, "at least you got one dance. Should we head home?"

"Yeah," I reply breathlessly.

He hands me my shoes and I swing them off the tip of my index finger as I walk down the stairs. "Put them on, Maren. There might be broken glass."

"I can't. Once you take off shoes that were too small, your feet swell to twice their previous size. That's just science."

He grins. "I'm curious about what scientific rule you're referring to."

"I am too, since I was terrible at science."

"Climb on," he says, glancing over his shoulder as he steps one stair below me. "I'll give you a piggyback."

I wrap my legs around his waist. "Excellent. This is just the outcome I was hoping for."

He laughs and starts walking toward the car, his hands banded around my calves to keep me in place, my voluminous dress spilling off to our sides. I rest my head on his shoulder and smile wide. Somehow it feels as if I got the night I wanted after all, the sort of night I'll never get again if I wind up with someone like Andrew.

It's only once I'm back in the cottage, alone, that I realize I just lived out Margaret's exact dance with William. On the very same porch.

I don't know if I'm really following in Margaret's footsteps or not, but it's probably time to find out what happened to her next.

June 24, 1916

William acted as if I was invisible all morning. Perhaps he's embarrassed about dancing with me last night, or perhaps it's simply that I'm so much younger than he is. Although Matthew Lessard is courting Ethel Brown and they're nearly ten years apart, while William and I are only half that. I was angry and went into town for the church social and let George walk me home. I finally admitted something to myself when I got to my room, though: I don't think I want to marry George. He's nice enough, but he has mentioned wanting to move upstate a few times now, and today he said he didn't understand why I would need to go to teacher's college since I'd just be having children. And that's true, but I'm not sure I want a husband who says it outright.

July 1, 1916

Tonight, at last, William came out to the gazebo. I've come out here more and more this summer, though the mosquitoes are terrible, and I think it was simply to be nearer his cottage. We talked about the book I was reading —*A Room with a View* by E.M. Forster. I'm quite enjoying it, while William insists Forster's new book is much better. Either way, it was a lovely talk, which he ruined while walking me to the door.

"You can't be serious about George," he said, and even though I've had the same thought, he had no right to comment on who I'm serious about as if I'm a child. I told him I was very serious about George and flounced inside, which I now regret. I wish I'd been a bit more dignified. I wish he'd give me a reason to turn George down instead.

For the rest of July, her journal is nothing but her discussions with William. They meet at the gazebo each night and discuss books, but he never indicates any interest in her at all. I'm as confused by this as Margaret. "Grow a pair, William!" I shout as I flip through the entries. "Make your move!"

And, at last, he does.

August 10, 1916

This was William's last night here. I was near tears all through dinner thinking I'd never see him again. After dessert, Mama sent me down to the root cellar to get a jar of plums. He was on his way to his cottage for the night as I emerged, but he saw me and then marched back my way, as if he was furious with me. And then he kissed me. He kissed me so hard that my back was pressed to the wall and I dropped the plums entirely but didn't care, and then he said, "Wait for me, and don't you dare marry George Graves," and then he marched back to his cottage as if he was still furious. But when I got to my room, I found the most glorious bouquet of roses beside *Howard's End*, the Forster book William likes best.

The roses. That overwhelming scent of roses, fresh from the garden, before I dissolved in grief.

Whatever happened to Margaret and William, it wasn't good. I shut the journal again, because I really don't want to know anymore. Yes, Charlie and I danced. Yes, he rescued the puppies. But he's certainly not going to demand I don't marry Andrew, nor would he ever kiss me the way William kissed Margaret, though I sort of wish he would.

Whatever parallels exist between my story and hers, I'm pretty sure they've reached their end. It leaves me sad for all four of us.

28

———

MAREN

I t's the day before Kit's engagement party, and I am still not in the Hamptons. My mother is livid, even when I explain that trying to get out there on the Fourth of July would be nearly impossible, and that I'm flying straight to the island's tiny airport in the morning.

"You're dragging your heels," my mother snaps, and she is right.

I *am* dragging my heels, because I'm probably not coming back, so I want to stretch these final moments out as long as possible. I've been in South Carolina for a month now, living vicariously through Margaret—or perhaps she's living vicariously through me—while my real life back in Manhattan withers on the vine. Harvey has threatened to give away all my clothes and says he's changed the locks on the condo. These are things I don't care about, but I bet if I spent enough time in Manhattan, I'd realize I *should* have cared.

But tonight, this last night with Charlie, is going to be magical. They're having a town festival for the fourth, with food vendors and fireworks and I've convinced him that we should bike into town. In part, because parking will be a nuisance, with the crowds, but mostly because I want to feel like a kid who grew up here. A kid who was here in the twenties or thirties. Maybe even a kid growing up now. I had a city childhood. I didn't bike anywhere, ever, unless we were off on vacation somewhere. The one time I asked Henry to let me and Kit bike somewhere—swearing we'd be careful and that we'd stay on the sidewalk—a homeless man exposed himself to us. I bought our ice cream and let Kit eat mine as well as hers, and she threw up on the way home.

I never asked again, but tonight I'm going to get a little taste of that life.

Charlie's waiting for me by the porch that evening in khaki shorts and a T-shirt. The simplest outfit possible, but I'm almost sickened by how handsome he is.

"You're wearing *that*?" he demands.

So, I guess the admiration isn't mutual.

I glance down at my red-and-white-striped sundress. "It's patriotic."

"It's *short*," he grouses. "We're parking these bikes outside town and walking in. I don't need every guy on the street trying to look up your skirt on that bike."

I shrug and climb on my bike. "Obviously, you've got a lot more experience perving on women than I do."

"I certainly hope so," he replies.

We start down the road that leads to town under the shade of the live oaks.

I wonder if Margaret ever biked on this road. *Did* girls bike back then? Maybe her brothers brought her in a Model T like William's, or possibly she went on horseback.

She was a beautiful girl. She must have married, even if it wasn't William she wound up with. She probably had kids. Loads of kids...People spat them out like rabbits back then and no one blinked an eye if you were married straight out of high school. So how did the house fall into disrepair, how did it fall into the hands of a bank, and why can't I find a trace of her?

We park the bikes outside town and walk in. The food trucks along the street sell frozen lemonade and barbeque and mac and cheese with bizarre toppings. I try a little of everything and make Charlie finish it. We shop at the vendors' stalls, where locals are selling things like crocheted toilet-paper covers shaped like ball gowns, and wood stumps carved and lacquered into hideous coffee tables.

"If you leave before the house is done," Charlie warns, "I'm going to decorate it entirely from shit I buy here."

I smile but I want to cry at the same time. I really, really need to stay gone when I head back to New York tomorrow...and I really don't want to.

Martha from the Stop-n-Shop has a little craft stand where she sells plants and herbs. I buy some lavender from her, and she grins from me to Charlie, who's now one booth over. "I knew that it was going to work out for you, hon. Good on you."

I don't have the heart to tell her how wrong she is.

When it grows dark, Charlie and I head to a hill where we saw other people spreading blankets as we biked in. The fireworks are a tiny fraction of what we'd see at home, but there's something more special about this, about sitting beside Charlie in the grass, our hands splayed side by side, his pinkie finger resting against my own.

I remember, suddenly, a different fireworks display. It was New Year's Eve and we were in Sydney with our parents maybe two years after they got married. Charlie and I had run off to the bar, and we'd slammed our first drinks and were waiting on our second ones when the fireworks started up. I turned to watch, and when I glanced over to see if our drinks were ready, Charlie was staring at me.

Not at the fireworks shooting off Harbour Bridge, but at *me*, with this thing in his eyes.

He looked away almost immediately, and then it was me, watching him, my heart racing. Wondering what it was that I'd seen. Wishing I could see it again.

I can feel his gaze on me again. I want to look, but I don't dare.

It would ruin everything, wouldn't it?

There's a *boom*, one that doesn't sound like fireworks, and lightning streaks across the sky. Parents glance at each other, and Charlie and I do the same. Do we run for shelter? Do we ignore it? The decision is made for us when rain begins to fall in slow, fat droplets. We gather our trash and the stuff I bought from Martha and run back toward the bikes, but by the time we've reached them, the rain's coming down so hard that I can barely see a foot in front of my face.

We bike back through the downpour, and lightning zigzags across the sky as we dump the bikes and run for my cottage.

Charlie follows me inside. The rain is thunderous on the tin roof above us, but the dogs are too exhausted to care. They barely raise their heads when the door slams shut.

"I've never been this wet in my life," I tell him, kicking off my shoes.

"As you've spent the past five years with Harvey," he says, pulling his shirt overhead, "this does not surprise me."

Air seems to still in my chest at the sight of him there, feet from me, rain dripping down his perfect chest. He's too large for my little cottage, suddenly, and too undressed.

"You can take the first shower," I force out, "since you're already half naked."

I wait until he's in the bathroom to strip out of my soaking wet clothes, put on my robe and curl up on the bed, thinking about today.

I've done crazy things for this holiday in past years, but in spite of how it ended, I think this was my favorite Fourth of July ever. I love Oak Bluff, but I don't think it was the town that made this one special.

The bathroom door opens, and I roll over to ask Charlie if he remembers the year our parents took us to Paris for the Fourth.

He's got a towel wrapped around his waist...and nothing else. Every word in my head vanishes at the sight.

Charlie, long and lean and muscular, tan from the weeks here and the shirtless workouts.

Charlie, and the look in his eyes as he glances at me on the bed.

If it wouldn't ruin everything, would he stalk across the room and untie the robe?

If it wouldn't ruin everything, would I let him?

His gaze sweeps from my toes and up, lingering on my face. As if he's considering it too. "All yours," he says, his voice rough, before he opens the door and walks back out into the rain. He didn't get his clothes. He didn't even get his shoes.

I cross the room and take in my reflection. I'm flushed. I look hungry and not for food.

Yes. I'd have let him.

Even if it *would* ruin everything, I'd have let him.

29

CHARLIE

I drive Maren to Hilton Head early in the morning to catch her flight.

"You're sure you don't want to come?" she asks, consoling Echo and Narcy as she puts them in the dog carrier.

Why the fuck is she taking the dogs? I told her I'd watch them. It bothers me.

"There's a lot going on here, Mare," I reply. I can't go. Elijah's working seven days a week to get us ready for inspection. There are very few valid excuses for taking off, under the circumstances, and *I've got to attend a party in the Hamptons* is not among them.

She forces a smile, kisses my cheek, and walks into the small outbuilding to check in.

I know it's for the best if we spend a weekend apart. Last night, finding her in bed with that fucking look on her face when I walked out of the shower, nearly did me in. It took every ounce of restraint to walk out her door.

But the moment she's out of view, the missing begins. It roars in my brain the whole way home, telling me I should have gone with her or convinced her to stay.

I pull up to the house. There's normally this small electric charge in my gut when I approach. Now, though, I feel nothing. Even with the new porch, it still looks like it's been abandoned. It still looks like no place I want to be.

I return to removing tiles in the upstairs hall bath and I'm still at it when Elijah finds me. "Is Maren around?" he asks. "I need to order the new appliances."

I scrub a hand over my face. "She just left."

He blinks. "She *left*?"

"She'll be back." I hope. She'd better fucking come back. I need her here. "Her mom is throwing an engagement party for Maren's sister, Kit."

"You're not going?"

I shrug. "There's a lot going on here. I'm not going to ask you to work all weekend when I'm not doing the same."

He frowns. "I just...that seems like it'll be sort of hard on Maren."

My jaw grinds. "Because of Miller?"

"Who's Miller?" Elijah asks, leaning against the counter.

I was assuming Maren had told him because why else would she need me there? "Miller is Maren's ex. He's engaged to her sister now. Why were you thinking it would be hard on her?"

"Jesus, Charlie," Elijah says. "She's going through a divorce and seeing everyone for the first time since the news came out, and as if that's not bad enough, it's happening at a party celebrating her sister's engagement to Maren's *ex*? That's..." He shakes his head.

I guess it does sound like a lot. I've heard Maren say a million times that she doesn't care and that she's happy for Kit, but it's still going to absolutely suck to have everyone watching her go through it.

"You're right. I wish there was something I could do, but—"

"Bro," says Elijah with an incredulous laugh, "there is.

Fucking go up there. Stand by her side. The same way she's been standing by yours."

It...never occurred to me that she'd want me there. It never occurred to me that I might help. But if our positions were reversed, she'd be the one person I'd want to lean on.

She shouldn't have had to ask me.

And I sure as shit shouldn't have said *no*.

I glance at my watch. I can still catch a flight from Charleston to JFK, but it's a Saturday, which means it'll take three or four hours to get out to Ulrika's house. If everything goes to plan, I might catch *some* of the party. If anything goes wrong, I'll spend a whole day traveling, miss the party, and look like a whipped asshole to everyone who knows why I really did it—namely, myself.

But I already know I'm a whipped asshole, so I guess that's not much of a loss.

30

———

MAREN

As far as I can tell, there is no one in the state of New York that my mother has not invited to this party—in our home which only possesses five bedrooms.

"Everyone thinks they're staying here!" my mother shrieks, pacing the wide-plank floors of the kitchen. "Where do they think they're going to sleep?"

I pinch the bridge of my nose. "Mom, you know that when you say *come to our house in the Hamptons*, people think you are literally inviting them to stay."

"Well, I wasn't, and now I'm short at least a hundred and sixty beds."

"If the party is successful enough," Roger says with a grin, "no one will need beds. Or they'll only need them *briefly*."

Charlie would be cheerful in precisely the same way if I were panicking. And it probably wouldn't work, just as it is not working with my mom, but it leaves me homesick for him already. "Roger, half the guests are over the age of forty. They are not going to be staying up all night, nor will they be using the beds for other purposes."

"Apparently, I have more faith in our age group than you do, hon. Maren, you'll stay up all night, right?"

I sigh. "It sounds like I won't have much of an option."

An hour later, Henry arrives. He pulls me out to the back porch before my mother can suck him into her madness. "How are things, kiddo?"

My smile is overly bright. One of those Anna Kendrick smiles that reeks of the force used to hold it up. "Just great. Thanks so much for your help with the dogs."

He frowns, as if my gratitude pains him. "Maren, I'm your father. Of course I was going to help with the dogs. You don't need to thank me. Is Harvey giving you any trouble? Don't lie to me about it."

My eyes sting. It's always like this, when Henry is kind, and I don't know why. Maybe because I have a batshit crazy mother whose only concerns are my weight and my income potential, and no matter what Henry says, I know he owes me nothing. "He's been kind of a dick," I admit, mostly to explain the tears in my eyes. "He's texting a lot, accusing me of stuff...with Charlie."

Henry narrows one eye and hesitates, as if he thinks I might admit what Harvey's saying is true. When I'm silent, he lets his hand rest on my shoulder. "I'll take care of it. You won't hear from him again."

I believe him. Henry never says anything he doesn't mean, and he certainly has the power to make it happen.

My mother breaks up the conversation, hands flailing as she accuses us of *acting like guests* and tells us to go help Roger find houses for the overflow. She then begins to wail about some rare fish the caterer isn't going to be able to acquire and gets indignant about the song list provided by the band.

I slip out of the house while she's off to either yell at or seduce the catering manager into giving her what she wants and go into town, simply for a break from the hysteria.

I enter the tiny, overpriced grocer on the corner and have just grabbed a Diet Coke—though I should apparently be buying a sleeping bag, which they don't sell—when someone calls my name.

I turn to find Andrew, tan and handsome, carrying a six-pack of Sapporo and a minuscule serving of prosciutto. He gives me a one-armed hug. "I had no idea you were in town."

He says this without reproach. He is not a man who reads into silences or failures to text. He won't pout and punish when he's displeased. He's so much better than Harvey.

"My mother is hosting a surprise engagement party for my sister and her fiancé. I just got in a few hours ago."

He smiles and holds up the Sapporo. "Me too. Going to my buddy's house and attempting to be a good guest. I had this whole idea in my head about what I'd bring, but they don't have half of it so..." He shrugs. "I guess I'm showing up like this."

A sweetly hapless male looking for a partner, one who won't assume the favorite grocer in town will be fully stocked on a Saturday in high season.

"So...I assume the party is tonight?" he asks.

I should invite him, I guess, but God, that'd just open up another can of worms. Multiple cans of worms. Half of my mother's friends would be texting everyone they know in Manhattan to say Andrew and I are a thing, and I'm not ready. "Yes," I reply. "Just family and some friends."

"Are you staying around afterward?"

Do I want to see him? I don't know. Things are already so chaotic. It's an impossible question to answer under the circumstances.

I nod. "Yeah. I'll be here for at least another day."

He gives me a half-smile. "I imagine that you're pretty busy right now, but could we try to get lunch tomorrow?"

I tell him that sounds great, except it *doesn't*, and I don't know why. Wouldn't ending up with someone like Andrew solve every problem I currently have? When I'm in Oak Bluff with Charlie, I forget the rest of the world exists. But it does, and it's a world I'm about to return to. I need to figure out how I'll move forward without the part of it that actually matters—him.

∾

Kit and Miller arrive mid-afternoon. She's tan from Turks and Caicos and glowing with joy.

My mother makes a huge fuss over Miller and gushes over the ring and Kit seems to shrink a little, as if she can make herself small enough that the spotlight will no longer find her.

Miller's hand wraps around her waist, tucking her into his side, shielding her. I wonder if they discussed the awkwardness of this situation on the way here.

This is, after all, the very place where Miller dumped me—apparently because he was in love with her. That I'd so thoroughly forgotten it until this second is proof that I'm over him, but no one is going to give me the opportunity to say this and wouldn't believe me if I did.

Kit has Miller take their bags up to one of the bedrooms and then grabs me as soon as our mother's back is turned to go sit on the back porch swing.

"This party is Mom's worst idea," she says, "and that includes the two years she failed to pay taxes."

I laugh. "I can't believe she implied to all the guests that they could sleep here."

Kit groans, running a hand over her face. "See, I wasn't even talking about Mom's incredibly poor planning skills when I said that. I just meant...this is awkwardly timed. I'm sorry you're being put through it."

I squeeze her knee. "I'm fine. Seriously."

She opens one eye and squints at me. "You *are* fine. Actually, you're better than fine. Why are you suddenly doing so well? You were miserable the last time you said you were leaving Harvey."

I shrug. "Helping Charlie with the house has been nice. So much more peaceful than being at home and I'm just...happy."

She studies me a moment too long. Kit, like Henry, is too smart for her own good. Smart enough not to believe, anyway, that some time out of the city would be all it took to solve my emotional turmoil. She's kind enough to let it go, however.

"Thank you for helping Miller pick the ring," she says, studying her hand. "God only knows what he would've picked if left to his own devices."

"What you should be thanking me for is that," I say, nodding toward the large, framed photo of Miller and Kit at Everest, which my mother plans to display. "Aren't you glad I made you get your hair highlighted?"

"Henceforth, I will assume I'm about to be proposed to whenever you or Mom is insisting that I get my hair and nails done."

"Mom insists that at least once a week. And I sort of hope this is the last time you're going to be proposed to."

She smiles with a quiet joy I can't help but envy. "It will definitely be the last time. Or at least it will be the last time I ever say yes."

That's what I want. I want to get engaged to someone knowing I won't regret it. I want to marry someone without a single impulse to run back down the aisle and hop into a cab instead.

I never got that, but not everyone does.

And while marrying someone like Andrew wouldn't inspire the last-minute terror I felt on the day of my wedding to Harvey —the feeling of *oh my God, how did I get into this? How do I get out of this?*—it won't be a thrill.

It'll feel a bit like settling.

We talk about Everest and the proposal, and eventually Kit goes upstairs to find Miller and I go to the hall bathroom to start getting ready for tonight. There's an emptiness inside me when I look in the mirror as I admit the truth to myself: what has sustained me these past few weeks was not some kind of newfound maturity on my end. It wasn't the peacefulness of Oak Bluff. It was Charlie. It was opening my eyes in the morning, excited to see him and the way my heart would hammer every time he shot me that lopsided grin. It was our meals together, in the humid summer heat of the back porch, and our bike rides, and watching him laugh as the puppies licked his face.

How much of all of that would have happened anyway, and how much of it is Margaret reenacting some piece of her past through me?

Not going back will break my heart. But how much harder will it be if I give myself another month with him only to wind up exactly where I am right now?

At seven PM, the party is in full swing, and I am in hell.

If I had a dollar for every time one of my mother's friends had gently squeezed my arm or looked at me as if I was the grieving widow tonight...well, I wouldn't be as rich as I am now, but I'd be well off.

I'm sure they all think it's kind on their part, this sympathy for a situation that doesn't bother me in the least. And the situation that *does* bother me—the fact that I'm wildly infatuated with my stepbrother, a man who wants none of the things I want—is one I can't breathe to a soul.

I'm in a beautiful yard, wearing a beautiful dress, surrounded by a group of women I know, yet I can't escape this feeling that I'm very small and vulnerable, and especially that I'm *alone.*

It's a pretty familiar feeling, one I've had since those earliest memories of Henry saying, '*I can't believe I'm a father*' when he held Kit for the first time. And in all the time I've spent with Charlie, I didn't feel it once.

Charlie wanted me there. Elijah did too.

And I left to come back to this bullshit.

"Have you seen Ellie Hermann and her husband?" whispers one of the women. "At each other's throats." I'm relieved they're not focused on me, but I don't love this conversation either.

"That marriage doesn't have long," says someone else. "Speaking of...did you hear about the Kellys?"

"He'd gotten into such good shape," says another. "That's always the first sign they're on their way out."

The conversation turns to someone's Birkin, and who's on Ozempic, then onto the amount of money a couple has donated to an event and how it's simply because he's trying to keep his dad out of jail.

They care so very much about everyone's place in the hierarchy. They'd all shove me down a flight of stairs if it pushed them further up.

I've never felt more on the outside than I do now. But...do I even *want* to be on the inside? Do I even care about the things these women are so viciously fighting to win? I don't think I do.

I excuse myself, knowing they'll talk about me next—my money is on "*Harvey left because she couldn't get pregnant*" or "*she never got over Miller*"—and cross the yard in search of someone I don't loathe.

Before I can find that mythical person, I'm cornered by Malia, one of my mother's old modeling cronies.

She pulls me to the side of the stage, her leopard-print caftan blowing over my arms as she clutches my biceps. "You've got to stay strong, Maren," she says. "I was in your exact situation thirty years ago."

I smile politely. "Oh, I thought it was more recent than that. Didn't you just get divorced last year?"

She shakes her head, waving a hand to dismiss the idea. "Not that. Divorces are a dime a dozen. I mean—" And here she looks over at Kit and Miller, who are currently on the dance floor, gazing at each other as if they're the only people in the world. "Not with my sister, thank God. But my best friend. He was the love of my life, and she swiped him right out from under my nose. They got divorced five years later, if that gives you any hope."

Wow. Okay, so she thinks I'm upset about Miller, *and* she thinks I want my beloved sister's marriage to fail.

"That sounds very different from my situation," I say mildly. "I'm thrilled for Kit. I wouldn't have it any other way."

"That's the spirit," she whispers. "You keep saying that to yourself and one of these days, it will start to feel true."

My smile flags just as the photographer snaps a photo of us. Great. That's going to be the picture the press runs with when they publish the story.

Maren Fischer's Secret Heartbreak they'll call it. A source will claim, somewhere in the body of the story, that I spent most of the night in the corner of the yard, being consoled, because Miller was the love of my life. Someone else will claim to have seen me in tears.

"I just hope that you've found another man before they start having children. I know that's something you wanted."

My stomach drops. It's already happening—I only ended things with Harvey a few weeks ago, but already people are acting as if he was my last chance at having a family, and perhaps my last shot at being loved. It's the exact sort of gut punch I don't need right now.

My mouth opens to reply just as a hand wraps around my

waist. I glance at the hand first, but already my heart is beating faster. Because I know that hand. I know its size, its possessiveness.

Charlie's lovely mouth presses to my cheek. "Do you mind if I borrow her?" he asks, pulling me away from Malia without waiting for her to agree.

I turn and throw my arms around him. "You came!"

He shrugs. "The signature cocktail sounded good."

I can't stop staring up at him. At his lovely face and his sweet dimples and those glowing eyes. I shouldn't go back to South Carolina, but my God, I'm not sure if I have enough self-restraint to stay away. All I want in the whole world is to be able to spy his face somewhere in the periphery several times a day and make sure he occasionally eats a vegetable. "I'm so glad you're here. Kit will be thrilled to see you."

"Kit doesn't give a flying fuck about seeing me," he says, glancing toward me and then away. "And I didn't come here for her."

He came because the situation would be tough on me. He came because he cares that much about my comfort. The smile on my face is so wide that no one here could possibly believe for a second that I am mourning Miller.

"Now the real question is this: why aren't you drinking?"

My mother has set up two bars—one on the porch and one at the back of the yard, near the massive boxwood hedges separating us from the shore. He pulls me to the bar near the house and orders gin and tonics for us both.

Laughter chimes from the champagne fountain to our left. To our right, dancers on the temporary parquet floor my mother had installed squeal as they come close to falling into the pool.

"I'm so glad you're here," I tell him, letting my head rest against his shoulder. "The woman I was just speaking to tried to console me by promising Kit and Miller won't last."

"It was lonely without you," he says. "I even missed your terrible dogs."

"I knew you loved them."

"Love is a strong word. It's more the way you miss hiccups when they finally stop coming."

I laugh as I take a big swig of the gin and tonic he's handed me. He's so full of shit. He'd die for my puppies, and he knows it.

"Where are they, anyway?" he asks, looking around.

"I put them in Mom and Roger's room so they wouldn't be underfoot," I reply. "Would you like to go see them?"

"Absolutely not," he says, "but we'd better make sure they're not tearing the place apart."

Again: he's so full of shit.

We take our drinks up to my mother's room and wind up sitting on the floor with the puppies in our laps, our backs against the footboard, while he tells me what I've missed during the twelve hours we were apart.

I tell him that everyone's treating me like I've just learned I've got a fatal illness and several people have referenced my dwindling fertility, and then Narcy knocks over my gin and tonic and we agree that the best course of action is to leave before my mother finds out we were up here at all.

Downstairs, we get more drinks. Ulrika tries to sideline Charlie and he excuses himself, telling her he wanted to talk to me about my dwindling fertility.

The night is saved. No, it's better than saved. I'm bubbling over with my happiness. The way the puppies act when I come home? That's how I feel when Charlie enters the room. Like I want to leap at him until he pulls me into his arms. And yes, it's dangerous and a variety of other bad things, but tonight I'm just going to allow myself to love it. Because he came here for me, and that fact alone has me smiling so wide no one could possibly think I was brokenhearted.

Not once, for the rest of the night, do I hear "you're handling this so well."

Or maybe it's just that I'm no longer listening to anyone speaking to me aside from Charlie.

THE PARTY RAGES on until the very early hours of the morning. The beds are entirely gone by the time we get inside—and so are the couches. Charlie pulls a big blanket out of the linen closet and grabs my hand, leading me down to the beach. The breeze is chilly, but once we're lying down —my head on his very warm shoulder and the blanket around us—I'm as cozy as I've ever been in my life.

"I don't want to fall asleep," I whisper, fighting my drooping eyelids like a toddler.

"Me either," he says, pulling me closer. It's been a perfect night, possibly my favorite night ever, and if I can just stay awake, I can...

The sun's first rays are in my face before I can finish the thought.

"Shit," he says, reaching for his phone, and then his shoulders relax. "I've got to go. I forgot to set the alarm."

Go? But he just got here. And I somehow had it in my head that he'd stay until I felt okay about him leaving again, but when is that day coming?

"Already?" I ask.

"I'm catching a ride with some guys heading to Kiawah in about an hour," he says, climbing to his feet and helping me to mine. "And I can't ask Elijah to work the hours he is and not at least be present."

I want to argue that he hasn't slept all night and won't be any use to Elijah this afternoon anyhow, but even if that's true, it would be unfair of me to ask him to stay. He already gave up a day in Oak Bluff to be here, and even if he's useless when he gets home, he'll wake up ready to go tomorrow.

I sigh in agreement. "I'll take you to the airport."

"You know," he says, pushing the gate to my mother's property open, "the party is over. I'm sure there's room on the flight if you just want to come back with me now."

As much as I long for sleep, I long for the peacefulness of Oak Bluff more. But it is not to be.

"I can't. I told Andrew that I'd go to lunch with him."

"Andrew," he says flatly. "How are you going to get back to the city by lunch?"

I shake my head. "He's here. In the Hamptons. I ran into him yesterday."

Charlie tenses, his jaw locked tight. "So it's a date," he says.

I shrug. "It's just lunch."

"I'd better go get my stuff together," he says.

I haven't done anything wrong by agreeing to lunch with Andrew. I am guilty anyway, and at the same time, irritated by the way Charlie is ruining our final minutes together. We walk inside. I brush my teeth while he changes and returns his suit to its garment bag. He holds out his hand for the keys as I walk to the car—I might object to it under other circumstances, but I just want to cure his sudden bad mood.

We drive in silence on the way to the airport. "Are you okay?" I ask. "You've gotten very quiet."

"Just tired," he replies. "So, when are you coming back down?"

My eyes flutter closed. I let the decision float away last night during the party, but it's probably time to reel it back in. Now that he's leaving, especially, it's hitting me how little I have in the world other than him.

"I don't know. My mom thinks I should do some go-sees and get my career started again. I guess it makes sense. I can't hide out in South Carolina forever."

I want him to tell me that he needs me, that a return to my career can wait. He could say that, and it would be true. I don't technically *have* to work. It's more about establishing a life for myself, a way to while away my hours until I...what? Marry? Give birth? Come up with a purpose of some kind? I should probably know the answer, but I guess I've got time to figure it out. Because Charlie doesn't tell me he needs me, or that my career can wait. He doesn't say a goddamn word.

We arrive at the landing strip and pull up beside the plane. I climb out and he does the same. He comes around to my side of the car and hands me the keys.

I wish we weren't leaving it like this after such a lovely night. The best night I've had in forever.

"Thanks for—" I gasp as he pushes my back to the car...and kisses me. His hand is on my jaw, his body pressed tight as a magnet to mine, and he is kissing me hard, as if he's been saving it up for a long time, and oh my God, maybe I was too, because this is something I never want to stop doing. There's this low rumble in his chest, a gravelly hum of want that has me melting, pressing tighter, needing—

He breaks the kiss suddenly, his breath coming fast, his eyes dark and focused. He has not released my jaw. He holds it in place, forcing me to meet his eye.

"Forget about Manhattan. Tell Andrew you're not interested," he hisses. "Then fucking come back to me."

He's gone before I've uttered a single word in response.

I RETURN to the house in a fog. Only a small part of it is sleep deprivation.

My fingers roam over my lips, seeking a trace of him there and finding it—my mouth is swollen from that brief kiss. I've thought of nothing else this entire drive.

My mother is just waking, and Kit is freshly showered and hunkered down at the table.

"Where were you?" my mom asks.

I'm not sure why there's always an accusation in her voice. *She's* the only one of us with questionable ethics.

Although...I did kiss my stepbrother a few minutes ago. So maybe my ethics aren't great either.

I press the pad of my index finger to my lower lip, longing for the pressure of his mouth, for his body—tight with need, all muscle and strength and heat—pressed to mine. "I just took Charlie to the airport."

"He left? Without even saying goodbye?! Well, isn't that just vintage Charlie? He doesn't think about anyone but himself."

"That's absolute bullshit," I snap, coming out of my trance at last. "He's constantly thinking about other people."

"Well, you *would* say that. You're the only other person he thinks about."

"That's not true."

She clicks her tongue. "Of course it is. Why do you think we elected you to go check on him when he stopped answering our calls?"

That's...crazy.

Or is it? Would he have shown that letter to anyone else? Would he have allowed anyone else to stay with him?

"You're the only reason he came to the party too, I'm certain," she continues. "Kit, tell her. Did Charlie come up here because he cared about the party, or did Charlie come up here because he thought the situation might be hard on Maren?"

Kit flushes. She truly no longer needs to feel guilty about this. I feel nothing toward Miller anymore.

"Don't drag her into this," I hiss. "There was nothing hard about this situation."

"Of course there was," Mom says. "You said so yourself. You

said everyone was going to be treating you like an Oscar actress who'd lost or something along those lines."

I huff. "I said everyone was going to be watching my reaction."

"And it was uncomfortable," she says with a smug smile, "so Charlie came."

And yeah...that *is* why Charlie came. But I don't need the whole family believing it. And I'm scared to allow myself to see this as part of a pattern, a consistent record of Charlie doing his best to take care of me when it wasn't his job. "Tell her she's nuts, Kit."

Kit grabs her coffee, plus the one she's just made for Miller. "It's too early for this conversation. Mom, Charlie isn't selfish." She turns to me with an apologetic smile. "Maren, he does care more about you than all the rest of us, and yeah, you're definitely, a hundred percent the reason he was here. It's kind of sweet."

"It's not sweet," my mom replies. "It's disturbing. Make sure he's not getting the wrong idea if you go back, which you should not. Let yourself be one of his many conquests and you'll ruin everything."

"Don't be ridiculous," I whisper, turning away as tears sting my eyes.

I have no idea what's going on right now. I don't know why I'm upset. I don't know why I have all these useless feelings for Charlie that can never turn into anything, and why he has these useless feelings for me.

I abandoned ship with Harvey, and that was a huge step backward. But to start something with Charlie? That'd be like taking a knife to the life raft too and jumping into the stormy sea.

Unfortunately, jumping into the stormy sea is the only thing that holds any appeal.

I blame Margaret, even if she's not here.

31

CHARLIE

I wanted her to come back so I asked her to come back—but there are times when the people you love are best served by dishonesty.

And that moment on the tarmac was definitely one of them.

I don't want the same things she does. I can't give her what she wants out of life. It's insane for her to give herself away to someone as boring and useless as Andrew fucking Murray, who might provide her with kids but will never make her happy.

But it would be more insane for her to choose me. I'm sure she's aware of it, and after the stunt I just pulled, what are the odds that she's even going to return?

And God, I shouldn't have kissed her because how am I ever going to forget the way she fucking *submitted*, the way her mouth opened? How am I going to forget that needy little sound of protest she made when I pulled away?

I get back to Riverbend and go straight to my cottage. I unbutton the shorts and reach into my boxers. I'm already heavy and swollen at the thought of her, at the memory of that sigh. I fist myself, imagining her lovely pink mouth, imagining her dropping to her knees and sucking me off as if there was nothing she wanted more. I come hard, my back falling to the door.

I get maybe two seconds of ecstasy, and then my eyes open. Fuck.

One more thing that didn't happen, that will never happen.

I'm just standing here like an asshole with come all over my hand, thinking about a girl I've wanted pointlessly for a decade, and will continue to want for a decade more.

And who am I kidding? It'll last more than a decade.

I shower, take a quick nap, and head to the house, where Elijah—in the middle of tearing out a rotting baseboard—does a double take. "That was fast."

I shrug. "I caught a ride home with some guys."

"Rich people," he says with a laugh under his breath. "Did Maren come with you?"

My grip tightens around the hammer. "I'm not sure if she's coming back."

His eyes meet mine and he climbs to his feet. "What did you do?"

"What makes you think I *did* anything? She doesn't fucking live here, and she's got to deal with her divorce." I'm way more defensive than I should be. Probably because he's right.

"Maren loves it here," he says. "And she wouldn't just *not return* unless you'd really fucked up."

Yeah.

"Fine," I tell him. "I really fucked up."

"Idiot," he mumbles, abandoning his tools and the baseboard as he walks away.

Yeah.

I go to the second floor and return to popping out the tile in the hall bath. What the fuck am I going to do? I don't want to be here without her, but I also don't want to be in Manhattan without her. Which is why I should never have agreed to any of this. I should have stayed in New York, working long hours, silencing every miserable thought in any way available to me— if you're empty long enough, you get used to it. You sort of forget what it's like to be full.

I remember now. I don't think I can go back to it.

But I still don't want anything Maren does.

Early in the evening, Elijah shouts up to tell me he's leaving, and I walk down to the porch. I'm still pissed that he asked me what I'd done to keep Maren away. Even if he was entirely correct.

He starts telling me the plan for tomorrow. Something about cloth-wrapped wire that didn't pass inspection and leaking ducts.

"You've also got to decide if you want to expand the bathroom in the primary," he adds. "I know it's an additional cost, but if you're thinking about flipping this place, no one's going to want a bathroom that small."

The scope of the job just gets bigger and bigger. *Why am I dumping every penny I've got into this bullshit? I don't want this house, and it'll never sell for what I've put into it. I did the whole damn thing for—*

The gravel rumbles ahead of us—a car approaching. Elijah and I both glance to the road just as a black town car swerves into the drive.

Two squirming puppies leap from the back seat, followed by Maren, blushing as her eyes meet mine.

What does it mean—that look? The fact that she's here at all?

"It appears," Elijah says quietly, "that you didn't fuck up as bad as we thought."

Echo and Narcy run up the steps and jump at my feet. With a reluctant smile I squat and pet them both while Elijah greets Maren and heads to his truck. I rise, a puppy under each arm, just as she reaches me.

"I picked up Thai," she says, holding a paper bag aloft, her gaze uncertain. "I assumed you hadn't eaten."

I don't have a clue what it means that she's here. And it's stupid and selfish, but...I'm so fucking glad I was honest on the tarmac. All that matters is that she's come back.

32

———

MAREN

What is happening right now?

I'm sitting across from Charlie at the small table on the back porch, politely eating my Thai food and drinking the chilled white wine he's poured in a glass, and I have no clue what's next.

He hasn't referenced the kiss. He hasn't tried to do it again. The air is heavy with hours of longing—and who am I kidding, it's been *weeks* of longing on my end—but maybe it's all in my head.

Who knows why he did it? Maybe it was just a ploy to keep me from making some life-changing mistake with Andrew, though he hasn't asked about him at all.

"Did you spend some time with Kit today?" he asks.

I draw a line through the condensation on my glass. "We got lunch before I left."

His gaze darts to mine as the words register.

There. I've admitted, sort of, that I cancelled the lunch with Andrew, but I'm suddenly too nervous to let it hang there or to hear what he says in response.

"They're looking at getting married next summer, but you know Kit...she isn't going to let my mom plan some monstrous wedding like I had. Odds are she'll just get pissed off and elope."

"Yeah," he says. And that's the last word spoken for a solid five minutes while we finish our meals.

Which is awkward. It's so fucking awkward.

Clearly, whatever was going through his head this morning has worked its way right back out. Which makes sense because obviously this, with us, is a terrible idea. It can't last—I'm not the future he wants, and he's not the future I want—and...he's going to be family for the rest of my life.

If something happened between us, we'd exchange a guilty glance any time someone made a joke about sex during the weekly family dinner. And when my eventual husband says, "Are you sure you've never been with Charlie?" the way my former husband did *all the time*, I'll either lie poorly or admit this monstrous truth. Eventually, it'll be so obvious that everyone knows, even my mother, at which point she'll break poor Roger's heart and wind up with another guy who holds her face to the floor to make her lick up spilled food.

I rise, nearly knocking my chair over in my haste. "Are you done?"

When he nods, I stack his plate on mine, and walk back into the kitchen, strung tight with both want and mortification. I turn on the water and rinse the plates. God, what a fucked-up mess this has become, and I should probably—

Charlie enters the kitchen and sets the wineglasses on the counter beside me.

And then...he's behind me, with his hands on my hips.

My breath stops entirely. His head burrows into the crook of my shoulder. His lips press to the skin right at the corner of my jaw, then lower, at that pulse point in my neck. I stiffen but don't stop him.

His cock presses to the back of my dress, as his hands slide upward to my breasts. His thumbs strum my nipples hard, as if I'm an instrument he's very proficient at. Air bursts from my throat in a single, shallow exhale. He grinds against my ass, and I have to grip the back of the sink to keep myself upright.

I need more. I widen my stance—I have never been this desperate for friction, for the hard press of someone pushing inside me.

"Say it," he demands. "Say you want it."

I swallow. I'd really rather not. I'd really rather just have it happen without ever taking responsibility for my part, but that's exactly why he's not letting it unfold that way.

"I want it," I whisper.

He grunts. The sound is involuntary, as if I've knocked the air out of him. His hand slides beneath the hem of my sundress and his thumb brushes over my clit, outside my panties.

Harvey's touch was hard and mechanical, as if he was pressing the doorbell of a home where a bitter ex-girlfriend resided. This...is different. This is Charlie, with his tight inhale and exhale, circling his thumb, releasing these small, sharp breaths, as if it's my hand on *him* when I'm not even touching him.

I was frozen with Harvey, but right now, I'm beyond pliant. I'm melted butter, too soft to be shaped into anything at all.

"Do you know how long I've wanted this?" he asks against my ear.

I can't form a word in response. I simply shake my head *yes*, then *no*.

"Always," he says. "From the day we met, I've wanted to watch you come on my hand. I could jerk off to the memory of this and nothing else for the rest of my fucking life."

My breath is frozen somewhere in the middle of my throat. I still half-expect him to give me that smug smile of his and laugh as he walks away, for him to make this joke on me. And yet those choppy breaths of his and the bulge pressing against me as he leans closer say that if the joke is on anyone, it's on us both.

Goose bumps prickle the back of my arm. My nipples tighten beneath the sheer cotton of my dress. "Look at you, not enjoying it," he says. "Look at the way you absolutely don't want me pulling those tight little nipples between my teeth."

"Fuck off," I reply.

His circling thumb pulls away. I whimper and he laughs.

"Go ahead and say it again," he says, dragging my earlobe between his teeth. "Tell me you don't enjoy sex."

"I...please."

"Please, what, lovely girl? Please stop? Please make you come?"

"Yes."

His index finger resumes the path his thumb traced a moment ago. Lighter now. As if he actually wants to prolong this. Or maybe he's just giving me time to realize I'm full of shit.

Which I was.

I don't hate sex. I don't dread sex. Yes, I want this to end because it's...wrong. But I also don't want it to end. Not unless it will start right back up again.

My legs spread wider. I'm so empty, so ready, grinding against that *log*—hard, long, thick—pressed to the cleft of my ass.

"Oh, fuck, Maren. You are so wet and tight for me. You are fucking dripping, swollen, dying to spread your legs for my cock, aren't you?"

I'm not sure if he's really asking, and I'm so close that I don't need to answer.

His finger stops moving. "Admit it," he demands.

"Yes," I gasp, and he pushes the panties to the side and shoves two fingers inside me. Three quick pumps, hitting something so perfect and—

"Oh God, Charlie..."

I come against his intrusive fingers. I come so hard that my knees bend as if I'll fall to the floor, as if the only parts of me worth keeping upright are the ones he's touching. He wraps a hand around my waist, holding me tight.

"That was exactly how I knew you'd be," he says. "Wet, ready, submissive."

I'm still trying to catch my breath. I want to argue that I'm not submissive, that it was simply an unusual situation, but...

I liked the way he took control. I liked how he made me answer him, how he threatened to withhold it if I didn't.

He seems to understand some things about me that I do not.

I lean backward just enough to press my ass to the tented front of his jeans, and air hisses between his teeth. "You have no idea how bad I want to push inside you right now."

"Then do it," I demand, grinding backward.

"I've waited too goddamn long for this," he replies. "Our first time is not going to be bent over a sink."

He turns me to face him, his hand on my jaw, cradling my face. "I'm going to shower upstairs. Be in your bed *ready for me* like a good little girl by the time I get there."

He kisses me hard before I can even agree, groaning as I palm him. "Go," he orders.

I should tell him he can't just boss me around, but I'm already outside, walking to the cottage like a good little girl.

I get inside the door with the dogs at my feet. They go straight to their beds, tired from the long day. I haven't showered since this morning, so I strip off my sundress and climb under the spray before it's even gotten warm. I scrub myself, wondering how this will go tonight. It's been so long since I was with someone new. What if I'm bad at it? What if I've lost my skills? What if every complaint Harvey ever had about my attitude, my body, or my sensuality was actually somewhat accurate?

The cottage door slams shut and I turn the water off. He's already in bed when I emerge. I shut off the light, clutching the towel around me as I walk toward him, scarcely able to get a full breath.

With the moonlight pouring through the French glass doors, he's clearly visible in the darkness, and I'm not sure what I expected of this moment, but it wasn't this, because Charlie, who never takes anything seriously...is watching me walk toward him as if this is something he's waited for his entire life. As if the fate of the world rests upon what is about to take place. I swallow audibly.

"We don't have to, Mare."

I drop the towel.

It's as close as I can come to getting on my knees and begging for it. Unless he asks me to, and then I'd probably do that too.

He draws back the covers and pulls me in beside him, warm skin to warm skin, his fingertips trailing from the curve of my waist to the curve of my ass.

"You're trembling," he says. "Are you nervous?"

I shake my head. I was, but now it's more anticipation than anything else.

"We really don't have to do anything," he whispers, so close now that his lips brush mine when he speaks.

"Yes," I reply, pressing my mouth firmly to his, "we do."

He releases a quiet groan and wraps a hand around my hip to drag me closer. He's still wearing boxers, but there's no disguising how hard he is against my abdomen. His lips move against mine, once and again, and when my mouth opens beneath his, it's because I can't stand for it not to. His hand glides up my sternum and his calloused thumb flicks one tight nipple so hard that I jolt as if I've been shocked. I arch toward him, suddenly desperate for friction. He inhales sharply when I grind against him, then rolls me onto my back, pressing me into the mattress. He's pinned me here, with one hand flat to my hip, while he sits back on his knees.

Denying me everything I was after a second ago, that hard press of him in the exact right spot and...Oh. God.

His fingers have slid between my legs. "God, Maren," he groans. "You're so fucking wet."

I wince. "Sorry. It's actually been a really long—"

"Are you seriously apologizing?" he demands, swiping a thumb over my lower lip. "Do you have any idea how hot that is?"

He leans over me as his fingers continue to slip over my skin, and when he pushes a single, thick finger inside me, I gasp.

He rests his forehead against my shoulder as if he's catching his breath. "Jesus. You're so responsive," he whispers, more to himself than me. "I fucking knew you would be."

Before I can reply, he's kissing me hard, pushing those long fingers inside me again, hitting some spot, some perfect, perfect spot, and when he moves lower, tugging at one nipple and then the other with his teeth, still hitting that spot, I turn liquid and dissolve entirely, arching into his hand as I come.

I'm still coming—I've just had the best orgasm of my life— but I'm already too empty, desperate for more than his clever fingers.

"Charlie," I plead, blindly reaching toward his boxers and wrapping my hand around him, "fuck me."

He thrusts once into my palm, almost involuntarily, with a barely audible groan and then pulls away, pressing kisses to my rib cage, to my belly button, to the inside of one thigh, and then the inside of the other. "Come for me one more time, Maren. Just like this."

"I can't, Charlie. I don't—"

His tongue flickers over my clit before I can finish my argument. It tingles along my spine, turning that ache into a solid *pang* of want.

He does it again. I don't come from this and I don't come twice in a row, but...his tongue is just as talented as his fingers were and it's too good for me to bother explaining these things just yet, at this precise moment.

His tongue flicks in hard, rhythmic pulses, followed by slow, languid licks. I clench the sheets, dragging air into my lungs.

One more minute, perhaps. Then I'll tell him he's wasting his time.

He pushes two fingers inside me, and suddenly he's feasting as if he's been starved for this, groaning as he tells me how wet I am, how much he loves it, how many times he's jerked off thinking about how I'd taste.

"I'm gonna fuck you so hard," he warns. "The second you come."

And that's what does it. His words murmured against me while his fingers plunge. I cry out, tugging his hair as I come, and two seconds later, he's moving above me and grabbing the condom he must have had waiting.

He rolls it on and then leans over, lining himself up. The tip of his cock is a hard, blunt press against me. His jaw clenches, and then he pushes in only an inch—his eyes falling closed, his mouth ajar. As wet as I am, as pliant as he's made me, I gasp at the burn—half pain, half pleasure.

"Is it okay?" he grunts, his jaw locked. "You're so fucking tight, Mare. So wet and warm and tight. I'm trying to go slow, but—"

He's struggling. He's struggling not to thrust in, and I'm struggling not to beg him to do it, even as I ask myself if this is actually going to work.

"Yes, just—" I don't have words for what I want. Perhaps

because I want more and also less at the same time. I grab his hips and he sinks in another inch, then another still.

"Fuck yes," he hisses. "Maren, it's so good."

I think he's shoved every ounce of oxygen out of me. It's so much. Too much? No, I'm adjusting, and it's—

He pulls out and thrusts back in, bottoming out at last. I gasp. I cling to him, throbbing, trying to hold him exactly where he is forever, but he's already pulling out and pushing in, pulling out and pushing in.

I wrap my legs around his back, demanding more, but he stops instead, wincing, his breath coming quickly. "I can't...I've wanted it for so fucking long. I'm going to finish too fast."

Charlie, who has slept with every model in Manhattan, is apologizing. Apologizing because he's going to come too fast. Apologizing because he wants me too much.

But I knew it was different with us before we even started. Because it's *us*, because he wouldn't have gone here with me unless he couldn't stand not to. It's different because I'm not some girl he can put in a cab tomorrow. Different because I think he loves me, even if he doesn't know it, and I think I love him too.

He holds my gaze as he begins to move again, cradling my jaw when he kisses me, sitting up to watch my body move below his, grasping my hips tight as if he's pulling me onto his cock at the same time he's pushing in. He stops when he gets close and then starts again.

It's so good. If it was possible for me to come again, I'd have done so by now. My muscles tighten as if it's going to happen anyway.

"I'm going to come so hard, Maren," he groans. "Are you going to take all of it for me?"

I whimper in response, nodding, my back bowing off the bed. The friction is so much, so intense, as if every nerve ending I possess is lining the eight or so inches he's currently hitting.

"That's right, you gorgeous fucking girl," he says, hips pistoning. He presses his thumb to my lower lip, holding my mouth open so I can't stifle my noises. "Come for me again."

And I do, just as he's commanded, only dimly aware of his groan, of the way he slams himself inside me as he explodes.

"Fuck," he hisses against my ear, with a few final, jagged pulses. We kiss again, sloppy and heedless, and then his head falls, burrowing into my neck as we both catch our breath, his body settling into mine.

It's another minute before I grow aware of the dogs' quiet snores, the cacophony of crickets and cicadas and water lapping against the shore outside. The moon is full, casting a golden path across the room. And then I realize that I, Maren Fischer—who can barely come *once*—just came three times in a row.

"Charlie?" I whisper, running my hand over the back of his head. "I guess I like it after all."

He laughs. "You'll like it even more in about ten minutes."

He removes the condom, ties it off and throws it into the trash can, then lies down and pulls me into his warm chest, which smells like soap and sweat and him.

Our breathing quiets. I watch the rise and fall of his ribs beneath my hand.

"I was worried I'd never see you again after that stunt at the airport," he says quietly.

"That *stunt* is the reason I'm here," I reply, pressing my lips to his chest.

"Then I wish I'd pulled it a decade ago." He rolls me to my back and takes me in for a long moment before his mouth lowers, a kiss to say what our words cannot.

This thing will be conducted without a single promise or reassurance or look at the future. I'm not going to tell him I love him and he's not going to say it back to me, because that exchange would weigh too heavily on us over the decades ahead, when we're sitting at a family dinner, married to other people.

It's probably the worst thing I've ever done, and I'm going to keep right on doing it for as long as I possibly can.

33

MAREN

It's for the best that the house is full of people and that Charlie is expected to work. Because otherwise, little would be getting accomplished.

I'm sleep-deprived, my body feels like one long bruise—and I just want more, which is not something I'd have said of anyone I was with in the past. He can't even cross my line of vision without my brain stuttering. It's far less about his loveliness—though, God, there's that as well—and more about the way he watches my face, about the things he says. *"I'm going to fuck that swollen little mouth of yours so hard the second this house is empty,"* he promised over breakfast this morning. It's about his jaw falling open just before he comes, as if the pleasure is so intense, he's forgotten everything else.

Is it different because it's Charlie or is it different because he's the one guy I know I can't keep? There's no winning him over, nothing to be done but enjoy these few moments I'm being given.

And how many more of them will I even get?

He's due in San Antonio soon. And the second he decides he's had enough of this, that's what he'll use as an excuse and I won't be able to complain. I've always known the day would come, right?

I'm in the hallway repairing the plaster, thinking about all of this, when he and Elijah pass me on their way outside. His gaze catches mine and my unhappy thoughts vanish. Instantly, I'm falling down a rabbit hole of things I want him to try, things I want him to do again, and wondering how long it will be until all these contractors are out of the house.

CHARLIE

If you keep looking at me like that, the crew's going to get a show.

I have NO IDEA what you're referring to.

Meet me in your cottage in two minutes and I'll explain it to you.

I can't drop my trowel fast enough. I head toward the cottage, trying to keep a normal pace just in case Charlie's watching—I refuse to look eager. And the moment I open the door, I discover he's already inside, already pulling me against him, his mouth on mine.

"We're out of condoms," I warn as he pulls my T-shirt off.

"No, we're not," he says, tossing a new box on the bed. "I had them delivered."

My head jerks from the box to him. "Charlie, in a town this size? They're all going to be talking about it."

He pops the button of my shorts and pushes them to the floor. "From Hilton Head, for twice the cost and a fifty-buck tip. Now, Maren, do you want to keep grilling me or do you want to get on your back?"

I get on my back, obviously.

~

I REMEMBER READING about honeymoons when I was a teen. I pictured some sun-soaked jaunt through Italy on a Vespa, one in which I inexplicably looked like Audrey Hepburn, which could never happen. I'm six inches taller than Audrey Hepburn, for starters.

We would sit on flower-covered terraces and my husband would hold my face tenderly and smile as I talked, as if simply listening to me made him happy.

My honeymoon with Harvey was…none of those things.

It wasn't in Italy, nor was it sun soaked, and really it was a business trip for him that he let me tag along on. We spent three days in Munich, and then he left me in the hotel alone while he took off for Frankfort because he really needed to talk to a guy, and it would be easier if he wasn't worrying about me.

There were no flowered terraces, and there wasn't much fondness. He'd glance up from his phone over dinner when I asked something, with a look I'd soon grow all too familiar with: tempered irritation. *I'm busy, you're interrupting, you clearly don't know what it's like to hold a real job, Maren.*

I wasn't imagining it. He soon began saying it aloud.

The only time he seemed glad I was there was when we got into bed, and even that was…bland. I'd slide between the sheets wondering if I'd made a mistake, wondering if his behavior all week was an anomaly (it wasn't) or a harbinger of things to come (it was), and I resented him for suddenly acting as if he liked me when he wanted something. I resented the sudden reappearance of his attention and charm, which I already knew would disappear as soon as he rolled off me, like a large, hardback book slammed shut. The man who'd claimed to love me would disappear again until the following night, until I was beneath him—not coming—wondering why I couldn't just be happy the way I was supposed to be.

I'm thinking about that week a lot these days.

No one would call our time at Riverbend a honeymoon. All

week I'm popping tiles off the bathroom floor or plastering over damaged walls while Charlie's rebuilding stairways and hanging new windows and doing just enough work on behalf of his firm that he can keep paying for this place.

Elijah doesn't want to put the A/C in for the upstairs until his guys have completed the flooring and insulation in the attic, which means that the only cool air for this massive house comes from the basement, and promptly spills back out the open windows, the swinging doors. We are sweaty and somewhat stressed. Things fall and break roughly every ten minutes. I've never heard so much profanity in my life.

And yet, I'm happy. I spend the days in this euphoric, anticipatory bubble, and the second the crew leaves, Charlie is picking me up and carrying me out of the house with my legs wrapped around his waist, telling me all the things he's wanted to say during the day but couldn't. Only half of them are filthy. I guess none of this would be happening if he had the normal array of Manhattan models and influencers to choose from, but I'm trying not to think about that.

And maybe there have been some things he's trying not to think about too.

I'm nestled against his chest—Charlie, unlike Harvey, is a cuddler. When we wake, he is wrapped around me, his leg draped over my thighs. He falls asleep with my back pressed to his stomach, arms holding me tight the way they are now.

"How did you leave things with Andrew?" he asks out of nowhere.

My brow furrows. Is he asking me about Andrew because he wants reassurance, or is he asking because he's hoping I have someone to lean on when this thing ends?

I roll toward him. "I told him I couldn't make it because I was in a hurry to get back here, and he kind of laughed and said he knew when you showed up at the restaurant that night, you were going to be a problem. But he's still talking to people about the house."

"Good," he replies. He runs a thumb over my lower lip. His relief is tangible. And because of that, mine is too.

I close my eyes, curling against him, but I can still feel his gaze on me.

"Go to sleep, Charlie," I tell him with a quiet smile. "We have to be up early."

His lips press to the top of my head. "I'm not tired."

I open one eye to peer up at him. "Should I tell you a story? That's how I used to get Kit to sleep."

"Yes," he says. "Something boring, but not as boring as Andrew."

I laugh and tell him a Greek myth, the sort I used to tell Kit when she was small. Just as I conclude, assuming he's asleep, he pushes me onto my back.

"Sorry," he whispers, pressing open-mouthed kisses against my skin. "But I don't think your voice could ever put me to sleep. It's sort of the opposite."

I smile in the darkness, running my hand through his hair as he slides down my torso.

These are the thrilling, sun-soaked, besotted, orgasmic days I've always wanted.

It can't last, but honeymoons aren't meant to.

Eventually, when he moves on and I marry someone who wants a family, I will go on a second honeymoon with someone else. My new husband will be kind, nothing like Harvey...but it could never, ever be this good again.

34

———

CHARLIE

Calls are coming in now, fast and furious. It's always like this, just before another round of funding begins. It's mid-July, and I should already be in San Antonio, gearing up. Instead, I'm sending junior VCs out in my place, simply because...

I could tell myself I'm staying for the house—technically it could get demolished any day now, though fucking *Andrew* claims we're safe for the time being— but even *I* am not that blind to my own motivations. I'm staying for the one reason I've stayed all along.

I'll have to leave by the end of August. There's no choice about that. And it looks bad that I'm not down there now. But days like this, with Maren, come once in a lifetime.

I'm getting these two months with her all to myself. It'll somehow need to be enough.

We take the bikes out in the afternoon, weaving along the lane that carves its way around the cove. It's hotter than hell, but the trees overhead provide enough shade.

I love everything about this: the breeze, the motion, the sight of Maren turning back to look at me over her shoulder with a grin on her face. Her shorts riding up on the bike seat, revealing the lush curve of her ass every time she pedals. I'm probably going to wreck, with the way it distracts me, but it'll be worth the time I spend in traction. When we've gone far enough, I lead her down toward the water and we spread out a blanket, drinking icy lemonade with chicken salad sandwiches for our dinner.

She stretches her long legs in front of her and leans back on her forearms, smiling in drowsy contentment. "I don't know why everyone doesn't live here," she says. "Every single person in Manhattan should be throwing their possessions in a car and moving this way."

"The need to earn a living might have something to do with it, trust fund princess."

She laughs. "I guess if everyone from Manhattan moved here, this wouldn't be what it is anyway, would it? It would be a million high rises and snarled traffic."

"You make it sound like you don't like New York, and I always got the impression that you did."

She shields her eyes from the sun as she glances at me. "I do. I mean, I like parts of it. I think I just need...a break. Like, a handful of times a year, I need something like this. Silence, no people, no traffic, no rules about wearing shoes."

"Lucky for you, I know a guy who owns this big fucking mansion he has no use for. You're welcome anytime."

She rolls toward me. "You really don't think you'll ever settle down? I mean, you said you don't like the puppies, but you clearly do. You don't think that you'll eventually feel like that about kids too?"

I stiffen. There's almost nothing I wouldn't do for Maren, but I can't give her false hope about this because my stance won't be changing.

"I know I won't." I meet her eye to make sure she's hearing me. "I know things haven't been easy for you the past few months. But you really have no idea how much worse it can be when kids come into the picture."

Her head tilts. "Then tell me. Make me understand it."

How do you explain the kind of grief my mom felt over my sister? And not just when my sister died, but from the second she got diagnosed? It was bottomless, infinite. It would seem to have hit its lowest point, and then it would get worse.

"My sister really wanted to go to Universal," I reply. "Harry Potter World. And by the time we went she was so sick it was like—" I stop, clearing my throat. "It was like she was doing it for us. She was so pale, sweating. And my mom was pushing her in a wheelchair and acting like it was the greatest day ever, but that night after Zoe fell asleep, she went into the parking lot, and I followed her because I knew something was wrong. She was on her knees. Begging God for help, saying she'd give up anything if He'd fix this. I've never seen desperation like that. And I loved my sister, but in that moment, I wished she'd never been born, just so my mom wouldn't have to suffer."

My mom was all smiles and optimism before Zoe got sick, just like Maren is now—trying to find the positive side to every equation. And Zoe's death stole that away. She still smiled at me, but there was no joy in it. I don't want that to happen to me. And I sure as hell don't want to witness it happening to Maren, because I love the way that she sees the world. I love the way she seems to reflect all its light back and make everything brighter.

"You don't think you could just be happy with the dogs?" I ask.

Her smile is sad. "I don't think I could."

It's a conversation I could have with anyone, but it also feels...like a bit more. As if we've both peeked through a door, surveyed what lays behind it, and are now acknowledging it's best left closed. Though I sort of wanted to enter the room.

Okay, I really, really wanted to enter the room.

"It's for the best," she says. "You'd be a terrible father."

"Worse than you can even imagine. I've been hiding my really bad side."

She grins. "Worse? I'm not sure that's possible. I already picture you feeding your newborns whiskey and testing their body fat by throwing them into the lake to see if they float."

"That's the first thing anyone's said to make parenting sound fun. Perhaps I've been too hasty in writing it off." I push her onto her back. I want her—I always want her—but mostly I want to forget the conversation we just had. I want to forget that we'll eventually come to an end.

She gives way, exactly as I knew she would. We could be in the middle of an argument for the ages and I'm pretty sure that if I kissed her and slid my hand between her legs, she'd be exactly like she is right now: pliant, willing, soaking through those little white cotton panties she's got on beneath her shorts.

I climb above her and strip off the shorts. We're on private property, sure, but we could still be seen if someone came by on a boat. I'm more than happy to risk it, and with the way she's reaching for my zipper, I guess she is too.

"Goddammit," I hiss. "I didn't bring anything."

She smiles. "There are other things we can do. Roll over."

I could come just at the thought of the way Maren gives head—eager and hungry, getting so turned on as she does it that she's dripping by the time I finish. But right now, I want to be inside her. "I'm dying to fuck you right now. Let's just go back to the cottage."

She bites her lip, flushing. "I got my test results."

I frown. "Huh?"

"Just before we left to come down here, I got an STI screen. I sort of suspected Harvey was cheating, but I was fine."

Oh. Fuck. What she's saying is that she can't get pregnant, and I can't catch anything from her, so as long as she can't catch anything from me...

It seems like a bad idea, but already I'm rock hard at the suggestion. I haven't had sex without a condom in over a decade. "Yeah?" I ask, already pushing my shorts down.

I position myself between her legs. Goddamn, even this feels amazing. Even this—rubbing the tip of my cock against her wet, tight cunt—is insanely good. So fucking good I have to close my eyes and think of something else momentarily.

"Jesus, Maren," I whisper.

Her legs spread wider. "Charlie," she moans, that half beg of hers.

I'd like to force her to say the words. I love watching Maren blush as she begs for it, using the filthiest phrases I can convince her to say. But right now? Fuck.

I just need to.

I push inside of her with a wordless gasp and just hold. It's so wet, so warm. Her walls cling to me, and Jesus Christ, I'm already close.

"This is going to be embarrassing, Mare. It's too good. I just can't…"

She smiles and pulls me down to her, wrapping her arms around me. "Then go ahead and come. And then do it again."

I slide in, again and again, helpless to stop. I kiss her hard, channeling all the words I can't say aloud into the motion. All too soon, heat bursts at the base of my spine and I am coming inside her, groaning her name.

She's so perfect. So fucking perfect.

I'd give almost anything to keep her with me forever.

Just not the thing she wants.

35

MAREN

It's been a month—a dreamy, drowsy month.

I've had more sex in the past thirty days than I've had, cumulatively, in my entire life. When I walk into Margaret's room, I feel nothing...and I think it's because I already feel *everything*. I'm giddy. I'm euphoric. And beneath it all is some grief, but I'm trying not to notice that right now.

Whatever it is Margaret wants from me, she seems to be getting it. There's no one but me when I look in the mirror.

I've nearly completed the kitchen redesign. Every time I forget that it won't be my kitchen, I come up with an idea to make it more spectacular. Every time I remember it will be the kitchen of Charlie's future wife, I want to shred the plans and refuse to help at all.

I'm in the middle of selecting tiles for the backsplash when my mom's agent calls. Even the flash of his name on my phone is an unpleasant shock. I should be thrilled, since it probably means he's got a job for me. Instead, I long to let him go to voicemail. To pretend in a month or a year, or whenever it is definitely too late, that I never got the message. But Charlie needs to be in San Antonio in a few weeks. He'll be gone through the fall, and it's not like I can stay forever.

"Do I have a job for you," says Scott. "How would you like to be this year's face for Marais & Wolfe?"

It's a good, high-profile gig. I actually like the clothes. Internally, however, I am already wilting. "When would they need me to start?"

"Well, they'd want you in New York this week just to get your measurements. There'll be a fitting later in the month, and then they'd need you in Barcelona at the start of September."

"Barcelona?"

"That's the best part. It's an around-the-world theme. You'll shoot in Barcelona, then do some appearances, followed by Phuket in early winter and get this—Antarctica next February. Crazy, right?"

"Yeah," I tell him, trying my best to inject a little enthusiasm into my voice. "Very."

I love Barcelona and Phuket. I've always wanted to go to Antarctica. I think what makes me sad about this isn't the job itself, it's that by the time I've visited all these amazing places, Charlie will be a part of my past.

"I don't want to go," I tell Charlie that night over dinner.

He stares at his plate for a moment before he answers. "If you didn't want to go, you wouldn't be going. I understand why you said yes, but let's not pretend you had no choice."

"I can't just *not work*, Charlie. I'm not trying to get pregnant, so how would that look?"

"Why do you care how it looks?" he counters.

I guess he might have a point. Why do I care? Because people I don't even like will talk shit about me? I guess that's only a small part of the issue. The bigger part is that I have nothing to return to when my time here ends, and those days are approaching rapidly.

"What happens when this is done, Charlie?" I ask quietly. "When I get back, I've got no home, no plans, no job. I need to feel like I've got something."

He doesn't suggest I stay with him. He doesn't say *why don't we buy another property and flip it? We're good at this.*

I don't even necessarily think we *are* good at it, but I'd agree simply to extend my time with him.

"Except you don't even like modeling," he says, "so what else do you like? Surely, at some point in your life, you thought about something other than babies."

I push the salad around on my plate. Even in my earliest childhood memories, I only recall taking care of Kit, five years younger than me and such a little handful. Taking care of her and relishing it. I sort of fell into modeling because it was impossible to say no when the opportunity arose. What else was going to pay me that well? It's not as if I have any skills.

But motherhood remained my real goal.

"Even when I was tiny, I just wanted something of my own. I'm not especially good at anything else."

"For Christ's sake," Charlie groans. "What about design? You clearly enjoy it, and you're so naturally good at it that people are constantly trying to get you to sell any place you renovate. Do you know how rare that is? To be really good at something that you also really enjoy?"

I hitch a shoulder. "I haven't gone to school for it though, and it's not like—"

"It's not like what?" he asks.

"My father is a pretty famous artist, my mother is a famous supermodel, my stepfather is a famous rich guy. Kit's going to be a doctor, which won't make her famous, but it's sort of better than being famous. It feels like I'm supposed to do something larger than life, and modeling is as close as I can get to it."

"Who the fuck do you need to impress other than yourself?" he demands.

It's a good question. I wish I could answer it. "Harvey would make fun of me if I tried to do it professionally."

"Fuck Harvey. Fuck anyone who tries to make your life less than it should be, and that includes me," he says, suddenly fierce.

He cares so much. More than anyone else ever has. He cares about me, and he even cares about the dogs, though he won't admit it—he's spent the entire meal feeding Narcy bits of his steak.

He'd make the best husband, the best father. And the only way to stop hoping for it is to leave here. Will the longing fade away fast, once I go? Will I wake after a week away from him as if I'm coming out of a trance, only to realize Margaret's hand was on the scale all along, making things more intense than they'd have been on their own?

"Do you ever worry that we're being...influenced? By the house, I mean."

His mouth twitches. "Influenced?"

"Charlie, we danced at the Graves mansion just like Margaret and William did. You kissed me just the way William kissed Margaret when he told her not to marry George. You went and got the puppies back from Harvey; William went and got the broach back from George. Margaret used to watch William exercising in the yard, and I used to stare at you doing push-ups—"

He laughs. "You still stare, but who could blame you?"

I ignore this. "You see my point, though."

"This is why hot girls are a menace," he replies. "Because if you *weren't* hot, I'd think everything you're saying was pretty weird. But you *are* hot, and therefore, it's simply quirky and sort of adorable. Rich men always wind up raising kids who decide to go into shit like performance art, and you know why? Because they got seduced into breeding with a weird girl they found adorable."

It's so deeply insulting, but I'm fighting a smile.

"So in this scenario, you're the smart man, and I'm the weird girl who's destroying your potential offspring?"

"We're not passing our combined genes on, so it's not an issue," he replies. "But yes."

On Thursday, I leave for New York to meet the ad director. At my mother's urging, I've agreed to stay for the weekend.

Charlie drives me to Charleston and never says a word about where things stand, or who I'll be seeing during my time in the city. Maybe he's looking forward to the break from me and has had his fill—he seems to hit that point pretty quickly with most females, and it's not as if we have any kind of agreement. For all I know he could be off to Smokies tonight to chat up the bartender with the teeth. I hope that he won't, but I've been wrong about people before.

Like the last guy I married.

He pulls in front of the terminal and we both climb out of the car. He meets me curbside and hands me my bag.

"So," I begin. And then I say nothing because there's nothing I can say and also too much to be said.

"So," he replies. "I'm not going to later find out you were hanging out with Andrew, right?"

I grin. He found a way to introduce the topic, thank God. "I don't know. Do I need to warn you about the bartender with the teeth?"

"Maren, I was never interested in the bartender with the teeth."

"You said she was pretty."

"She wears that Pink Floyd T-shirt all the time," he says. "A, I hate Pink Floyd. B, I bet she can't name a single song by them. She's just wearing it because it's trendy."

I laugh. "That's incredibly picky, Charlie."

"Do you want me to be *less* picky?" he asks, wrapping his hands around my hips.

What a ridiculous, roundabout way to discuss exclusivity without ever having to say it aloud. Because if we *did* say it aloud, we'd both be forced to recognize how pointless it is when this isn't going to last.

"No." I'm not entirely able to meet his eye. "I don't want you to be less picky."

His lips press to mine. "Maren," he says. "No matter how picky or not picky I am, there isn't a chance I'll be doing anything except waiting for you to come back to me."

I'm flooded with relief, my heart soaring high. We can't come to anything, but it's enough that he's mine right now.

KIT and I are in my mother's large, lovely kitchen, seated at the hundred-thousand-dollar lava stone table while my mother paces, wineglass in hand, telling Kit why she can't have fewer than four hundred wedding guests.

"Do you want to tell her, Maren," Kit says, "or should I?"

"Mom," I say, "Kit is rebellious by nature and Miller will do anything she asks because he's so sickeningly whipped, so if you keep pushing her, she'll just elope, and you'll be lucky if you ever meet your grandchildren."

"You wouldn't dare," my mother gasps, sloshing wine from her glass as she rounds on Kit.

Kit looks up with one brow raised. "What have I ever done to make you believe that, Mom?" she asks. "Plus, I'm returning to medical school, my fiancé's in the middle of starting a new company, and I hate most of the people you would want to invite anyway, so I already have all the inducement I need to elope, and you trying to get me to agree to your flower selection and some crazy seven-color dream board you've created—entirely in colors I hate, I should add—is exactly what will send me over the edge."

My mother's hands go to her hips. "Teal and chocolate brown are this season's black!"

"I wouldn't want to get married in black either," Kit replies. "Call me crazy."

"Fine," Mom says, throwing up her hands. "If you're so much smarter than me, I won't trouble you with my assistance."

She flounces off toward her bedroom and Kit and I laugh.

"What are the odds she's not going to *trouble me with her assistance*?" Kit asks.

The odds are zero. Ulrika will be back to planning within the hour as if this conversation never occurred. "You're not really going to elope, are you?"

She groans. "No. Miller says we need to have a wedding so he can watch Dad cry."

I laugh. "That's not really the best reason I've heard for a wedding."

Her smile is sweet and secretive, a smile I might've been jealous of a few weeks ago but suddenly understand to the depth of my soul. "That's what I said, and he said there were a few other reasons he wanted to marry me in front of everyone, though it was mostly about that."

I never dreamed I'd use the word *silly* to describe Kit, because even as a toddler she acted like a small, angry adult, but it's as if Miller has brought out some young, unjaded part of her. I love it. Half of Manhattan thinks I'm angry about this situation when I'm actually just grateful it's happened the way it has. If he hadn't dated me first, they might not have met. They were meant to be, and if anything, I'm glad I got to play a part.

Ulrika returns to the kitchen only a minute later, triumphant because she's just secured "the end-all, be-all wedding planner of the century."

That didn't last long.

And then she points one long-nailed finger at me. "I'm setting you up with that friend of Roger's while you're here. Saturday night. He wants to take you to Le Bernardin, which seems like a good sign." She rubs her thumb to her forefingers. So the sign she's referring to is money.

"Mother, I am not going out with a friend of Roger's," I say firmly.

"He's not Roger's age, though honestly, Maren, you're in your thirties now. It's time to start making some concessions. He's fifty-three. Maybe fifty-four. Still young enough to start a second family but not so young he'll be picky about it."

"Jesus, Mom," Kit groans. "I need you to say all that again on tape so I can play it for Maren's eventual therapist. It'll explain everything."

"I'm not going out with Roger's friend," I repeat. "I'm not going out with anyone."

"Fine!" Mom huffs, throwing her hands in the air. "You can just move in and be a spinster and take care of me and Roger in our old age! I won't help you get out of this mess, and we'll see how much you like what you're left with!"

Kit laughs as Mom exits the room. "What are the odds she's not going to keep trying to *help you out of this mess*?"

I grin, trying not to let on how much the threat bothered me, how worried I am that this could be one more way my life and Margaret's potentially follow parallel paths.

I ask about the apartment she and Miller have just rented in Charlottesville. She asks about Charlie's house and commends me for helping him with it. I feel guilty accepting her praise—I am doing very little to help Charlie these days outside of things that involve my vagina.

I tell her about finding the journal, and William, who wouldn't admit he loved Margaret until the very last minute.

Her head tilts. "It's funny. When you describe him, I keep picturing Charlie."

I try to not read too much into the way she seems to study me as she says it.

"So, what happened to them?" Kit's too practical to believe the giddiness and grief I've felt in that room could mean something. Love has softened her a little—she might be more polite about it than Charlie is—but she'd still think it was nuts.

I shrug. "I stopped reading. I can't find any of their descendants, and I met someone at the club who said 'old Miss Ames' lived there when he was a kid. Plus, Charlie said some past owner of the house was found dead in this shack that used to stand on the property. I don't want to find out that Margaret died alone."

Kit's head tilts again, as if she's seeing things in me I can't even see in myself. "It's not like you can control the outcome. Wouldn't you rather know a sad truth upfront than spend the rest of your life waiting for it to destroy you?"

She's talking about the journal, but it's true of this thing with me and Charlie as well, isn't it? I'm not looking at anything too closely.

I'm waiting for it to destroy me instead.

36

———

CHARLIE

I have dinner with Elijah and some of the crew in town that night. The bartender Maren mentioned swings by with drinks on the house for all of us and slides me her number. Elijah smirks as I crumple it up, but I don't owe anyone an explanation.

I get back to my cottage and prepare for bed with Echo and Narcy right at my heels, something that used to annoy me, but no longer does. "You miss your mom, guys, huh?" I ask.

I know the feeling.

I've never been a guy who calls a woman for no reason, but I just want to hear Maren's voice. I want to hear how her day was, and probably get pissed off by whatever idiotic stuff Ulrika's said to her. I want to tell her about the girl at the bar, slipping me her number, and that I threw it away.

If I didn't know better, I'd say that I might be acting like a man who was ready for a commitment.

Where are you now?

MAREN

Bed, but don't get any ideas. My mom is right
down the hall.

I'm calling.

"I need my bedtime myth," I tell her, and she laughs.

Maren has this encyclopedic knowledge of Greek mythology, and every night, I get her to tell me a story. I'm pretty sure she could tell me a different one daily for a hundred years, and I'd never tire of it.

I like the sound of her voice, the yearning there when the story is sad and the excitement over the rare story that ends happily.

Sheets rustle on her end of the line. I picture her long, smooth legs sliding inside them. "My mom's going to hear me telling you a myth and know something's up."

"Then tell her to mind her own fucking business. Actually, do it right now anyway. Then lock that door and take off your clothes, and we'll move this to FaceTime."

"I'll just tell you a myth," she says. "It's less likely to result in Ulrika storming out of the house and threatening to leave your dad."

I push my shorts to the floor and climb into bed. "Let's hear it. Who's Hera mad at this time?"

She laughs again. "No Hera. Tonight I'm telling you about Atalanta, who'd only marry a man who could beat her in a foot race."

"I hope you're not planning to do something similar," I cut in. "Almost *anyone* could beat you in a foot race."

She tells me to shut up before continuing.

This dude fell in love with Atalanta, apparently—I'm not sure why because her obvious competitiveness is a little off-putting—and asked Aphrodite for help, so Aphrodite gave him three golden apples. He threw the apples during the race, Atalanta stopped to pick each of them up, and he won.

"She sounds easily distracted," I tell Maren. "Bad wife material."

"I like to think," she replies, "that Atalanta secretly wanted him, too, and just decided to let him win."

It's on the tip of my tongue to ask which of us is Atalanta in this scenario, except that implies we'd be heading to marriage.

"At least it ended happily," I say instead.

"Not really," she replies. "They later were caught having sex in a sacred temple and were turned into lions."

Most of these stories don't have a happy ending, so I shouldn't be surprised.

"I wish you weren't staying the whole weekend," I admit.

"Same," she says softly.

"Then just fucking come home," I tell her, before I remember that she's the one who's home or acknowledge that I'm acting like a complete pussy. "Please."

"Okay," she says. "I will."

And I no longer care what I look like, because whatever it was...it worked, and she's coming back to me.

37

———

MAREN

I go to my meeting with Marais & Wolfe, leaving my bags with the front desk. They take my measurements, then lead me into a conference room to discuss the concept with the ad director.

She's accompanied by several people in suits with vague job titles, who tell me what being the face of the brand will entail. There will be the standard clauses: I can't change my hairstyle, and my measurements must remain the same.

There's also an additional one: they want weekly weight checks in their New York offices.

I push the paperwork away. "*Weekly* weight checks?" I ask.

They glance at each other. "Well, your weight seems to have fluctuated a bit since your modeling days. We just need to make sure you're on the right course."

God, I hate this industry. No wonder my mother is so obsessed with her own weight and mine. She's had an entire lifetime of this bullshit. And sure, I understand why most people would go along with it—the money's good, and the work, once you hit a certain level, isn't all that taxing.

But I don't need the money, and this is bullshit.

"I live in South Carolina right now," I tell them, rising to my feet. "So it looks like this isn't going to work out."

"We may be able to strike the weight thing," says one of the women. "Let me reach out to legal and—"

"When you've fixed it, let me know," I cut in, because I'm not wasting an hour here while legal tries to come up with a new way to make sure I'm a sample size two for the rest of my life. "But I've got a plane to catch."

Maybe they'll decide I'm too uncooperative. Maybe they'll decide that whole ten pounds I gained while trying to get pregnant is so repulsive they can't take the risk. I really, really don't care. I just want to get back to Charlie.

When I land in Hilton Head, he's waiting, leaning against the rental car. I texted him the whole flight down about the meeting. He raises his sunglasses and grins as he pulls me against him, his hands palming my ass. "Have I ever told you how much I love those extra pounds?" he asks.

He shows me exactly how much he loves them when we get back to the cottage, and then he passes out, which makes sense —a full day of physical labor tends to be more tiring than a one-hour meeting and traveling by private plane.

I lie awake, hearing Kit's voice in my head, asking if I wouldn't rather know a hard truth than spend my whole life dreading it. I wish I could forget the question entirely.

But if Margaret and William don't get their happy ending, it will tell me nothing I don't already know about me and Charlie.

There are no happy endings here either.

I pick the journal up where I left off, using my phone's flashlight to read. There are several entries that say little—the boys are gone. George Graves is writing her, and she wishes he wouldn't because his letters are "dreadfully dull," and she bets William would write interesting ones if he ever chose to write her, which he does not.

Over Christmas, the boys return, minus William, who's

gone to his aunt's house. They talk of nothing but the battle of Verdun and the coming war—which all of them are inexplicably eager to be a part of.

December 25, 1916

It should have been lovely with all the boys home, but truth be told, I was a bit sad. I thought William might at least send me a letter at the holidays, but Sam brought nothing home and barely mentioned him. Papa asked how William's enjoying law school, and Sam said he doubted he'd even get to finish, with the war coming.

December 26, 1916

I turned eighteen today and Mama gave me that broach —the one William recovered for me last summer. I burst into tears and told her I was crying from joy, but I wasn't. In truth, I've never been so sad. Sam announced over dinner that he's engaged to a pretty girl from Columbia named Millie. We wondered where he got off to yesterday and it was there, to ask her! Mama and Papa are going to Columbia for the New Year to meet her family and make arrangements. Ruby Wilson got engaged this week too. It feels as if I'm being left behind.

December 27, 1916

We were all sitting around the table when Ruth came in and said William Howard was at the door and should she invite him in. Mama made a place for him, and all I could do was stare through the entire meal while he stared at me.

Mama scolded me for not eating and I told her I needed some air. I walked straight outside without my coat and only a minute later, William followed me. I meant to be very grown up and dignified, but instead I burst into tears.

"Why didn't you write me?" I asked, and he pulled me close and kissed me.

"I could hardly write without your father's permission, could I? And he wouldn't grant it until you were eighteen. He'd said as much last summer."

And that's why he is here! To get Papa's permission to court me. He'd driven all the way from Atlanta. It's the most romantic thing ever.

Margaret is secretive about the months that follow. She alludes to William's romantic letters and how much she misses him, but it's as if what transpires between them is too private to even be put into words. I sort of get that. I wouldn't want to risk someone reading about most of my moments with Charlie either, though I suspect my moments with him are a lot more X-rated than hers were with William.

When war is declared in April, Sam marries Millie in a very small ceremony and brings her back to Riverbend. Most of the boys enlist in the army, but William chooses the Marines, as they're training at Parris Island, which is closer to Oak Bluff than the other bases. Margaret sees him most weekends, and they talk about how they'll marry as soon as his tour is done. He won't marry her before he goes, the way Sam did Millie, because he doesn't want to leave her a widow if the worst happens.

I no longer see much of Charlie in William, but I guess the excuses to avoid marriage line up.

Charlie wakes just as William is getting ready to ship out and nestles against me. "I thought you didn't want to know how it turned out?"

"I changed my mind. Except William's going off to war, so I might have been right in the first place."

His hand glides over my bare hip. "So are you going to read it to me? If he's going off to war, I'll probably cry."

I bury my grin into my pillow. "That's okay. I like a guy who's in touch with his feminine side."

Charlie's hand tightens. "*Feminine* side? I can show you exactly how feminine it is, if necessary."

I thrill at the prospect and have to struggle not to show it. "All I'm saying is that there's nothing wrong with showing some emotion," I reply, setting the journal on the nightstand.

"I think it's pretty sexist of you to imply that showing emotion is *feminine.*"

"I think it's pretty sexist of you to criticize me when I'm just trying to let you know it's okay to cry."

"Ah," he nods, rolling me beneath him. "So when a man criticizes a woman it's sexist, but not when a woman criticizes a man? Different rules for each gender—isn't there a name for that?"

I pull his mouth to mine. All he's done is climb above me and I'm already wet. "Stop arguing. Save your energy for those unshed tears."

"Oddly enough," he says, pushing my thighs apart, "this discussion has me wanting to expend my energy on something else entirely."

He pushes inside me without warning, knocking the air from my chest, knocking all thoughts of William from my head.

There is only Charlie and nobody else. I can't imagine it will ever be any other way.

38

MAREN

There are two important calls the following week: one from Marais & Wolfe, dropping the bit in the contract about weigh-ins. I guess it's good news, though it does mean I've got to be in New York for a fitting one week from today and Barcelona not long after.

The second call, which matters far more to me, is from Andrew.

"I've got some good news," he says when I pick up the phone. "I did a little investigating, and that developer? He's done this to several other people. There's actually a lawsuit being brought against him for trying to use a loophole to take some Native American land in the center of the state."

I'm slow to see how any of this helps us. A guy who'd try to take land from Native Americans isn't going to feel *worse* about taking it from a moderately well-off venture capitalist.

"So is the lawsuit going to stop him from doing it to us?" I ask.

"No," Andrew says. "But I've now got several reporters looking into the story. Once they start investigating which government officials have been helping him along, people won't be able to back off fast enough. I've also got a representative down there promising his staff is looking into your situation. Give it a week, and the state will reverse everything it's said to date."

Wow. Andrew has often said he *hopes* something will work, or that it's *possible*. I've never heard him say it definitively like this.

"It sounds like you think it's really going to work out," I whisper, stunned.

"It one hundred percent is going to work out, Maren. I'd stake my life on it."

I sink back into my chair. I can't believe it's about to solved, just like that.

"I can't thank you enough for helping us," I tell him.

He laughs. "I can think of some ways, but given that you're still in South Carolina, I imagine Charlie would object."

My shoulders sag with relief. I suspected I'd made my feelings clear enough when I canceled our lunch in the Hamptons, but this confirms it. "Yeah, he probably would."

"Look, Maren. I just have to say something. Based on his reputation, he doesn't want any of the things you do, unless something's changed."

I swallow hard. That's the ugly truth, isn't it? The truth I have been reluctant to face. "No, nothing's changed."

"I'm sorry," he says. "And you know I'm interested, but that's not why I'm saying what I'm about to: don't let him waste too much of your time. I let Kristen waste far too much of mine, and it's probably my greatest regret."

Also true. Whether Charlie and I say it aloud or not, this is a waste. It will go nowhere.

"Thanks," I reply. "I know. I'm fully aware that this…is ending."

"When you're ready to move on, I'm here," he says.

I tell Charlie what Andrew said about the house and

Charlie simply rolls his eyes. "I don't see why he couldn't have put it in an email," he grouses, jealous of a phone call about the house my friend is helping him save for *free*.

I can't believe he's the same guy who pretended to have an eleven PM Zoom meeting with Tokyo in order to get two girls out of his apartment.

The person he is with me—and to some extent, the person he's always *been* with me—feels like the real one. But when we go back to New York...who will he be then?

Two days later, we get notified by the state that the house is no longer condemned. There's not going to be an inspection at all.

We don't need to be here, then. We're completely off the hook. I wait for Charlie to suggest he should really get to San Antonio, should really go into the office, and he says neither.

But the end is coming, either way.

So I finally buckle down to read Margaret's last few entries.

August 10, 1917

William was given several days' leave before he ships out. He went to say goodbye to his mother but spent his final day here with me. He'll sleep in the shack tonight, which seems insane, given that all the boys' rooms are empty.

We had such a lovely day together. He kissed me again in the shadow of the house and told me not to see him off in the morning because it would be too hard. He said he's marrying me the day he gets back, out in the gazebo if possible, though Mama will probably want a church wedding, and he gave me a ring that belonged to his grandmother. Just a tiny emerald ring, but I love it more than I'd ever thought I could love anything. Now he's sleeping out along the water, yards away, and...why are we wasting these last hours? I pray the war ends quickly, but there are no signs of it, and they say that a million boys were killed at Verdun. A million. How is such a number even possible? If the worst happens, how bitterly will I regret spending this night away from him? What am I trying to preserve when everything I have belongs to him?

August 11, 1917

I went to see William. He asked why I was there and I will say no more here, but I'm glad. No matter what happens, I'm glad I did it.

So she slept with him. She must have. I'd love this were it not for one thing: that previous owner of the home, the woman who left her mansion and died in the shack where my cottage now stands. Increasingly, I've suspected it was Margaret and now I'm nearly certain.

I scan ahead. She and William exchange letters. She writes him daily while his tend to come in batches of five or ten. They start off cheerfully enough—the biggest issue is lice, which is what she hears from her brothers as well. *I want to believe all this,* she writes, *yet...a million boys dying in a single battle. So many lives lost. And that's how it happens, isn't it? A million boys writing home to their mothers and sisters and sweethearts, complaining of lice and rain and rations and then...they're gone, as if they were never there at all. Five people I love are there. Plus all the boys I went to school with. What are the odds that they'll all come home? That they won't simply be taken in a single battle?*

And then, it happens.

December 1, 1917

Sam is dead. We learned it weeks ago and I couldn't bring myself to even write the words here until now. Sweet,

sweet Sam is dead. I can't imagine a world without him. Papa is so quiet now, so gray. Mama as well. Sam's death has broken them, and I fear they can't be put back together. Millie returned to her family in Columbia—a war widow when she barely got to be a bride. He's buried somewhere in France, but Papa says we'll give him a headstone here too, when Mama's better.

Margaret decides she won't leave for teacher's college after all. Her parents need her close. There are more letters from William, less cheerful ones. His closest friend lost both legs, and William was inches away when it happened. He sleeps with Margaret's photo next to his heart and says he wishes now they'd married, selfish though it would be, because very few of them will come out of this alive.

She receives word that his regiment is moving toward Belleau Wood, in the north of France, and then, it begins: day after day of Margaret asking, "Why hasn't he written?" and consoling herself with reports of slow mail and batches of letters arriving months later than they should.

I turn the page. More questions. More suggestions that a mail boat was blown up, that the fighting is too heavy for news to leave at all, and then...the journal just stops. I flip through the blank pages and toward the back is tucked a small, folded letter, one that's been read many times.

I unfold the letter—it's dated just a few days before William left for the front.

Dearest Margaret,

I'm writing you now from the attic of my aunt's home and will leave this in my mother's care, only to be sent on to Riverbend if the worst has happened.

There's too much to say and also very little. The important bit is that I have loved you with my entire soul, and you made the few years I got brighter than I'd ever dreamed years could be. I knew I loved you that very first night. Do you remember it? You seemed to hate me for some reason—I'm not sure I ever asked why—and I made that joke about your yellow dress to bring you down a peg, while thinking I'd never seen anyone so lovely. You were too young and I knew it, but seeing you fritter all that beauty and intellect away on George Graves killed me. I tried so hard to stay away from you, but I couldn't quite manage it.

It was in my best interest, because the minutes I've had with you have meant more than every other minute I've had put together, but if you're reading this, I'm not sure it was in yours.

Don't grieve for me, because I intend to find you again. Do you remember those myths you loved? Baucis and Philemon. Hero and Leander. What they had in common was that they found each other in death, and we will too.

All my love, William

I curl up in bed and weep. I weep for Margaret and William, for Sam and Millie, for all the other boys that didn't come home. I guess I'm crying for me and Charlie, too, because already I can feel the end coming.

Eventually, I rise and go outside with the dogs at my heels, heading for the hill Charlie once mentioned, the high point of the property. I knew he was right, that the graves were probably there, but I didn't want to look.

I climb, pushing through the underbrush, until I finally reach them. Seven graves, all in a row. The four boys, all of them dead within a year of each other. Helen Ames, who died in 1964 and her husband Richard, who died the next year. And finally Margaret, who died September 12, 1993.

She died on the day I was born.

A chill crawls up my spine...and yet I've known there was a connection between us since I first walked into the house. In some ways, it's not even a surprise.

Was it her they found in that shack by the water? Did she say goodbye to the end of a long, unhappy life in the place where her sweetest moments transpired?

I go into town and buy a couple things I don't really need at the Stop-n-Shop. The real reason I'm here is to talk to Martha, or anyone else who might know what happened to Margaret in the end.

She greets me with a wide smile and her typical comments about the weather before asking how that cute friend of mine is.

"He's good." I blush, then lean into the counter. "Hey, you don't happen to know anything about the people who built Riverbend, do you?"

Her mouth purses and her brow furrows as she considers the question. "Not too much. I think it was a big family—a bunch of boys who were lost in the war, maybe?"

I nod. "Charlie said somebody died there. I'm just trying to figure out who it was."

She laughs. "I'm guessing a *bunch* of people died there. If you scare easy, I wouldn't think on it too hard."

I hitch a shoulder. "It's not that so much. But Charlie said that someone went down to the shack to die. It's sort of weird, right? I was just trying to figure out who it was."

She starts scanning the paper goods I've stacked before her. "I guess you've tried the Internet?"

I hold open a bag so she can drop the stuff in. "Yeah. I can't seem to find anything. I know when it might have happened, but that's it."

"What about microfilm?" she asks. "Go to the library in Beaufort and ask for microfilm from the local newspaper around the time it happened. That might shed some light on the situation."

I thank her and head to the car, throwing the stuff in the trunk before I text Charlie to tell him I'm going to be late.

THE LIBRARIAN in Beaufort is enthusiastic. "I love when people actually know about microfilm," she says, so I don't mention that I'd never heard of it before today. "Most young people think they can just find anything online and if they can't, it doesn't exist."

As it turns out, however, old copies of the *Oak Bluff Daily Record* were never digitized.

My shoulders sink. *Another dead end.*

"I do have physical copies if you don't mind combing through them," she adds.

My eyes spring open. "Yes, that would be perfect. I'm looking for information about someone who died on September twelfth, nineteen ninety-three. So maybe the two weeks from that date?"

It takes her an hour to locate the correct year, and then the correct month. Eventually, she drops a big box of newspapers on the table before me. Three days after she died, I find the headline:

Margaret Ames, 95, Found Dead on Property

Margaret Ames, one of Oak Bluff's oldest residents, was found on Tuesday by concerned friends after she failed to show up for church on Sunday.

Miss Ames, who never married, was the youngest of five children and lived at Riverbend her entire life. Tragically, her four other older brothers all died during World War I, a loss her parents, Judge Richard Ames, and his wife, Helen, never recovered from. Miss Ames is said to have lived with her parents until their deaths in the 1960s, and then remained in the house alone until she was found this week.

Miss Ames's body—found clutching a bouquet of dried roses— was recovered after nearly a full day's search of the house and prop-

erty, and was eventually discovered in a small shack "in great disre-pair," according to someone at the scene.

Her location contributed greatly to the difficulty in finding her, but foul play is not suspected.

"The heat alone would have killed her," said Betsy Squires, a longtime member of the Oak Bluff Methodist Church. "I can't imagine why she would have gone out there."

I curl up in the hard wooden library chair and cry with my face pressed to my knees. I'm weeping for Margaret and William, yes, but also myself.

Not everyone gets a happy ending. Sometimes you just get one tiny moment of joy in a very long life, and you cling to it forever. I guess I already knew this—I just thought I might be an exception.

I'm pretty sure I won't be.

39

MAREN

All night I have dreams that begin happily then bleed into nightmares. A nice moment with Charlie, down by the water, turns into discovering Margaret dead in an abandoned shack.

A baby is crying, and Margaret pats my hand and says, "That's Millie's, not ours."

Kit's getting married, but when the priest announces they're husband and wife, it's Charlie and that girl he danced with the night of the country club ball who turn toward the crowd.

I toss in bed and when I finally wake sometime just before dawn, my stomach is churning.

Charlie remains asleep beside me, not budging as I throw back the covers and race to the bathroom, barely skidding to a stop in front of the toilet before my stomach empties.

When it's blessedly over, I let my face press to the cool tile floor, too weak and shaky to stand. I hope it's simply food poisoning as opposed to the flu. There's too much going on between my Marais & Wolfe contract and our final days at the house for me to be sick in bed all week.

I manage to brush my teeth, then slide back to the floor, too weak to continue standing. A minute later, Charlie enters the bathroom, wearing not a stitch of clothing. Even as sick as I am, I'm still able to appreciate what an absolute work of art he is: lovely and large and muscly. All mine for not much longer.

Yet another reason I can't afford to lose any days to illness.

"Jesus, Maren, what happened?" asks Charlie, squatting beside me.

"I threw up," I whisper.

He laughs as he lifts me into his arms off the floor. "Yeah, I put that part together, hon. Let's get you back into bed."

I weakly shake my head, then press my face to his cool chest. "I don't want to get you sick. I should sleep somewhere else."

"I'm far too strong and masculine to get sick," he says.

I laugh shakily. "I'm no doctor, but I'm not sure it works that way."

I'm too tired to fight him, however, as he tucks me back under the blankets and though I want to talk to him, I drift off to sleep, exhausted.

The next time I wake, the sun is out, and Charlie's fully dressed with his hand on my shoulder. "Drink, Maren," he says, his brow furrowed as he hands me a glass of something bright red. "You need electrolytes."

Reluctantly, I accept the glass, though I really just want to go back to sleep. "I think I'm better. Just tired. It was the chicken. I was worried I hadn't cooked it enough. You're not nauseous at all?"

He pushes the hair back from my face. "I told you. I'm too manly to get sick."

I give him a halfhearted smile. "Oh, right. I forgot."

"If you weren't sick, I'd have a very reasonable and not at all selfish way to make you remember."

"Maybe you should do it anyway. Then you can claim I was healed by your cock."

"I intend to tell everyone that regardless," he says. "You think you can eat something? I made soup."

My heart swells like a cartoon character's. "You cooked?"

"Don't give me too much credit. I added one cup of water to a can of Campbell's and shoved it in the microwave. I doubt it's getting a Michelin star. But stay put and I'll go get it."

I push off the covers. "Honestly, I think I'm fine. I can go to the house."

He rests a hand on my shoulder. "Stay in bed. Just in case. I'll be right back."

He rises and turns toward the door, and my eyes fill. Why can't he want the things I do? Why can't he want marriage? Why can't he want to fill that big house with children? He'd be so good at it, at all of it, and there's no one alive I'd rather do it with.

Not everyone gets a happy ending, yet I can't seem to stop wishing I'll get mine.

By midday, despite Charlie's insistence that I remain in bed, I get up and persuade him to go for a walk around the lake with me. That night, he doesn't succumb to my repeated assurances that I'm perfectly fine until I've undressed and climbed into his lap.

Eventually, he agrees that it was probably the chicken.

In bed, as we start to doze off, I list the things I want to get done tomorrow. So many things, to make up for how little I've accomplished today.

I fall asleep dreaming about measuring for the kitchen counters and wake drenched in sweat and gagging. This time, I remain in bed, hoping the nausea will pass so that Charlie doesn't rush off to play Mother Hen again—not that I minded.

It does pass after a moment. But what the hell? I was fine yesterday afternoon but ate very little last night just to be on the safe side, and now I'm back at square one.

I run through every catastrophic possibility first, and

quietly climb out of bed and splash water on my face in the bathroom. I'm drawn and gray beneath my tan, with circles under my eyes. I open the cabinet, wondering if we have anything for nausea...and my gaze lands on the box of tampons I bought ages ago because my period was due.

It still isn't opened.

What the fuck?

I've gone for so many years now *hoping* for a missed period, then didn't even notice when it actually happened. I'm late. Three weeks late? Four weeks late?

I'm significantly late.

I reach up and cup my breasts. They're tender. They've been tender for two weeks now, and I...I don't even know what I thought that was. I suppose I assumed it was all the attention they'd been getting from Charlie.

Is it possible? After years and years of trying, have I wound up pregnant with the last man in the world who'd want me to be?

It doesn't seem possible. How could it be? The fertility doctor ran a nearly infinite number of tests and told me point-blank it couldn't happen on my own. Did he lie? Was he mistaken? Or is this some magic created by the house?

Maybe it's one of those pregnancies women get where it's all in their head. Except those happen to women who were actively thinking about pregnancy, whereas I'm someone who basically forgot about it for six weeks straight.

And there's also this quiet joy inside me anyway—a joy that says by some miracle...it's actually true this time.

There's no way I'm going back to sleep. I grab my clothes and sneak out of the cottage, changing in the predawn light before I go out to the car.

The Stop-n-Shop is open already. Martha is almost always there, and I trust her. She'll have plenty of opinions about this, but she won't share them beyond the two of us.

I wave to her and go to the back of the store where the pregnancy tests are kept.

She smiles when I reach the register. "Well, this is an interesting turn of events."

"It's probably nothing," I argue. Mostly because if she gets excited, then I'll get *more* excited, and it'll hurt that much more when the second pink line never appears. I've lived it so many times over the past few years I don't know how it's even upsetting when it happens.

"It's not nothing," she says, squeezing my hand. "I've been wondering for weeks. I figured you were just keeping it a secret."

I freeze. "How? How could you know?"

She shrugs. "You've just got that look. Definitely having a girl."

She couldn't possibly know any of this, but yeah...I think she's right. I think I might be pregnant, and I sort of feel like it's a girl too.

I take the test in the powder room of the main house. I've taken a million tests at this point in my life for no reason at all. My period would be a day late and I'd be rushing off, too excited not to check. I hold the stick under the stream of urine, counting to five. And when I've finished counting, I pull the test back into view, watching as pink washes over the white screen. The control line appears immediately and I'm waiting for that other line as if my life depends on it.

"Don't get your hopes up, Maren. It probably means nothing, and it's for the best if..."

My brain goes silent. I didn't have to wait a minute. There's a second line, as dark as the first, almost instantaneously.

I am pregnant. I am definitely pregnant.

After all my years of doing everything right so that I'd have the perfect pregnancy, it happens now? I've been drinking, I've been running, I've been eating like shit. "You're already a terrible mother, and it's barely begun," I whisper, and I'm weeping but smiling at the same time. It's really going to happen. Maybe. I'll need to take a blood test. I guess I'll need to see a doctor. I'll need to discuss it with...

Charlie.

God. How the hell am I going to tell Charlie?

HE COMES into the house with a brow raised, glancing at the table laid out with enough food for ten people.

"I made breakfast," I tell him.

He pulls me against him. "I see." His mouth presses to the top of my head. "How do you feel? All recovered?"

My breath catches. *I could tell him now. I should tell him now. But he's just woken up and it can wait, right? It can wait until he's fully awake, and he's had some food.*

"Totally fine," I reply.

His hand palms my ass, and he gives it a light slap. "Then you really ought to be back in bed instead of in here, fully dressed. We've only got thirty minutes until the guys arrive."

I laugh. "Breakfast will get cold."

I know he's thinking he'd rather get laid than fed, but he gives in with a reluctant smile and sits at the table.

I take a seat across from him, forcing down a little fruit, though nerves have demolished any appetite I might have had.

I watch the way his long fingers lift the fork, the way his beautiful mouth closes around it, the way his blue eyes catch mine. If I could pick anyone in the world to be my child's biological father, it would probably be him, and if he could pick any outcome in the world, it would be to not father anyone at all. It's a miracle, and it's also deeply unfair to him—he thought I was this sure thing. It's as if I've tricked him. Hopefully he won't actually believe that but God, who knows?

I'll offer him the option of bowing out. As much as it hurts to imagine leaving him, if he doesn't want to be a part of this, I'm not going to force his hand. I'd go elsewhere, claim I conceived through IVF, and he'd need never get involved. Except we aren't two strangers who'd never see each other again. There'd be holidays and family dinners and every occasion in between. Kit's wedding, the birth of her children, our parents' birthdays.

Is he really going to watch his own child—a child who might look just like him—running around the room at Christmas and pretend it isn't his? Of course he won't. He'll feel duty-bound to help raise the kid, and probably to make an honest woman of me, too, once I'm no longer married to someone else—and that would make me so incredibly happy, but only if it wasn't going to make him incredibly miserable.

Which it obviously would.

40

CHARLIE

Maren makes the next trip to New York in a single day and is home again by bedtime. I ask, just before we fall asleep, what her favorite Greek myth is.

"Orpheus and Eurydice," she says. "But it's kind of sad."

"They're all kind of sad. How the fuck did you end up memorizing them anyway?"

"Henry gave me this big colorful book when I was a kid with all the Greek myths. Gorgeous illustrations. I still have it, actually. I read it cover to cover, again and again, and then I read it to Kit when she was old enough."

Thanks to the moonlight, I can just make out her smile...the way she always smiles when she talks about Kit. I suspect that's where Maren's obsession with having children began, because she's way more of a mother to Kit than Ulrika has ever been.

"Okay, tell me about Orpheus and whoever the fuck he was in love with, who undoubtedly turned out to be a witch or a goddess who punished him for something dumb."

She laughs. "Eurydice, and no, she wasn't a witch or a goddess. She was Orpheus's wife, but she was bitten by a spider and Orpheus was so grief-stricken that he went to the underworld after her. He was a musician, so his music calmed Cerberus, the three-headed dog who guards the underworld, and that allowed him to get by."

I glance at Echo and Narcy, both snoring in their sleep. "Realistically, it seems like it should have taken a little more than that to get by a three-headed dog guarding the underworld. That wouldn't even work with *your* dogs, and they're not smart."

She pinches my side. "Shut up, Charlie. Anyway, the gods took pity on him and said his wife could follow him out of the underworld, behind him, provided he never looked back once, but then he looked back, and she was lost to him forever."

"That's...heartbreaking," I groan. "Why the hell is *that* your favorite?"

"I don't know." There's something melancholy in her small smile. "I think maybe I just always wanted to believe it was possible to have someone love you that much. Love you so much that he'd go to the underworld to come after you."

Because she didn't get that with Harvey. She hasn't gotten that with anyone, and she deserves it more than any woman alive.

I want to tell her that I'd travel to the underworld after her. I know that I would, without question. The only reason I don't say it aloud is because of what she'll be wondering in response: if I'm so crazy about her that I would travel to the underworld to retrieve her, why won't I just commit?

So I say nothing, and she falls asleep less happy than she was before.

I'd like this to last forever. It's already falling apart.

I REACH across the bed when I wake with my eyes still closed, my hand eager to find the soft curve of Maren's hip, or her waist, or a breast. I'm not picky. I just want to find her beside me. My hand hits the sheets instead, and my eyes open.

What the fuck? Since when does Maren wake before me, and several days this week at that? I reach for my phone. Have I overslept? But no... It's six in the fucking morning, and she's already gone. This would be an ideal scenario with any female but her.

I head for the main house, inexplicably cranky when I find her in the kitchen making breakfast.

"Why are you up so early?" I ask, trying but failing to hide a touch of disgruntlement. "I wasn't done with you."

She glances over her shoulder from the stove with a smile that doesn't entirely reach her eyes. "Sorry. I wasn't feeling great."

All my irritation vanishes. I cross the room and wrap my arms around her waist from behind. "What's going on? You shouldn't be cooking if you don't feel well."

She swallows. "No. I'm fine now. It passed."

I get the feeling that she isn't telling me the truth about something. "Why are you making that many eggs?" I ask, nodding toward the pan.

She shrugs, continuing to flip them. "Some for you, some for me."

There's something...wrong. I can't put my finger on it, but I know her, and something has changed. "You hate eggs."

There it is again, that look on her face, conflicted. Lying to me over something as stupid as eggs. "I figured I ought to try to get more protein."

"So let me get this straight: you got up because you were sick and came in here to make me breakfast?" I force a laugh to cover my irritation. "You're going to make someone a perfect wife."

I'm not even sure why I said it. Perhaps simply to remind myself that I am not what she wants for the long-term, to let her know that I get it. But her face has fallen, so I wish I'd just kept my fucking mouth shut.

"Aside from the pregnancy issues," she adds quietly.

"There are plenty of men, like myself, who think that a wife who can't get pregnant is sort of an ideal situation..." It's something I've been thinking for a while but haven't had the balls to put out there. "You really like design. Maybe it would be enough. Design, a decent marriage. You know, instead of having kids? Because seriously, kids ruin everything."

It was not exactly what I meant. It was the coward's way of saying, *If you think it could be enough, then I'd like to be the person it's enough with.* But she's blinking back tears at the mere *idea* of not having kids, which means my stupid fucking fantasies about this situation continuing were exactly that—stupid fantasies.

"I really want kids," she says quietly.

I already knew that. But fuck if it's not a punch to the gut anyway. I've wanted something I can't have for a very long time, and I'm going to go through the rest of my life still wanting it.

41

———————

MAREN

Charlie heads off for his run after breakfast, so I'm alone in the kitchen when Elijah strolls in and finds me crying. His cheerful whistling comes to a sharp halt when he sees me.

"Who died?" he asks, and I look up at him with bleak eyes before I cover my face again.

"I'm pregnant," I whisper. I don't know why I told him this thing I can't tell anyone else. Not any of my family, whose first question would be about the child's parentage. Not the baby's father, who considers fatherhood a fate worse than being murdered.

Elijah's hand lands on my shoulder. "Hey now, it can't be all that bad. I thought...didn't you *want* to be pregnant?"

I nod, still crying. I did. So much. But not like this. Not by losing every other thing that makes me happy, by which I mean Charlie. "It's just...a fucked up situation."

"Because you're having your brother's kid," Elijah says.

"He's not my *brother,* and he's...wait, how did you know?"

Elijah releases a quiet laugh. "You two are the only people in the world who think it's *subtle*. What did Charlie say?"

I freeze, then dry my eyes on the sleeve of my shirt. "I haven't told him. I don't know if I can, so please don't say anything. You know what he said once? That my infertility was the sexiest thing about me. I mean, he was trying to make me feel better, but he also meant it." I release a sad laugh and hiccup on another sob. "He really, really doesn't want kids. He's going to feel tricked."

He gently leads me to a chair and encourages me to sit before he crouches in front of me. "Maren, you know him better than that, and you've got to tell him. You know that he'll do the right thing."

"That's the problem, though. I don't *want* him to do the right thing. I want him to be as thrilled as I am, and he won't be. He'll be the opposite."

I don't want to condemn Charlie to that life, and I don't want to condemn myself to marrying a guy who never wanted any of the things I did in the first place. It would be easier just to do it alone.

He rises and begins to pace, his hands linked behind his head. I suspect he doesn't like my answer, but also knows I'm correct. "So, what are you going to do?" he asks.

I really have no idea. Charlie made it pretty fucking clear this morning where he stands on having children—and it's where he's always stood. So I either tell him and make him miserable or...I find a way to let him off the hook.

If I leave, if I go away for a year and have the baby somewhere thousands of miles from Manhattan, I might be able to pull it off. I can lie about the birth date or just say she arrived early.

Will Charlie believe that? I don't know.

Or...I suppose there's Andrew. He was ready to be with me in any way he could. Does he want me enough to pretend someone else's kid is his own? Do I want to protect Charlie enough to go along with the ruse, to marry some guy I like but barely know? I'm so tired right now I can't even think straight, but I'm not going to think any straighter here with Charlie breaking my heart every time he comes into view.

"I'm going to Barcelona early," I say, sitting up straight. "And if I can come up with a believable way to let Charlie off the hook, that's what I'm going to do."

42

———

CHARLIE

I spend the day with Elijah down in the basement, fixing the most recent water damage and going over this morning's conversation in my head. I'm not sure what's going to happen when I'm in San Antonio and she's in New York. I know for a fact that I'm going to lose my fucking mind if I have to watch her with someone else. But I also know that I can't give her the things she wants.

"What's up with you today?" Elijah asks. "You're contemplative."

"*Contemplative*?" I ask. "Is that from your word-of-the-day calendar?"

"Contemplative and also a fucking asshole," Elijah adds.

I shrug. "I had a weird conversation with Maren this morning. Something's going on with her."

"Something like you're sleeping together and basically functioning like husband and wife while pretending you're not together?"

I could deny it, but why bother? He'd know I was lying. Anyone who has ever seen me around Maren probably would realize it was a lie. I can barely keep my hands off her. "Yeah. Something like that."

"All I'm gonna say before I pretend we never had this conversation is that you'd better lock that down before someone else does."

If there was some way to lock it down, I would've done it a decade ago.

I go upstairs to shower before I hunt for her. She's usually found somewhere downstairs with the dogs at her heels, but when she's not there, I go to the cottage.

The door swings open and I freeze at the threshold.

The dogs are gone. The bed is stripped. A single sheet of paper rests on the mattress.

> *Charlie,*
> *I'm dropping the dogs off at home and heading to Barcelona early. I've loved these weeks with you here—I've never been happier—but we both know that it can't last. It's time for me to move on with my life.*
> *Much love, Maren*

I sink onto the bare mattress and put my head in my hands. Was it something I said this morning? Whatever it was, I wish to God I hadn't said it.

And how exactly is she planning to move on? With another guy? With *Andrew*?

I'm furious, but can I actually blame her? She's been nothing but clear about what she wants from the start. She's a traditional girl—she wants marriage and kids and more pets than any family should own. And what did I give her? Not a fucking thing. I've fallen at her feet for the past decade, I've rarely told her no, but I still never offered her the things she actually needed from me.

I storm out of the cottage with the letter in hand just as Elijah's opening the door from the basement.

"Did you know about this?" I demand. "Did you know she was leaving? Is that why you gave me the third degree this morning about locking it down?"

"I knew she was thinking of leaving," he says, letting the doors slam behind him. "What did you expect her to do, Charlie? She's not the kind of girl you treat like a dirty secret."

"Fuck you. I never treated her like that."

"Yeah?" he challenges. "So I guess that means you must've had a talk with her about where the relationship was heading? I guess that means you made it official somehow and I just missed the announcement?"

I scowl at him. "We were happy the way things were, and I didn't want to ruin it. I didn't want to mess with a good thing."

"I'm not trying to rub salt in the wound, bro, but that's the kind of shit a guy says about a mistress or a dirty secret. You've made yourself known to her as the guy who wouldn't settle down, and I'm guessing you never once indicated that something had changed. I mean, *has* it changed? Because if you're still that guy and you still can't make a commitment, you should just let her move on with her fucking life. If there's some guy willing to ditch everything to meet her in Barcelona, then just let her go."

I crumple the note in my fist. "Is that what she told you? That she's meeting someone there?"

He shrugs. "She said something like that, but I wasn't really listening."

So she left me to go be with Andrew. She climbed out of our bed and left me for *Andrew* mere hours later. And why wouldn't she?

Elijah's right. I should let her go on with her life.

Going to the underworld for somebody takes balls.

I didn't even have the balls to tell her I'd consider doing it.

43

———

MAREN

I drop the puppies off with Kit and head not to Barcelona, but to Paris, dropping my bags in a locker at Charles de Gaulle since I won't be here long.

I looked up Belleau Wood online after I finished Margaret's journal. There were twenty thousand casualties total, half of them American—the biggest battle involving US soldiers since Appomattox. The French renamed the area *Bois de la Brigade de Marine*—Wood of the Marine Brigade—in honor of the US Marines who fought there. William's regiment, the fifth, was later awarded the Croix de Guerre by the French government. Many of the soldiers are buried at the Aisne-Marne American cemetery nearby. I'd like to see if he's there. I'd like to finish the story.

The train to Belleau takes an hour, the Uber to the cemetery another ten minutes. It's so close. So easy to get from one place to the next. If William had lived in another time, he could have reached Margaret in eight hours. Or he could have been the coward he accused George of being and just never have gone to war at all.

But of course, he wasn't a coward, and he didn't live in

another time, and everything I'm wishing for them is pointless. They're both long gone.

I locate his name on the cemetery directory:

William Thomas Howard
Atlanta, Georgia
5th Regiment

It takes a while to find his grave. I set the bouquet of roses I bought beside it.

"I have no idea if you're living on in Charlie or if this is all in my head," I whisper. "I have no idea if Margaret is living on in me. I sort of think so, but Charlie would call me Professor Trelawney right now if I said it, or explain that this is how hot girls are a menace." I laugh and then choke back a sob. "But if you are living on in him, I think he'll wind up with a happier story, even if it's one that I'm not a part of. And my ending is happier than Margaret's, even if it's not the exact one I wanted."

The breeze blows my hair, and I look up at all the identical graves. Two thousand American boys whose stories all ended unhappily.

Two thousand boys who broke their parents' hearts.

Maybe those Greek myths I read obsessively as a kid were trying to prepare me for the hardest truth in adulthood: most of our stories are sort of unhappy ones, in the end.

"I hope you were right about Hero and Leander," I tell him. "Maybe you had to wait for another life. And I guess I'll wait for the next one too."

I WANDER the streets of Barcelona, which is every bit as lovely as I remembered, but I think I prefer a crumbling mansion, nearly obscured by live oaks. I think I prefer a place, any place, where

Charlie's smile is the first thing I see. And that isn't happening here.

I wander the tiny alleyways of El Born for hours. An ambulance comes through, and I flatten myself to the wall so it can pass, then walk in back as it moves at a snail's pace behind the crowd.

Maybe it will lead me somewhere, somewhere that makes sense of things.

I love Charlie. I'm so in love with Charlie.

If he'd ever once said, *"Can't you just be happy with what we have?"* before I discovered I was pregnant, I'd probably have said, "*Yes.*" But he didn't say it then, and really...he never made it clear that he'd be in this for the long haul, even when he did say it, which was way too late.

A sign on the garage door of an art gallery says,
JUST IN CASE NO ONE
TOLD YOU TODAY:
HELLO!
GOOD MORNING.
YOU ARE DOING GREAT.
I BELIEVE IN YOU!!
GREAT BUTT

This faceless person behind a garage door is attempting to be kinder to me than I'm capable of being to myself. I don't know why that makes my eyes sting.

God, I've fucked up so badly. I've gotten my fondest wish only to discover that I want something else just as much. A couple months ago I'd have been overjoyed by this turn of events, and a part of me *is* overjoyed, but I'm also so sad at the same time. Because I once only wanted one thing from the world: a baby. And now I want two mutually exclusive things: this baby I might be carrying and its father, and I can't have both.

I stumble upon an old church. You can barely turn a corner

in Barcelona without bumping into a cathedral more magnificent than anything at home. Inside, lining each wall, are these amazing tableaus for the saints. Not paintings but actual carved and painted saints. In front of one, a woman is on her knees weeping, clutching a candle.

You have no idea how much a child can break you, Maren.

Charlie was right. Perhaps this woman prays for a sibling or a spouse, but most likely it's a child. My hand rests on my abdomen. I already love this baby enough to die for it.

Of course it will break me if something goes wrong down the line, if I lose her. Of course that's terrifying. But doesn't he understand that when you love someone that much, the terror is worth it?

I've only been aware of her existence for a handful of days, and already the terror is worth it. I just wish I wasn't going to be bringing her up alone.

I go to a restaurant, determined to ignore the sense that I have failed my child already. Trying to ignore this paralyzing loneliness. If I act as if I don't care, then maybe I won't. Isn't that the way it's supposed to work? I'll experience all the pleasures of the city in order to let it fill that empty space inside of me, then return to New York slightly less broken?

"Uno, por favor," I tell the hostess.

She says something too quickly for me to understand, but I'm fairly certain it was *no husband?* Apparently, New York isn't the only place where they will treat you like a pariah for dining alone.

I shake my head. "No. Uno."

She leads me to a table out on the street, and though I want to enjoy this meal, I sort of feel as if the damage is done—I now feel heartbreakingly, conspicuously alone, which is ridiculous. How many people have come here for business and had to dine alone? I certainly cannot be the first. Will it be lonely for my daughter or son, though? Will it be enough to only have me?

Or would she be better off with a father of some sort? A kind man, like Andrew, who will smile when she speaks, and admire her crayon drawings, and give her away at her wedding?

I don't even have to ask the question. Of course that would be better for her.

And Andrew might even be okay with it.

The food, when it arrives, is probably delicious, but I taste nothing as I weigh the possible solutions in my head. Andrew is kind. He'll be a good dad and a decent husband. He'll make my child's life better, and he'll let Charlie off the hook, so he really solves every problem aside from one: I'm head over heels in love with someone else, and I think that's never going away.

I walk back to the hotel slowly, struggling not to cry. This entire trip was a fucking failure, some misplaced gambit to have my own *Eat, Pray, Love* experience in which the necessary life lessons are delivered in a timely fashion, and I go home happy with my choices. But all I've learned is that food tastes like nothing when you're sad, even if it's good food, and that sometimes acting in someone's best interest will break your heart.

I check the time. It's noon at home. As good an hour as any to ask a man who's never even kissed you how he feels about raising your stepbrother's kid.

I step through the lobby doors, bracing myself to call Andrew. *The worst he can say is no, I guess, and for my daughter's sake, I'll sink a lot lower than this. I'll just—*

A man steps into my path. A large, livid man with circles under his eyes.

A man I've longed for desperately for the past forty-eight hours and never expected to see.

"Charlie?"

He looks past my shoulder as if expecting someone else and swallows, his jaw set hard.

"How did you know where I was?" I ask.

"You've been sharing your location with me for months," he

bites out. "And it took flying to three fucking cities to catch you, so let's have a chat."

I nod, wide-eyed as I look around me—at the subdued staff dressed in head-to-toe black, the vibrant palm wallpaper behind them. "Here?"

"In your *room*, Maren," he growls.

I don't know why he's so angry with me. Is it the way I left? I only did it because I wouldn't get through a drawn-out goodbye without crying.

He wraps a hand over my elbow, steering me toward the glass elevator.

"Floor," he barks. I hit five and, in spite of what a dick he's being, I press my face to his chest. Because this is all I've wanted since I took that pregnancy test, all I've wanted since I arrived, all I wanted when I saw the woman clutching the candle, all I wanted while I ate alone. I wanted my face pressed to Charlie's chest and his arms wrapping around me the way they are right now.

Even when he's furious, he still wants to comfort me.

"Why'd you leave like that?" he whispers. "Just tell me the fucking truth."

Am I really going to continue lying about this? I wanted to spare him. I have no idea what to say. "I needed to think."

"About *Andrew*?" he asks. There's no mistaking the accusation in his tone.

I nearly laugh. He thinks I left because of *Andrew*? He must have no idea how crazy I am about him to even suggest it. Yet... we both know Andrew offers something he does not. So maybe he's got a reason to be jealous.

"No," I reply. "Not really."

He stiffens but says nothing as we exit onto my floor. Inside the suite, he scowls at the broad terrace, at the glass cake plate stacked high with macarons. "Little nicer than Riverbend," he grumbles.

Is it? It never occurred to me. The entire time I've been here, all I've longed for is a cottage with insufficient air conditioning and noisy dogs sleeping nearby while I curl up against Charlie.

I open the doors to the wide veranda and walk out. When I start to take a seat on the cushioned sofa facing the room, he snatches me to him, pulling me into his lap. He's still mad, but he wants me close.

I love that and I hate that, both.

"Okay, please tell me what you're doing here a week early if it's not 'really' about Andrew."

"I came here to have my *Eat, Pray, Love* moment," I tell him. "I thought I was going to learn life lessons and come back with my head on straight and able to see things more clearly. Why are *you* here?"

I expect him to make some surly comment about Andrew. To my surprise, he pushes my hair out of my face and pulls my mouth down to his. "Because I don't want to spend a single night without you. And I never again want to discover through a fucking *note* that you're gone."

"I thought you didn't want to be attached to anything."

"I didn't," he says, and my heart sinks. "But it appears I already am, so it's too fucking late to take it back. I'm attached, Maren. I'm here. I'm not leaving unless you tell me I have to go, and to be honest, I'm probably not leaving then either because I'll keep trying to win you back."

I press my face to his shoulder and begin to cry. How badly did I want him to tell me this for weeks, only to hear it when I've got to ruin everything? I'm not going to stick him with the precise life he's always sworn he doesn't want, even if I think he'll change his mind in a couple decades with someone far younger than me.

"Charlie, we don't want any of the same things. It's the house doing this, trying to reenact a sad old story. It'll pass eventually."

He shakes his head. "Are you serious? Because I kissed you when I got jealous? Because we danced together? Because you liked to watch me doing push-ups?"

"You've got to admit it's weird, all the similarities," I argue.

"No, I don't. Has it ever occurred to you that this is how people act when they're in love, Maren? That for as many similarities as you've found, I can name twice as many differences? Was Margaret also married to a twit? Was William about to start a new arena football team? Did he inherit a mansion? Did Margaret run off to Barcelona without explanation?"

"Well, she *couldn't* go to Barcelona. There was a war going on..."

He laughs, pressing a kiss to my head. "You're missing the point, which is that my life and your life are wildly different from theirs, and we happen to have a handful of things in common because that's how people behave when they're head over heels—and many of the biggest moments happened with the house hundreds of miles away. Our first kiss for instance. Or the fact that I felt like this a decade before we ever went down there."

My head lifts. "You did?"

"I did. From that first day I met you in the Hamptons. You know I did. I asked you to run away with me on your wedding day, remember?"

I stare at him. "You never...you never implied you meant it like that."

He holds my gaze. "You *know* I did."

I wince. Maybe, but it hardly matters at this point. There are a thousand different directions our relationship could have gone, but I can't take this back. I can't wish I'd chosen another course because look where this course got me.

I take a deep breath and raise my chin. "Charlie, I'm pregnant."

He freezes. His hands are still on me, but I swear they've

suddenly lost their warmth. "Pregnant," he repeats, as if it's a death sentence.

I nod. "I'm so sorry."

"Whose is it?" he asks, his voice quiet and controlled.

I gasp, audibly. "What kind of question is *that*?"

"What kind of question do you fucking think it is, Maren? If you flew halfway around the world to fucking see *Andrew*—"

"I'm not here to see Andrew. Where the hell did you get that idea?"

"Elijah said..." His voice trails off and I fill in the blanks: Elijah implied I was here to see Andrew because he knew it would send Charlie flying here in a jealous rage.

Charlie blinks as he meets my gaze again. "So...that would mean...it's mine?"

I swallow hard to fight the lump in my throat. "Yes, idiot. It's yours."

He's so frozen. So stiff. I rise from his lap, and he doesn't even seem to notice I'm gone. He buries his head in his hands. He's now picturing the two of us, losing a child. The two of us on our knees in a hotel parking lot, asking God for something He's not going to give us.

"I know this isn't what you want," I say quietly. "I've been trying to figure out what to do—if the best thing would be to disappear for a year or so and let you think it was IVF or something else."

I don't mention the solution involving Andrew—it seems like more than he needs to know. Though he barely seems to hear what I'm saying, so perhaps he wouldn't hear that either. I only realize now that there was still some tiny piece of me holding out hope for a different outcome, picturing him learning I was pregnant and being surprisingly okay with it.

I was being all Maren about it again. Dreaming up a best possible outcome in place of the realistic one. Even when I was telling myself I'd call Andrew…I was still hoping Charlie would pull through.

And he's not going to.

"Charlie, you don't need to be involved. I can do this on my own."

"So you weren't planning to tell me?"

My eyes close. "I tried. I tried the other day, and you went on your rant about how kids ruin everything. So I came here to think."

"Were you, or were you not, going to tell me?" he demands.

"I was trying to do the kindest thing, Charlie. You've been pretty open about how this is the worst possible outcome, so yes, it occurred to me that I could just disappear for a while and pretend the kid was someone else's. Possibly." *Probably.*

"I need to think," he says, and then he gets up, walks back into the room, and out the door, closing it softly behind him.

Just like that. I gave him terrible news and he handled it even worse than I'd imagined he would. So is he thinking about whether he's going to force himself to become a part of this? Or is he wondering how he can politely extract himself?

I curl into a ball on the corner of the long bench and press my face to my knees, feeling far more alone than I did before he arrived.

I have a father who left before I was born. A stepfather who was kind but didn't really think of me as his kid. An ex-boyfriend who fell in love with my sister while he was with me. An ex-husband who stopped wanting me before the ink was dry.

"It's just going to be us," I whisper to my daughter, resting my hand on my stomach. "And maybe we're better off that way."

I go into the room to pack. There's an early morning flight direct to JFK and I'd rather wait overnight at the airport than spend the next eight hours listening to Charlie explain all the ways this isn't what he wants.

I'm still crying, but I'm also furious, because...*what the fuck?* How am I possibly so egregious, so terrible, that every man in my life wants something or someone else? Wants a different daughter, girlfriend, wife?

"You need to *think*?" I demand, though he's not here. "You need to fucking think? Take all the time you want. Take your whole fucking life. We don't need you anyway."

I turn off location sharing, growing angrier by the moment.

"Fuck you," I say loudly. And that's to all of them. To my dad, to Henry, to every guy my mother was ever with who hit her or hit *on* me. To Miller, to Harvey, to Charlie. They all brought me as much heartbreak as they did joy, and my daughter and I don't fucking need any of them.

There's a knock.

I stomp across the room, sliding the chain in place before I open the door because he had his chance and he's not coming in now.

"Go away," I tell him. "I don't need this. I've got my own money, and I don't want you involved, so just go away."

"Maren," he says coolly, "you will open this fucking door right now, or I'll jump onto your terrace from upstairs and throw a chair through that sliding glass door."

I'd like to call his bluff, but he'll probably do it, and he'll break half the bones in his body in the process.

I unlock the door and step back, swiping away the tears on my face. "I—"

He shuts the door behind him, and then his hands cradle my jaw. "I made you cry," he whispers.

"Everything's making me cry," I sob. "You're not special."

He laughs. "You're a lot like Kit when you're triggered, you know that? But I love you anyway." And then he kisses me. He kisses me hard enough to steal my breath and make me lose track of every last thing I was about to say. For a second.

And then I remember.

"Stop." I pull away. "You can't just walk off and come back and say you love me, then decide you don't love me enough and walk off again. I'm done. I'm tired of this. I'm tired of men deciding I'm not enough. So please go. I'm just—" Exhaustion roars into me like a tornado, out of nowhere. "I'm really tired."

"Then lie down," he says, leading me to the bed and frowning at the open suitcase there. "Holy shit, Maren. Were you about to fucking take off again? How many places do I need to chase you?"

He pushes the suitcase off the bed, and I'm too exhausted to even get mad. I guess I'm not going to the airport. I'm just going to cry myself to sleep and figure it out tomorrow. "I don't want you to chase me. I stopped sharing my location."

I place my head on the pillow, and he lies down with his face next to mine.

"I'm sorry," he says. "I'm sorry I took off like that. It wasn't my finest moment. But it was a lot, and I had to catch my breath before we had this conversation."

I let my eyes fall closed, swallowing hard before I say what needs to be said. "We don't have to have *any* conversation. You don't want kids. End of story."

He frowns. "I didn't want your dogs either, but I seem to have adjusted."

It isn't enough. He's trying, but it isn't enough. "I don't want you to just go along with this, Charlie. I had a father who felt like he was tricked and took off almost immediately. I'm not doing that to my kid."

"*Our* kid," he corrects. "Ours. Look, hon, you're exhausted and I need to process this, so go to sleep and maybe by the time you wake up, we'll be in a better place. I love you. I just need a minute to adjust, okay?"

"Okay." Something settles inside me. Nothing he's saying means he's enthusiastic about this...but I can at least believe he *will* be. So we'll try it and see. And if he changes his mind, I'll deal with it. I've dealt with it before. "I can't believe you came all the way here because you were jealous of Andrew."

He hitches a shoulder. "I like Barcelona. If you'd gone to Siberia, I might've tried to figure it out over the phone first."

"You'd still have come for me in Siberia."

"I'd still have come for you, no matter where you went," he says, his lips close to my ear. "Even if you'd gone to the underworld."

UNDER OTHER CIRCUMSTANCES, we might have stayed in Spain a bit longer. I'd have dragged him into all kinds of museums he wasn't interested in, and he'd have demanded sex in exchange. But...other issues are more pressing.

We need to see a doctor. We also need to admit we're together. *If* we're together. Charlie is saying the right things, but I haven't seen a smile on his face that wasn't forced since the second he learned the news. A good night's sleep didn't do much for either of us.

We get on the next flight back to NYC and go straight to my doctor. A blood test confirms that I am, indeed, very pregnant, and an hour later, she's sliding a sonogram wand over my abdomen.

Charlie squeezes my hand. I see nothing on the screen, but then...there's a flicker.

"Huh," says the doctor.

Charlie's hand tightens. "Is something wrong?"

The world begins to cave in on us both. His worst predictions are already coming true.

She glances at him, then me. "Here's the heart," she says, pointing to a flickering little light. "That's the first baby."

I swallow. "First?"

"Right," she says, grinning. "And over here, this is the second baby."

"Twins," Charlie says blankly as the color drains from his face.

Twins. Wow. When we get pregnant by accident, we *really* get pregnant by accident.

"Your worst fear," I tell him. "So, is it worse than being murdered?"

He's white as a sheet. "I don't know," he says. He forces yet another smile. "I've never been murdered. But yes, I assume it's worse."

I'm not sure he's joking.

I let Marais & Wolfe know that my measurements are changing and that I will definitely be gaining a lot of weight as we ride back to his apartment. Charlie is utterly silent the entire way.

Once inside, he's kind and he's considerate. He asks me what I'd like for dinner and suggests I stay off my feet, as if I'm already in labor. But what he isn't is *pleased* or *enthusiastic*. And that's the only thing I really need from him right now.

I fall asleep early, and when I wake at three AM, he's no longer by my side.

We're supposed to be telling the family at dinner, sixteen hours from now. I no longer think we should. Charlie's doing his best not to be like my dad, not to act like a guy who got tricked into a situation he wants nothing to do with.

He just can't quite pull it off.

44

———

CHARLIE

I'm ruining this.

I'm ruining what I've got with Maren. I'm also ruining this dream she's held for most of her life. And if I don't fucking snap out of it, she's going to leave.

I sit in my leather armchair in the dark, sipping a glass of whiskey. I'm not trying to get drunk, and I'm not trying to escape this situation the way I once would have. I'm just trying to calm down enough that I can fall asleep, because maybe with a good night's rest, this all won't seem as daunting as it does.

My mother would be so disappointed in me if she could see this. She'd tell me every year she spent with Zoe was richer because of it, that wishing those years away is like wishing you'd never had a fortune you eventually lost, or never viewing a glamorous destination because you couldn't return to it.

I slide into bed beside Maren just as light is filtering through the blinds and watch her sleep. Hers is the one face I have always wanted to see on that pillow. The face I drank in whenever she wasn't aware I was watching.

I don't believe in ghosts or an afterlife. I also don't pray. But my eyes fall closed, and I quietly beg someone—my mother? God? the universe?—to intercede.

Please don't let me ruin this.

When I wake the sun is high, and the apartment is silent.

"Maren?" I call, and there's no response. I walk into the living room, but it's empty. Her purse is no longer on the foyer table.

My head whips left to right in a panic. Her carry-on is still in the bedroom, and I don't see a note, but...she's definitely gone.

I grab my phone where it's charging and text her.

> Hey, where are you?

She doesn't reply. When I go to check her location, it's no longer available to me.

Fuck, fuck, fuck.

What if she left? What if something happens to her, and I have no idea where she is? And she's pregnant. *Those are my fucking kids she's carrying. She can't just take off. I deserve to know that my children are safe.*

Everything that happens to her is happening to *them*. If she's thirsty, they're thirsty. If she's tired, they might suffer with her. I just need to know...

I sink back into the same leather chair I was sulking in only a few hours before. "God, I'm such an idiot," I say aloud, burying my face in my hands.

I'm not reluctant to be a father. I'm fucking petrified. And I'm petrified because I want them, and I want her, and there's something superstitious inside of me that says it's all too good, that everything you love will cause you pain and that I love too many things now.

But I can't stop loving them, and I won't wish them away because already these three people—one I've met, two I'll know soon enough—have made my life a thousand times richer than it was a few months ago. Richer than it's ever been.

I start to type. *Maren, please tell me where the fuck you are. I'm so sorry, but I'm panicking and...*

Before I can finish the message, there are keys in the door, and the dogs come racing toward me with Maren behind them. I charge across the room to where she stands, dropping her purse and keys on the table, and wrap my arms around her, my head buried in her hair.

"Turn on your fucking location sharing," I say gruffly. My voice cracks, and she tries to step backward but I don't allow it. After a moment, she relaxes against my chest.

"I just went to get the dogs," she whispers. "Are you okay?"

I nod. I'm so much better than okay. And as I stand here, with her in my arms, I know that *this* is what my mother wanted for me—not some restored house, but a restored *son*, one who was willing to love things again. One whose life could be just as rich as hers once was. "I love you," I tell her. "And I love them."

She pulls back, glancing up at me. "The dogs?"

"No," I reply. "Okay, maybe them too. I love all five of you."

I can feel her smile against my chest. "Good. We're going to be around for a while."

45

MAREN

The dinners my mother holds at the club used to be the highlight of my week. I thought I just loved being around my family, but...I haven't missed them at all since I left for South Carolina. I think I just loved being around Charlie and couldn't admit it to myself.

But even Charlie can't save *this* get-together.

"I'm going to be sick," I whisper to Charlie in the cab. His eyes widen. "Not literally."

His sigh of relief is so loud that the cab driver looks in the rearview mirror to check on us. "Maybe don't use that expression until you're past the throwing-up stage of pregnancy. And tonight will be fine."

"You should be just as worried as I am," I tell him. "My mom's going to use this as an excuse to leave your dad. And then you'll be comforting him while I'm keeping my mom from running off with a junkie or a Tinder scammer."

His lips press to the top of my head. I'm not sure what happened to him this morning, but ever since I got home with the dogs, he's been fully in. We're running late because he was researching preschools, and when I pointed out that we had a while, he said, "*Maren, we really don't.*"

"We have a secret weapon," he tells me.

"We do?"

"Not one but two grandchildren."

I hope he's right, but I'm not positive. My mom seems more the type to be upset that she's old enough to be a grandmother than the type to be thrilled by it. It also means the end of my modeling career and perhaps the end of my trim waist. Those were the two things about me that my mother liked best.

Everyone is seated at the long table in my mother's favorite room. There are my two favorite stepdads—Roger and Henry, who are now best friends. Henry's girlfriend, a twenty-four-year-old publicist that Charlie slept with first. Kit and Miller, the fiancé who's also my ex. Which makes Kit the only female who hasn't slept with *multiple* men here.

This room is already flooded with weird overlaps. And we're about to introduce the weirdest of them all. We greet everyone, but my mother is already on edge.

"I thought you couldn't leave South Carolina, Charlie," she says with more than a hint of accusation in her tone. "Here, Maren, come sit by me."

Charlie snags my hand, holding me in place, and the room goes entirely silent.

My mother rises to her feet, knocking a wineglass off the table in her haste and sending red wine splaying across the rug. "Absolutely not," she gasps. "Absolutely not."

"I *knew* it," Kit says to Miller. "And you said there was no way."

"Maren, you idiot!" my mother screams, dramatically lifting the plate in front of her and smashing it. "Charlie never stays with anyone, and now the family is ruined! I can't even—"

"Ulrika," Charlie warns, "raise your voice to my future wife again or call her another name, and you'll *really* see a family dinner get ruined."

I raise a brow. "Future *wife*?"

He huffs in exasperation. "*Obviously*. We'd have done it anyway, eventually, but my children aren't going to be bastards."

"I don't think anyone even uses that expression anymore, Charlie, and I don't want—"

"What?" shouts Kit. "Back way the fuck up. Children? What *children*?"

I bite my lip, trying to hold in my tears, but they spill out anyway. "We're pregnant."

"Oh my God," Kit says, leaping from her chair and hugging me, with Roger and Henry on her heels. I'd feel like an idiot for crying, except they're all crying too.

"This is so amazing," says Henry, his voice cracking. "I can't believe I'm about to be a grandfather."

The tears pour then. I'm not going to tell him why. I'm not going to tell him that I've been carrying around this memory of something he said twenty-seven years ago like a stain. Because whatever he said, he's erased all of it now.

My mother is the only one who isn't over here. She remains standing at the end of the table, pale, cheeks sucked in. "This is a disaster and you're all acting as if—"

Roger steps away, standing between us and her, as if he can shield us. "Ulrika, for once in your damn life, don't make this about yourself. She's having a baby. Our grandchild. You always said you wished we'd have a child, and now we sort of are."

"Grandchildren," Charlie corrects. "We're, uh, having twins."

"Twins?" my mother repeats faintly, sinking into her seat, her eyes suspiciously bright. "God, Maren, you're going to gain *so* much weight."

"Jesus, Mom," Kit gasps.

"I'm gonna kill her," Charlie hisses beside me.

But I just laugh through my tears. I'm pregnant, Charlie is by my side, most of the family is thrilled, and my mom is already back to worrying about my weight.

It's a far happier ending than I ever thought I'd get.

46

CHARLIE

By the time Maren's divorce is finalized, she is extremely pregnant.

It would have taken a lot longer. There was a period of time when Harvey was making noise about how he was owed part of Maren's trust fund and a lot of other bullshit. In that respect, our accidental pregnancy was a blessing: because once we'd subpoenaed the fertility doctor, we discovered that it was Harvey who had the issues, and the doctor told Maren she was infertile at his request.

It's still unclear why Harvey did it. He tried to blame the doctor, then said he was scared Maren would leave him if she thought he was the problem. My guess? She was easier for him to control when she thought the fault was hers. Either way, he quickly signed every paper Maren's lawyers set before him when we threatened to take it public.

We go to Riverbend on the day the divorce comes through and are quietly married in the backyard by a justice of the peace, with only Martha and a smirking Elijah there as witnesses.

That night, we sit on the porch swing, Maren's head resting

on my shoulder. "This is probably not at all the wedding night you pictured. No wedding night lingerie. No sex."

Maren wants to deliver back in NYC, so we can't risk doing anything that could send her into labor.

"I never pictured any sort of wedding night," I remind her, "so this seems like a pretty good one to me."

She glances up. The fact that I worshipped her for the decade before she was mine isn't quite enough to keep her from worrying.

"I know what you're thinking," I tell her. "You've got to stop."

"But...I sort of forced you down a path you didn't want to be on, you know?"

I squeeze her hand. "You pulled me off a dusty path through the desert, a path I was fucking miserable on, and brought me here." I nod ahead of us to the lane canopied by oak trees, heavy with Spanish moss. "My world was so empty I could barely summon the energy to pretend I was happy. And now it's so full that my greatest fear is losing a single inch of it."

She presses a kiss to my cheek. "Even if you've got to help your wife remove her shoes in a minute because she can no longer reach her feet?"

I grin. "Even then."

Because when Maren's referring to herself as my wife, everything else is irrelevant.

And when that pregnant wife *yawns*, I tell her I'm carrying her up the stairs to bed.

"You are not carrying me, Charlie. My weight has doubled since the last time we were here."

"I think I'd have noticed if your weight doubled, and I guarantee your *mother* would have," I reply, swooping her up in my arms. "And you're forgetting how strong and manly I am."

She looks at me from beneath her lashes. "I'm unlikely to forget how strong and manly you are, Charlie."

I raise a brow. "You know, when you use that voice, I start thinking about sex. Have you changed your mind?"

"There will be no orgasms. For either of us."

"Fine," I reply. "I just won't let you finish. Every time I sense you getting close, I'll stop."

"Neither of us has that much self-control."

This is undoubtedly true. "I'm going to remind these twins every night for the rest of their lives that I didn't get laid on my wedding night because of them."

She laughs. "You should. Kids love being forced to picture their parents as sexual beings."

"It's for the best anyway," I reply. "I don't want your ghost watching our marriage get consummated. Because it's going to be filthy when it happens."

"How filthy, Charlie?" she asks, and her cheeks are flushed, and her color is high.

"Maybe I can show you once," I offer.

I wait for her to insist, again, that it can't happen, but she gets a half-smile on her face instead. "One time probably can't hurt," she says. "But I really do need you to help me ditch these shoes."

I slide to the floor, unbuckle her shoes, and push her dress up around her waist. "Tell your ghost to look away," I warn, smirking as I spread her thighs. "I don't think they did this back in her day."

47

———

MAREN

SIX YEARS LATER

We arrive at Riverbend on a warm mid-April day. I breathe deep as soon as we step out of the car. Though we spend most of the year in New York, our holidays and summer break are always spent here. It feels more like home to me than anywhere else.

The twins—petite female versions of Charlie—unbuckle themselves and scramble out, with the dogs at their heels, while I lift Rosemary—blonde like me but with Charlie's ability to fall asleep anywhere. She buries her face into my neck drowsily while Charlie, carrying our five-month-old in her car carrier, bends down and presses a kiss to the top of my head. "I hope that deep breath you took was a good one, because it's probably the last rest you're going to get this weekend."

I smile. "Wait, are you trying to tell me that Easter weekend with the entire family plus three young kids and a newborn won't be restful? I wish you'd said something sooner."

He places his free hand on my back as we move toward the stairs. "It's mostly putting up with your mother that I'm worried about. She makes one comment about your weight and it's over."

I laugh. It hasn't happened in five years, not since I gave birth to the twins, and Charlie flew into such a rage it hasn't come up since. Yet he's still mad.

"I'm used to my mom. It's just the idea of playing hostess to ten people aside from us that I'm worried about."

"Maybe the house ghost can help you with hosting duties."

I elbow him with a laugh. Even after everything that happened, Charlie still does not believe the house is haunted. As long as Margaret doesn't mind his disbelief, I don't either.

Martha, who watches the house when we're gone and helps us when we're in town, swings the door open, and the twins dive at her.

"My girls are home at last," she says, with tears in her eyes as she holds them close. I rest my head on Charlie's shoulder, grateful that we hired her. She is far more of a grandmother to them than Ulrika, who actually suggested that I might want to switch the twins from breast milk to skim milk because they were getting too heavy.

They were two months old at the time.

By the time Charlie and I get into the house—its refinished floors gleaming in the sunlight—the twins and Rosemary are already out of it, rushing toward the grassy backyard where we are planning to play croquet this weekend at last. Charlie starts assembling the goal he brought so the girls can practice their soccer drills, and I laugh at his disappointment when they decide they'd rather spin until they're dizzy and fall on top of each other instead.

He shrugs and takes the seat beside me. "I'll let them get it out of their systems."

"We've got all weekend," I laugh. "Plus, you know, the next thirteen years."

"We really don't, though, hon," he says, lifting Mae out of the car carrier as she wakes. "Did you read that article I sent you? If they're not on travel soccer by age nine, they've got virtually no chance of being recruited."

I doubt the version of Charlie I first came here with years ago—the one who drank himself stupid most nights and couldn't remember who he'd brought home—would recognize himself these days, but I do. Charlie has gone full #GirlDad, but he always had that side—sweet and fiercely protective, and hell-bent on keeping the people he loves happy...and getting them recruited by Ivy League colleges, if possible.

Mae begins to fuss, her tiny pink mouth sucking at air. "You keep focusing on getting them into Stanford while I feed this one," I say, lifting her as I rise.

"Stanford isn't even an Ivy!" he calls. "Read the article!"

He runs into the grass just as the twins start kicking the ball and I head upstairs to Margaret's room, which is now our nursery.

Two cribs sit along the wall where the mirror was— between me and Kit, there is almost always at least one baby in the house and often two, as there will be this weekend. She and Miller just had their second child in January. I take a seat in the rocking chair, slipping down the flap of my nursing bra, and Mae latches on greedily. I slowly rock the chair back and forth while she drinks and then falls into a sated sleep, her mouth still ajar.

I stare down at my beautiful daughter as I fix my shirt, marveling at how it all worked out. I love our life, but just as importantly...Charlie does too. Every time he smiles at me over our sleeping children's heads, I see it in his eyes. He's already talking about having one more kid. He really wants a boy, but I suspect he'd be pretty happy with five daughters.

Provided they go to Harvard. On full scholarships.

I close my eyes for just a moment, feeling the weight of my daughter in my arms, with her quick sleeping breaths, and suddenly…a trickle of quiet contentment eases through me. Not *my* contentment, though I'm very content.

"Thank you, Margaret," I say aloud. "Thank you for all of this."

Charlie would say it was my imagination, but I swear I can feel her pat my shoulder—as if in seeing me get my happy ever after, she's finally gotten hers too.

THE END

For a bonus scene revealing the day Charlie and Maren first met from Charlie's point of view, subscribe to my newsletter here (ebook) or by visiting the "bonus" tab at www. elizabethoroark.com. Learn more about Elijah's book, arriving December 2025, on the next page.

MY FAVORITE FAKE ROMANCE

Faking it never felt this good.

Dr. Easton Walsh thought she'd be showing up to her best friend's wedding with a dazzling ring and a fiancé everyone wanted to Instagram. Instead, her boyfriend dumped her over what was supposed to be a proposal dinner and the only man offering her a lifeline is the last one she'd ever choose: Elijah Cabot. Her best friend's older brother. The guy who broke her heart once already.

He'll help make her ex jealous...All she has to do is help him drive his grandmother across several states to the wedding. Easy.

But the fake relationship is starting to feel real, and the longer the trip goes on, the harder it is for Easton to remember that Boston—and her carefully built life—don't include Elijah. Especially when her ex starts dangling threats that could derail her career if she doesn't come back to him.

Now Easton has to decide: risk everything for a second chance at the one man she shouldn't want...or keep playing it safe, even if it means losing the best thing that's ever happened to her—again.

Available December 11, 2025. Preorder here.

ACKNOWLEDGMENTS

I have an amazing group of friends/beta readers who never fail to give me the best feedback. Maren Channer, Michelle Chen, Katie Friend, Katie Meyer, Jodi Marten and Jen Owens...thanks as always for your love, encouragement and suggestions.

Valentine PR - there are too many of you guys now to list without accidentally skipping someone, but thank you! You make my life a million times easier...and it's only because of you that I actually do all the shit I'm supposed to when releasing a book.

Thanks so much to my editor, Lauren Clarke; my agent, Kimberly Brower; Laura Hidalgo for the designs and Christine Estevez for proof-reading and keeping me on track.

Thanks to Deanna, Katie and Sallye—the only people who could convince me to double fist frozen g&ts; to Laura Pavlov, with whom I could discuss shiplap for hours; and Patrick, Lily and Jack for spending so much money that I have to write books, even when I don't feel like it—yes, boys, I know it's mostly Lily.

ALSO BY ELIZABETH O'ROARK

The Summer Series

5 angsty surfer standalone romances

The Devil Series

4 funny, angsty, grumpy-sunshine, enemies-to-lovers romances

The Langstrom Brothers

Coach-student and best friend's girl romances.

The Parallel Series

She's been dreaming about him since she was small. And now, weeks before her wedding, he's appeared in real life.

ABOUT THE AUTHOR

Elizabeth O'Roark has a bunch of degrees she does not use and gave up working as a medical writer to craft grumpy, alpha heroes and the flawed women who love them. When not writing, she likes to spend time with her three kids, who are now teenagers and wish she'd find a different way to spend time. Visit her at www.elizabethoroark.com for book updates, bonus novellas and special editions of this and other titles.